NEW BEGINNINGS AT ROOKERY HOUSE

ROSIE HENDRY

New Beginnings at Rookery House

Copyright © 2025 by Rosie Hendry
ISBN: 978-1-914443-41-1

This is a work of fiction. All characters and events in this publication, other than those in the public domain, are fictitious and any resemblance to real persons, living or dead, is purely coincidental.

All rights reserved. No part of this publication may be reproduced, stored in a retrieval system, or transmitted, in any form or by any means, without the prior written permission of the publisher.

Published by Rookery House Press
Cover design by designforwriters.com

For David,
with love and thanks.

CHAPTER 1

Rookery House, Norfolk – February 1944

Thea Thornton gazed up into the inky blackness which was peppered with countless pinprick stars. The immensity of the night sky made her feel tiny, her worries small and insignificant compared to the many momentous and important events happening under its vast canopy. The world was at war! And yet even so, her own concerns weighed heavily on her shoulders tonight. She needed to work out what to do for the best and somehow put her mind to rest.

Rather than going straight indoors after she'd finished checking the animals, Thea had lingered outside despite the cold, wanting to take in the sights and sounds of the countryside at night – and to give herself time to think. The stars and a waning moon gave just enough light for her to make her way.

As she drew in a breath of wintry air that was fragrant with damp earth, a movement caught her eye. It was a barn owl, its feathers painted a ghostly white by the pale moonlight as it flew past her heading for the meadow – but she didn't hear a thing as its wingbeats were silent.

A rustle through the grass told her that Bess, her brother Reuben's sheepdog, was returning from wherever she'd been exploring. Thea was looking after Bess while Reuben was out with the village Home Guard. The dog watched the barn owl too, her head turning to follow its flight path. When the owl had disappeared from view, Bess gave Thea an alert, quizzical look.

'Come on then.' She touched the dog's back. 'Let's go and watch it hunt, shall we?' She led the way to the gate leading into the meadow and leaned her arms on the top wooden bar. Bess followed at her heels and sat down beside her, leaning against Thea's legs.

Thea could just make out the owl slowly quartering up and down in search of prey. Back and forth it went before suddenly stalling in flight, twisting and then plummeting to the ground. Moments later it took off and flew away towards a distant oak tree. Thea couldn't tell if it was carrying a catch, or if it was regrouping for another hunt, but either way it was going to have a long night of activity.

Thea was sure her night was going to be a busy one too – searching not for mice or voles, but for a solution. With the barn owl gone, her thoughts had already returned to the problem that was plaguing her.

Nancy was pregnant. And that meant she would be leaving her job in the garden at Rookery House and Thea would need to find a replacement for her. There was far too much work for her and Flo, their Land Girl, to manage between them, even with the help of those willing and able to lend a hand.

Thea felt foolish that Nancy's news had taken her so completely by surprise. After her husband's leave from the army last December... Thea now thought she might have anticipated the result. It was an exciting time for Nancy, her husband and their two young girls and Thea was genuinely pleased for them. A new baby coming was life-changing. Granted, it was unplanned, but it would be welcomed and much loved when it arrived.

Thea smiled and stroked Bess's ears. Nancy was a good mother and had risen to the challenges of being evacuated out to Great Plumstead from her home in the East End. She'd even transformed herself into a gardener and become – after a shaky start – a hard and reliable worker and a fixture in the garden at Rookery House. Thea was going to miss her, but she needed to find someone to take Nancy's place, and the sooner the better.

Rather like the barn owl had done when it was searching and scanning the meadow, Thea began casting her mind over the village, searching for likely candidates, but without success. There wasn't anyone she could think of who had the right credentials and was available.

She sighed. Maybe she should try another approach. Nancy hadn't had any gardening experience other than volunteering on the WI allotment and had surprised Thea by asking for the job. It had been a risk to take her on after Alice, Thea's niece, had left to join the WAAF, but it had paid off.

Was Thea ready to take another gamble on someone? And who?

Before she could answer her questions, Bess, who'd been sitting patiently beside her, leapt to her feet and, with her tail wagging fast, trotted off in the direction of the house. Reuben must have returned. This was confirmed moments later when her brother, dressed in his Home Guard uniform, appeared with Bess bounding along in front of him. He headed towards Thea.

'Hettie said you were still outside. Are the animals all right?'

'Yes, they're fine. I was just enjoying the night.'

'It's a beautiful one, crisp and clear.' Reuben joined her, leaning on the gate. 'I hear Nancy will be leaving.'

'Yes. She's not sure when yet. Depends on how she feels and what she can manage. But whenever it is, I need to work out how I'm going to replace her. Ted's always been good at helping when Nancy's had time off because one of her girls was unwell, but I can't ask him to come every day. I don't think he'd want to, what with his own garden to tend. And it's a *lot* of work...' Ted was her housemate Hettie's close friend and a retired head gardener. He'd given Thea invaluable advice and help since he'd moved back to the village, but she didn't want to impose on him to become a full-time worker.

'There is another option, one we've talked about before...' Reuben said.

He let the words hang and Thea knew exactly what her brother was suggesting.

'That I should apply to have an Italian POW,' Thea answered.

It was something they'd discussed when Alice left. Thea had been against it then, and when Nancy asked for the job, she hadn't had to give the Prisoner of War option any more thought.

'The POWs we have helping on the estate are good grafters and nice fellas,' Reuben said with conviction. He worked with POWs on the farms belonging to the Great Plumstead Hall estate and Thea knew he rated them highly.

'It's the language difficulty that still bothers me. You've said yourself that they don't all speak English. The few that can have to translate for the others. I would only need one man here and if he didn't understand any English, then it would cause difficulties,' Thea explained. 'We're busy enough as it is without having to stop and work out how to show someone what to do every time, then double-check they understand in case they start pulling up crops when they were supposed to pull weeds. I just worry it will create extra work and be more trouble than it's worth.'

'You could ask for a POW who speaks English,' Reuben suggested.

'I *could*, but that doesn't mean I'd get one.' Thea sighed. 'I just don't seem to be able to settle on a solution, though I need to do so soon. I want to let Nancy know I'm prepared and ready for when she wants to finish work. I won't let her endanger herself or the baby by carrying on when she should stop. It's a real concern.'

'Don't let it worry you; it will be sorted out one way or another.'

'I know, but sometimes…' Thea hesitated, turning to her brother. '*Sometimes,*' she repeated, 'it feels like a heavy burden keeping this place running. When it's me having to make the decisions. It can feel – lonely.' She heard her voice crack and it surprised her because she hadn't thought that her feeling was so strong or upsetting to her.

Reuben put his hand on her shoulder. 'You're not alone. You've always got me to help, and the others are here for you too.'

'I know. And thank you, Reuben.' Tears pricked at the back of Thea's eyes and she pressed her lips tightly together, determined to hold them in. 'I'm just tired and overreacting,' she said, after a moment. 'It's been a long day.'

Reuben gave her a concerned, searching look, then squeezed her shoulder before taking his hand away as if deciding, she thought, that his dependable, strong sister was back to being herself.

Thea wasn't so sure about that though, because suddenly expressing her feelings like that had given her more than a surprise – it was a shock. She was glad when Reuben changed the subject.

'I heard some other news tonight that will shake things up around here.'

'More than Nancy leaving?'

'I reckon so.'

'Then you'd better tell me and get it over with,' Thea said.

'The RAF is leaving.'

Thea gasped.

'And the Americans are coming in their place.'

'*What*?!'

'They're taking over RAF Great Plumstead.'

'When?'

'We weren't told. I suppose it will be in the next month or so. There are already some American airbases in our county so they'll be keen to add another one as soon as they can.'

'That means Elspeth and Marge will leave,' Thea said, thinking of the two young Waafs who'd stayed at Rookery House for a couple of weeks while their accommodation was finished at the aerodrome. They'd become part of the extended family, often visiting, and would be missed. 'We'll all be sad to see them go, especially Hettie.'

'That's the way it is for them. They must head off to where they're sent. Having Americans arrive in the village is going to cause a stir though.'

'It will,' Thea agreed. 'And yet another change because of the war.'

'There's one certainty in life and it's that things always change. Nothing stays the same for ever,' Reuben said sagely. 'We just need to cope with things as and when they come along. Who knows, it might be a good change for the village. For us, even.'

'We'll see.'

Thea turned her attention to the meadow where she could see the barn owl was searching once more.

Just like me, Thea thought. I'm searching too. For a replacement for Nancy. And for... what?

And with that question in mind, she bade goodnight to Reuben and Bess and made her way back towards the warmth of Rookery House.

CHAPTER 2

Prue pedalled her bicycle past the row of shops opposite the village green, then turned into the lane leading to her sister Thea's home at Rookery House. She had spent the morning in Wykeham, volunteering at the Red Cross Prisoner of War Fund shop. Since its opening last summer it had been a great success, raising money from donated second-hand goods and handmade items. Every penny they took went to help the Red Cross send more parcels out to POWs.

As much as she always enjoyed her shifts working in the shop, today she'd been distracted by the problem facing her sister. She wanted to help Thea find a solution and for some reason couldn't push it to the back of her mind, even while she'd served customers, restocked shelves and chatted with the other volunteers. Maybe it was because the gardening job had first been done by Prue's son Edwin before he left to work for the Friends Ambulance Unit. Later on, her daughter Alice had enjoyed working in the Rookery House garden until she'd volunteered to become a Waaf and do her bit for the war effort. Finally Nancy, who boarded with Prue, had replaced

Alice. It seemed a family affair almost, and so perhaps it was no wonder Prue was wracking her brains about who she might put forward for the job next.

Rounding a bend, she could see the Victorian property up ahead, standing on its own near a wood that was home to a large flock of rooks from which Rookery House took its name. Thea had lived there since she'd moved back from London in the summer of 1939, not long before the outbreak of war. Prue recalled her delight at having her sister living close by once more. And it wouldn't be too strong a statement to say that Thea's return had been life-changing for Prue.

Thea had supported Prue through so many challenges, from finding homes for evacuee expectant mothers and children to taking in Waafs who needed accommodation at short notice. Her sister had also supported Prue's children when their father Victor was at his worst.

There had been fun times too. The pair of them loved working together manning a WVS canteen, pitching up at sites across the county wherever they were needed.

Prue suddenly recalled the night they had taken the canteen to Norwich after it had been bombed and many parts of it were on fire. The sights they'd seen! The city they'd known had been irrevocably changed, with familiar buildings destroyed.

Prue let her bike slow almost to a stop as a wave of emotion flooded through her. Her husband Victor had been killed in the Norwich Blitz. Prue had seen him pulled from the home of his mistress. It was an image she could see clearly in her mind and one she knew she would never forget. Thea had been there with her and Prue was grateful for that. Even though the sisters were as shocked as each other, they had got through and moved on together.

More memories of that day and the aftermath came

rushing back but Prue forced them down with a shudder. She would not think about that, or him. Victor was in the past where he belonged. Prue had more pressing things to deal with. She sped up and turned her bicycle in through the open gates of Rookery House.

After dismounting she wheeled her bike round to the rear of the house and leaned it against the wall of the scullery. Opening the back door into the kitchen, she called out a cheerful 'Hello!' and stepped inside where she was met by a welcome warmth from the range and the delicious smell of baking.

'Auntie Prue!' two children's voices chorused.

Thea's evacuee children, eight-year-old George and his sister, ten-year-old Betty, stood at the large wooden table, one on each side of Hettie, making shapes out of pastry. All three looked as if they were enjoying themselves. Hettie was a perfect grandmother figure, although she'd never had children of her own. After retiring from her job as Cook at Great Plumstead Hall, she'd moved in with Thea and had wholeheartedly embraced living with all those who'd found their way here too, not least Betty and George.

'You look like you're having fun,' Prue said, giving the children a warm smile.

'Auntie Hettie's letting us decorate the top of the pie for tonight's tea.' Betty pointed a floury finger at the pastry-covered dish standing in the middle of the table.

'It's going to be marvellous,' Hettie said. 'You two carry on making your shapes while I put the kettle on. Do you have time for a cup of tea, Prue?'

'I'm not sure yet. I need to speak to Thea. Is she about?'

Hettie stepped towards Prue and spoke in a soft voice. 'Is everything all right?'

'Yes. I just want to talk to Thea about what she's planning to do about replacing Nancy.'

'You've come at an opportune time – there's been an interesting development on that front. It happened this morning and Thea's gone to speak to Reuben about it. But I'll let her explain.'

'She's over at Reuben's house?'

'That's right, he's back from work now with Saturday being his half day. Go and find them,' Hettie told her.

Intrigued by the older woman's cryptic words, Prue went outside and headed towards her brother's home, which was in a converted railway carriage sited in the grounds of Rookery House, near the orchard. He'd moved in not long after Thea, having been widowed the year before. Thea had asked him to come and live in the house with her and Hettie, but Reuben liked his independence, so living nearby in his little house was a suitable compromise. It was near enough for them to look out for each other but gave Reuben his own space.

Approaching the small house, which still had the look of a railway carriage but with a sturdy veranda built around it, she saw the door at one end open and her sister come out.

'Thea!' Prue waved to attract her attention.

'Oh, hello.' Thea headed towards her.

'Hettie told me where you were. She said there's been a development and you've been discussing it with Reuben?' Prue gave her sister a questioning look. 'Have you found someone to take over from Nancy? Only I was thinking if you haven't then maybe I could help. I couldn't manage as much time as she does now but I'll do what I can as and when I can fit it in.'

'And how would you do that? Shall we conjure up more hours in the day?' Thea raised an eyebrow, the corners of her mouth twitching into a smile.

'I know I've got a lot on, but...'

Thea put a hand on Prue's arm. 'What would I ever do without you?' she said, smiling affectionately at her sister. 'And as always, you're putting my needs over yours. However, I know full well that you're busy enough as it is with all the things you do and you already don't make enough time for yourself.'

'I'd enjoy working with you and Flo...' Prue began to protest but stopped when Thea firmly shook her head.

'No. You need time to do your own thing. Life isn't all about work. Even when there's a war on,' Thea added ruefully.

Prue let out a long sigh. 'Very well, I give in,' she said, grinning. 'And I'm sure you're right, though what I'd do with a few hours' time off I have no idea. I like keeping busy, always have.'

'I'm sure you'd find something,' Thea replied. 'And in answer to your question, yes, we have found a solution for replacing Nancy when she leaves. It's rather serendipitous. I just needed Reuben to agree, because I'll need his help, and he has done.'

'Agreed to what? He's not going to take on Nancy's role, is he?'

'Of course not, let me explain.' Thea hooked a strand of her curly brown, chin-length hair behind her ear. 'I had a telephone call from my friend Julia this morning – remember she's a Quaker living in London and is involved with helping refugees? It was she who asked me if Anna could come and live and work here after Edwin left.'

Prue nodded, recalling how Anna, a Jewish German refugee, had arrived at Rookery House in the early years of the war. Unfortunately Anna had been arrested as an enemy alien and taken to a camp on the Isle of Man. Thea had worked tirelessly to get Anna released, explaining to those in charge that she should never have been imprisoned since she was no threat to the country, having fled the Nazi regime herself. Anna was now teaching at a boarding school in Wiltshire.

'Does Julia have another refugee who needs a new home?' Prue asked.

'Not exactly,' said Thea. 'She's asked if I could take in a Dutch Professor.'

'Ah!' said Prue, then frowned. 'Is he – if it is a 'he' – going to come and work in the garden like Anna did? A Professor?'

'No, he just needs somewhere to convalesce after an illness. He'll be doing his own academic work while he's here and will pay for his bed and board. The problem is we don't have a spare room in the house. I can't have anyone staying in the dining room as Marianne uses it for her sewing, and any short-term visiting guests stay in there. The only option was for the Professor to sleep in Reuben's smaller bedroom but eat his meals with us in the house. Reuben's agreed to that.'

'But how does that help with replacing Nancy?' Prue asked, trying not to sound impatient.

'Because the Professor can speak Italian!' Thea's face lit up. 'He can act as our translator. Which means I'll be able to apply for an Italian POW and not have to worry in case he can't speak English. It's a huge weight off my mind.'

'And mine!' laughed Prue, relieved. 'When's the Professor coming?'

'Next week. He's called Max Van Gelder. Julia says he's been teaching at a university in London for the last ten years. He's originally from Amsterdam.'

'I'm so pleased it's all going to be sorted out,' said Prue. 'Nancy will feel much better – she's been ever so worried about leaving her job with no one to take her place, especially as she's not sure how much longer she'll be able to carry on working.'

'I'm hoping we can get a POW as soon as possible so he will overlap with Nancy, then she'll be able to finish whenever she's ready.' Thea put her arm through Prue's and they started walking towards the house. 'Yesterday, after Nancy told me she was expecting, I had no idea what I was going to do, and now an unexpected solution has turned up and we'll have a Dutch Professor joining us at Rookery House! Life is full of surprises.'

'I've never met anyone from Holland before,' Prue said thoughtfully. 'Do you know what he's like?'

'Julia said he is a very nice person and they've been friends for many years. She's an excellent judge of character. I don't think she'd send anyone to live here unless she was sure they'd fit in. By the way, have you heard the other news?'

'No, what else has happened?' Prue halted and looked at her sister.

'Reuben found out last night that the RAF is leaving and the aerodrome is being taken over by the Americans.'

Prue gasped. 'That's a big change!' She shook her head in amazement then said, 'With the Americans arriving and your Dutch Professor this village is about to become more international. It might do us good.'

Thea laughed. 'Reuben said something similar. Though I doubt the Americans will affect us much here at Rookery House. We might see them walking about sounding like actors from the pictures but we've no room for any to come and stay here, like the Waafs did.'

'I've seen some American servicemen in Norwich. I must say they look very dashing in their stylish tailored uniforms,' Prue said as they walked again. 'You can't miss them.'

'Great Plumstead is in for a shake-up with smart American servicemen walking about,' Thea mused.

'Just think how the evacuee expectant mothers created a

stir when they turned up, with their East End accents and ways of doing things, their fashionable clothes... and I'm mainly thinking of our lovely Gloria!'

'Gloria has been a breath of fresh air,' Thea agreed.

'She certainly has.' Prue fondly remembered the arrival of the expectant mothers at the beginning of the war. They'd been sent to Great Plumstead by mistake, after the village had been told to prepare for evacuee children. 'It turned out marvellously in the end,' said Prue.

'It did.' Thea agreed. 'Marianne and her daughters, Emily and Bea, would never have come to live at Rookery House if evacuee children had arrived that day.'

Prue nodded. 'I'm grateful to whoever made the mistake of sending them to us. They've become an important part of the village and because of them we've got The Mother's Day Club and all the good work it does for us and the war effort. Change and new people can be a very good thing.'

'It can,' Thea agreed as they reached the back door of the house. 'And change is coming, so we might as well embrace it.'

Prue smiled as she followed her sister inside. Her most pressing worries were gone and news of the newcomers to Great Plumstead and Rookery House filled her with curiosity and excitement. What would they bring to the village and its people? And to her?

CHAPTER 3

'We don't know where we'll be sent to next,' Marge said, shrugging her shoulders. 'We haven't a clue.'

'And even if we did, we wouldn't be allowed to say,' Elspeth added in her soft Scottish voice. 'I'm sorry we'll have to just up and leave, Hettie, but we have no say in the matter. That's why we grabbed the chance to come and see you today.'

Hettie gave the two young Waafs an understanding smile. 'I know you can't give me details but you mustn't mind me asking. We are all going to miss you both when you go.'

'And we'll miss you all too.' Marge poured some milk into her cup of tea and stirred it in.

The two Waafs had arrived at Rookery House a short while earlier, having got this Sunday afternoon off from their work. Hettie had been delighted to see them arrive and as always was taking the opportunity to feed them up, knowing that the food they were served in the aerodrome's cookhouse wasn't very appetising.

'There you go. Tuck into that.' She passed a plate with a generous slice of ginger cake to each of them.

'Thanks Hettie.' Elspeth gave a sigh of appreciation. 'You are the best cook I've ever had the pleasure of knowing. It's been a privilege sampling your magnificent creations.' She took a bite of cake. 'Mmmm – it's delicious, as always!'

Hettie chuckled. 'It's good to be appreciated.'

'Oh, we do appreciate you Hettie, and not just for your cooking skills,' Marge said. 'You've become a dear friend, welcoming us from the moment we arrived here. It has felt like we've had a home away from home and we've been very lucky to get to know you and have Rookery House and everyone here as a new family. I'm going to miss it terribly.' Marge's voice caught and she blinked away tears.

Hettie reached across from her seat at the end of the kitchen table and patted her arm. 'It will only be a farewell for a while. I hope you'll come back and see us one day. And who knows, you might not be sent that far away.'

Marge managed a watery smile. 'We will come back.' She glanced at her fellow Waaf.

'Definitely,' Elspeth said with feeling, her mouth full of cake.

'We'll write from wherever the squadron ends up,' Marge said, 'and let you know where we are. Don't worry, we'll keep in touch.'

'How soon are you going?' Hettie asked.

'We can't tell you *when* exactly… but it *is* soon,' Elspeth said. She gave Hettie an apologetic smile. 'That's why we *had* to come and see you this afternoon. To give us a chance to say goodbye.'

Hettie got the message – the two young women, along with the rest of the squadron, would be leaving imminently, within days, she presumed. With the need to *keep mum* as the posters said, they couldn't – and shouldn't – tell her more than they had.

'I'm glad you came,' Hettie told them. 'It would have been sad for us three not to have a last get-together.' Hettie picked up her teacup and held it in the air. 'A toast in tea, wishing you both good luck at your new aerodrome, wherever that may be. And to our future meetings.'

The two Waafs raised their own cups and echoed what Hettie had said, before taking a sip of tea.

'What do you think about Americans coming to the village?' Elspeth asked.

'It was already a big change for us having RAF Great Plumstead built and seeing all our airmen and women move in and be about the village, the aeroplanes flying around and off at night then back in the early hours. The war has changed things in so many ways and it's about to do so again.' Hettie smiled. 'We'll have to wait and see this time – it might be interesting having Americans here.'

'It might!' laughed Elspeth.

'We must remember though,' said Hettie, 'that it's not just us villagers that will be affected. Think of how far the Americans will have come from their homes. It's going to seem very different for them, going to a strange country with new ways. From what I've seen of America at the pictures, it's not like here at all. That film we saw, *The Mask of Zorro*, it was all hot and dusty and looked nothing like Norfolk.'

'Oh, *The Mask of Zorro* and Tyrone Power!' Elspeth said in a dreamy voice, putting a hand on the front of her blue Waaf tunic over her heart. 'What a wonderful film and such a dashing hero.'

Marge rolled her eyes. 'You and Tyrone Power. It's just as well that picture came to the end of its run or we would have seen it even more times.'

Hettie laughed, recalling how, when she and Ted had gone

to see it at the pictures in Wykeham, the two Waafs were there too, watching it again after loving it so much the first time.

'Not all of America is how it was in *The Mask of Zorro*,' Marge said. 'We've seen films set in New York and it's all tall buildings, straight streets and traffic. Busy, noisy and bustling.'

'It will seem strange for them until they get used to it here,' Hettie said.

The back door opened and George, Betty and four-year-old Emily came rushing in, bringing a blast of cold air with them.

'Marge and Elspeth!' Betty cried, launching herself at the Waafs. Emily and George did the same.

'Where have you all been?' Marge asked, putting her arm around George.

'On a walk to the woods,' the little boy said. 'We saw some deer. They looked at us and then ran off.'

'Hello!' Thea said as she came in through the back door with Marianne who was carrying two-year-old Bea in her arms. Flo arrived right behind them.

After everyone had said their greetings, and coats, hats, scarves and gloves had been removed, they all settled at the table with food and drink and the conversation returned to the departure of the RAF squadron.

'I'm going to miss my pals,' said Flo, smiling wistfully at Marge and Elspeth. Being of a similar age, she had immediately become friends with the two Waafs when they'd come to stay and the three young women had often gone out dancing or to the picture house together when they'd had the chance. 'Will the Americans move in as soon as you leave?' she asked.

'Sort of.' Marge told her. 'From what we know, there's going to be a handover ceremony to transfer the aerodrome into the American's charge. An advance party will then prepare the place for the arrival of ground staff, aircrews, planes and so on. They might want to alter what's already there to suit themselves and do things their way and that will take time.'

'I should think so,' Marianne said, steadying the cup Bea was drinking from, the little girl sitting on her lap.

'It could be weeks or months, it all depends on what they need to do,' Elspeth replied.

'The Americans fly their planes during the day,' Thea said. 'Some mornings we've seen them come together from other aerodromes, gathering in the sky above like a whole host of buzzards before they head off on their missions.'

'Sounds daft going in the daytime when they can be more easily spotted,' Hettie said, with a shake of her head. 'At least our planes fly at night when it's harder to be seen.'

'They have their reasons, I suppose,' Flo said. 'We'll probably see and hear them going and coming back while we're out working in the garden. That will be one change.'

'Will we see them when we're at school?' George piped up, having finished his piece of cake.

'Perhaps.' Hettie exchanged glances with Thea and decided it was time to change the subject with little ears listening. 'Did you want to show Elspeth and Marge the new piglets who arrived this week?' She directed this question to George.

'Yes!' His face lit up. 'They're lovely. Would you like to see them Elspeth and Marge?'

'We would,' Marge told him enthusiastically. She and Elspeth were used to being shown new arrivals when they visited. 'I remember your new chicks and baby bunnies – and I would love to meet some piglets!'

'We might not get the chance to see *any* animals where we go next,' Elspeth added.

George's eyes grew wide. 'Then we'd better go now!' he

said, and without further ado he led the Waafs from the kitchen, the others – even Emily and Betty – smiling after them.

∼

When the time came for the Waafs to leave later that afternoon, everyone gathered in the back garden of Rookery House to say farewell. The two young women received warm embraces from each of the children and adults, with Hettie last of all to give them a tight squeeze.

Hettie found her eyes filling up. 'Let us know where you go,' she said, finally releasing Marge, 'write to us often and we'll write back and keep you up to date with how things are here.'

Thea threaded her arm through Hettie's. 'Remember,' she told the Waafs, 'you'll always be welcome here at Rookery House at any time.'

'Thank you all. We will miss you.' Marge's eyes were bright with tears.

'It's been a joy to be part of your Rookery House family,' Elspeth said. 'Thank you.'

'Safe travels and look after yourselves!' Hettie called as she watched the two young women mount their bicycles and pedal out of the gate, turning towards the village with a final wave.

'Are you all right?' Thea asked as they lingered for a moment, after the others had drifted away back to the house.

Hettie nodded. 'I don't like saying goodbye.'

'I know. I hope we will see them again sometime and stay in touch. People come and go all the time these days. I suppose it's always been the way of things, but this war has sped everything up.'

'Hasn't it just?' Hettie agreed. 'Elspeth and Marge leaving and the Dutch Professor arriving this week. An Italian POW soon after. And Americans.'

'No chance of getting bored around here, is there?' smiled Thea. 'At least it keeps us on our toes.'

Hettie sighed. 'I'm supposed to be retired, taking life easier after years of working all hours...'

'That will be the day when you take things easy.' Thea gave her a knowing look which made Hettie chuckle. 'You love being busy and involved. New people, fresh challenges, you thrive on it.'

'That's true enough,' Hettie said proudly, 'and I wouldn't have it any other way.'

CHAPTER 4

'Could you meet him for me, please? He's arriving on the one o'clock train,' Thea asked, her voice coming down the telephone wires from Rookery House. 'Only they're desperate for me to drive the ambulance today. There's no one else available who can do it. I know it's bad timing with Professor Van Gelder arriving this afternoon.'

'Of course I will,' Prue replied. 'I have nothing planned that can't wait.'

'Thanks so much.' Her sister sounded relieved. 'I had it all organised and then got a call from the hospital. I'll be home as soon as I can. Hettie should be back from her shift on the WI market stall by mid-afternoon so she'll be able to give him something to eat and drink.'

'Don't worry, everything will work out fine. I look forward to meeting the Professor.'

'I hope you like him. If he's a friend of Julia's, then he must be nice. I trust her opinion. Right, I must go and collect the ambulance. Thanks again. Bye.' Thea ended the call.

As Prue replaced the telephone receiver, she did a quick

rejig of her plans for this afternoon. She'd been going to spend it doing some sewing in the workroom along with other members of The Mother's Day Club. Now she would cut her sewing time short to make sure she was waiting at the station at one o'clock to meet the Professor from the Norwich train.

She returned to the kitchen where Nancy and her two daughters, ten-year-old Joan and eleven-year-old Marie, were having breakfast. Sitting down at her place at the table, Prue finished spreading blackberry-and-apple jam on her piece of toast, which she'd abandoned a few minutes ago to answer the telephone.

'Is everything all right?' Nancy asked, dipping her spoon into her bowl of porridge.

'Yes, that was Thea. She's been called in to drive the WVS ambulance today but was supposed to be meeting the Professor at the station this afternoon. I'm going to meet him instead and take him back to Rookery House,' Prue explained.

'What's a Professor?' Marie asked, her expression curious.

'Someone who's done a lot of studying and learning,' Nancy told her daughter. 'He works at a university in London, so Thea told me. Sounds like 'e's a very clever man.'

'What's a university?' Joan asked.

'It's a sort of school only for grown-ups,' Prue explained. 'With work that's much harder.'

Joan pulled a face. 'Harder than the nine times table?'

Prue and Nancy exchanged an amused glance.

'Much, much 'arder,' Nancy said. 'But *you* still need to learn your nine times, miss. There ain't no getting out of that.'

Joan let out a groan.

Prue sympathised with the girl who struggled learning her times tables and the nine times she was supposed to be working on now was proving a challenge.

'You'll get there.' Prue gave her an encouraging smile.

'Learn a couple of the nine times each day and before you know it, you will have mastered them all.'

Prue arrived at Great Plumstead station with five minutes to spare before the train was due in. Although these days it was more likely to be late than on time, what with passenger trains often having to make way for those carrying things for the war effort. She pushed her gloved hands into the pockets of her coat to keep warm. It might be sunny today but it was cold and crisp, the sky a washed-out blue. There'd probably be another frost tonight as there was last night, Prue thought, watching her breath plume in the air.

She'd left a group of women from The Mother's Day Club busy working back at her house with Gloria in charge should they need anything. They'd had a batch of airmen's holey socks come in this morning for mending with a request that they please be done urgently. No reason had been given for the urgency but everyone knew the airmen were leaving the aerodrome soon. Gloria had suggested the men were wisely taking the opportunity to get all their pairs of socks in good order while they could. Wherever they went to next, they might not have the services of people willing to mend their socks for them, as they had here in Great Plumstead.

'They'll miss us when they're gone,' Gloria had predicted. 'So let's get their socks mended to our highest standards an' give 'em something to remember us by!'

Everyone had immediately stepped up to the task, putting aside their original sewing plans to spend the afternoon darning. Prue had left them working their way through the pile of socks. And of course, chatting merrily as they worked.

When the train came steaming into Great Plumstead five

minutes late, Prue thought that, since the start of the war, she'd got used to meeting strangers at the station. First to arrive were the expectant mothers on the day war was declared. Later on came mothers and children fleeing the bombing of the Blitz. On each of those occasions she'd had others with her to help – members of the village WI or Mother's Day Club. This time she was alone and was here to meet just one person. It should be straightforward, with no mix-up as had happened when the expectant mothers had arrived.

As the passengers for Great Plumstead disembarked, Prue scanned them, searching for Professor Van Gelder. All she knew was his name and her imagination had filled in the rest, picturing him as a studious-looking, older man with grey hair, round wire-rim glasses and wearing a tweed jacket. But there was no one of that description. The only likely candidate was nothing like Prue had imagined – but he'd spotted her staring and was walking towards her, carrying a large suitcase in one hand and a smaller, square case in the other. He smiled at her tentatively.

'Are you Thea Thornton?' His voice had a slight, lilting accent.

'No, that's my sister. I'm afraid Thea's been called away to drive an ambulance so she asked me to come and meet you instead.' She held out her hand to him. 'I'm Prue Wilson.'

He put down his cases and removed his hat, revealing dark brown hair with a few strands of silver at the sides. He gave a small bow of his head before replacing his hat and shaking her still outstretched hand, his dove-grey eyes meeting hers. 'I'm Max Van Gelder. I'm pleased to meet you, Mrs Wilson.'

Prue gave him a welcoming smile. He was nothing like she'd imagined and certainly much younger – she guessed he was a similar age to her, so somewhere in his forties. He had a calm air about him, his eyes curious and thoughtful. 'Welcome to Great Plumstead, Professor Van Gelder.'

'Please call me Max.'

'And do call me Prue.'

'Prue... is that short for something?'

'Prudence,' she admitted, disliking the sound of her full name on her tongue.

He nodded. 'But you prefer Prue?'

'Definitely!' she said. 'The other is...' she waved her hand. 'Too long, too fussy.' And what her late husband Victor always insisted on calling her. Victor was the only person who had, apart from his odious brother, even though they both knew full well that she disliked it.

'Prue it is.'

'I'll take you to Rookery House and Thea will see you there later. She's sorry that she couldn't be here to meet you as planned.'

'It's fine, I understand. I appreciate you stepping in instead.' Max picked up his cases and fell into step with her as she led the way out of the station. 'Does your sister often drive ambulances?'

'Now and again when she's needed. It's for the WVS. Thea drove ambulances in France during the Great War so has the skills and experience. Most of the time she drives a WVS canteen and I work in there with her,' Prue explained as they walked along, leaving the main part of the village behind and heading towards Rookery House.

'Julia speaks highly of Thea.'

'Rightly so,' Prue agreed. 'My sister is an amazing person and has achieved a lot in her life. I'm very proud of her.'

'I look forward to meeting her. Do you have other siblings?'

'One younger sister, Lizzie, and I had two brothers,

William and Reuben. William was killed in the Great War. Reuben survived and lives near Rookery House. You're going to have a bedroom in his home. It's small but cosy.'

'I'm very grateful to have a room and be able to live out in the countryside for a while.' Max glanced at Prue and smiled.

'Thea said you're here to convalesce.'

'That's right. I had pneumonia and my doctor recommended I get out of London for some cleaner air to aid my recovery. My work I can do anywhere.'

'It's certainly fresher here.' Prue breathed in a lungful of cold, clean air. 'I hope it helps you recover.'

'I'm sure it will as I could smell the difference as soon as I got off the train. There's no smoke from thousands of chimneys in it. It will be good for me here.'

'What work do you do at the university?' Prue asked.

'I'm a Professor of languages. At the moment, I'm doing a lot of translation work,' he explained.

'Thea told me you can speak Italian.'

'That's right, and French, German and passable Spanish too.'

'And Dutch,' Prue added.

He gave a wry smile. 'And Dutch, of course. How about you?'

'Oh, nothing like that. I can only speak English. They didn't teach us any languages at the village school here.'

'I was fortunate to have the chance to learn them,' Max said. 'It's given me an interesting career. I enjoy travelling to other countries so being able to speak the language is useful.'

'I've never been abroad but I'd like to one day. It would be good to experience other places and meet the people.' Prue's mind drifted to where she might visit first if she had the chance. Paris perhaps, or the south of France? Or how about the snow-topped Swiss Alps? Places she'd read about and wished to see for herself.

'I hope you do go abroad when it's safe to travel again.' He sounded sincere.

'We'll see. But we need the war to be over first.' Prue spotted the chimneys of Rookery House, reminding her of what she was supposed to be doing now. Pushing fanciful dreams of travelling aside, she pointed ahead. 'Not far now. That's Thea's house.'

Walking in through the gate a few moments later, Max halted and surveyed the red-brick Victorian house. 'It looks a lovely home.'

Prue stood beside him regarding her sister's house. She was so used to it she rarely took much notice of how it looked. As if seeing it through fresh eyes, she took in the ground floor bay windows on either side of the front door and the row of three sash windows on the upper floor. 'It is a lovely place. Thea always loved it from when she was a child. She used to say she'd live here one day. It took many years but she eventually got her dream. Reuben's home is rather different, though in a lovely spot in the garden. It's round the back. Would you like to follow me there now or have a rest and some refreshment first?'

'Lead the way,' Max said with enthusiasm.

Prue led Max around the house. She pointed out the back door as they passed by. 'Everyone goes in and out of that door into the kitchen. The plan is for you to have your meals in there with the others. You're in for a treat as Hettie's an excellent cook – she was the Cook at Great Plumstead Hall before she retired so is highly skilled. Plus, rationing hasn't hit so hard here as in London. At Rookery House they produce and grow most of their own food.'

'I look forward to it. In London I ate a lot in British

Restaurants. They were fine and it was simpler than doing my own cooking. But I'm sure Hettie's meals are far better.'

'They definitely are!' Prue gestured towards Reuben's, which stood about fifty yards away from the main house near the orchard. 'There's your new home for a while. It's a converted railway carriage. My brother's made a good job of altering it into a comfortable place to live.'

'How interesting, and a clever idea,' Max said appreciatively as they approached. 'This is an excellent dwelling, well made, with a lot of care put into it.'

'There are quite a few railway carriage homes about, as it's an easy and less expensive way to make a house. Thea would have had Reuben go and live with her, but he's a quiet man and preferred this rather than the hustle and bustle of Rookery House, which is sometimes bursting at the seams with all those Thea gives a home to,' Prue explained.

Max smiled at her. 'I am the same as Reuben. I like quiet too and am a peaceful person, I think. Reuben's place will be perfect for me.'

'Come on in.' Prue led them up the short flight of wooden steps to the end door. 'It's very cosy,' she added, opening it and leading the way inside. 'I've always liked it in here.' She gazed around the main living room, which had a stove with two armchairs by it. There was a table to one side and a kitchen area. 'This is your bedroom.' She opened a door leading off the living room and motioned for Max to go in.

He stood looking about him at the single bed, the chest of drawers and table and chair under the window. It was neat and compact. Turning to Prue, he smiled. 'This will do nicely. I can work at the table. My typewriter,' he gestured at the smaller square-shaped case which he'd put down on the floor, 'is noisy so I shall only use it while Reuben is out.'

'I know you'll be welcome in the main house anytime too.

Not just for meals. Although as I've said, it can get quite busy – you might be glad of having a quiet place to retreat to.'

'Perhaps, but I enjoy the company of others too. Who else lives in the house?' Max asked.

'There's Thea and Hettie, who I've told you about. Flo's a Land Girl who works in the garden here. Then there's Marianne; she came as an evacuee expectant mother and has two daughters, Emily and Bea. Thea also looks after two evacuee children, George and Betty.' Prue counted each of them off on her fingers. 'So eight in total. They're all lovely people and will welcome you. Now, can I get you anything to eat or drink before I go?'

'No, I'm fine, thank you. I'll unpack and settle in.'

'Hettie's due back soon and no doubt will come and find you. I expect you'll get a tour around the garden, grounds and main house soon. I hope you'll be happy here and recover well.'

'Thank you, I'm sure I will. I appreciate you coming to meet me at the station – thank you, Prue.' He held out his hand to her.

Prue shook it, giving him a warm smile. 'You're welcome. I'll see you again sometime.'

'I'll look forward to it.' Max returned her smile.

Releasing his hand, Prue thought that if her instincts were right, Max would make a positive addition to the Rookery House family. She might have only spent a short time with him but she had a good feeling. Her years of being married to Victor had attuned her to people's characters and moods – especially their negative ones. From what she'd seen so far of Max, he was easy-going himself and had put her at ease too. She was sure he was going to fit in well and looked forward to getting to know him better.

CHAPTER 5

Thea's day of ambulance driving turned out to be a longer one than she'd expected so the evening meal at Rookery House was finished by the time she got home.

'Here she is now!' Hettie greeted Thea when she opened the back door and stepped into the warm kitchen filled with the aroma of delicious food.

As her stomach rumbled, Thea realised how hungry she was. She'd had little opportunity today to snatch more than a biscuit and a cup of tea since breakfast.

'I'm sorry to be so late. There were more patients to move than planned.' Thea gave her friend an apologetic smile.

'Don't worry, you're here now. I've kept your meal warm for you.' Hettie got up from the table and went over to the stove to fetch it.

'Thank you,' Thea said gratefully before turning her attention to Rookery House's new resident – the Professor. He was seated at the table with Flo. Marianne must have taken the children into the sitting room after they'd finished eating as the youngsters liked time to play quietly or have some stories read to them before bedtime.

'Hello, Professor Van Gelder.' She reached out her hand to him. 'Welcome to Rookery House. I'm sorry I wasn't here to meet you this afternoon.'

'No need to apologise. And please call me Max.' He stood up and shook hands.

Thea returned his friendly smile, noticing what kind eyes he had. 'Max it is then,' she replied. 'And please call me Thea.'

'Prue told me you'd been called away to drive ambulances. I hope all went well.'

'Yes, it was a productive day, thank you, just an extra busy one.'

Hettie put down a hot plate of stew, mashed potato and carrots for Thea. 'You must be hungry so tuck in.'

'That looks wonderful, thank you Hettie.' Thea sat down beside Flo and ate, savouring every tasty morsel while Hettie added a bowl of apple pie and custard for Thea's dessert.

'Max has already had a guided tour of the garden,' Hettie informed Thea as she returned to her seat at the table. 'Flo, Marianne and the four children showed him around earlier.'

'George and Betty were rather keen to give Max a tour as soon as they got home from school,' Flo added with a grin. 'I don't think we missed out a single thing, from observing the distant beehives to walking around Primrose's byre, and everything else in between!'

'It was excellent and most informative,' Max said. 'I even stroked Primrose – which was the first time I've ever touched a cow. Young George told me he'd never seen one before he came to the village.'

'It was the same for most of the evacuees from London,' Hettie said. 'Coming to live in the countryside has given them a whole new experience of life. It's been remarkable to see how well George and Betty have settled in. I think they love it here now.'

'They do,' Thea agreed, still working her way through her meal while she listened.

The conversation flowed back and forth between them as Thea ate. Hettie and Flo told Max about what went on in the village, explaining all about The Mother's Day Club and how Great Plumstead Hall had been turned into a hospital, and that Evie, who used to live at Rookery House, was a nurse there. When Hettie and Flo started to clear the table, Max stood up to help.

'Leave it to us.' Hettie waved her hand at him to sit down again.

'But I would like to help,' he said.

'You can another time. It's your first night here so we'll see to the clearing up and dishes. But there'll be plenty more opportunities to help with it the future if you're willing.' Hettie chuckled. 'An extra pair of hands is always welcome at Rookery House.'

'Then I will start helping tomorrow – it will be my way to say thank you for a delicious meal. Prue already told me you're an excellent cook, Hettie, and she was right,' Max said.

Hettie's cheeks grew pink. 'My pleasure. I enjoy cooking.'

'If you'll excuse me, I will return to Reuben's house. It's been a long day and I'm tiring. My energy hasn't fully returned after my illness.' Max stood up. 'Goodnight all and thank you for making me so welcome.'

'You must rest to help you recover properly,' Hettie said sympathetically. 'Sleep is a great healer.'

'Can I walk with you back to Reuben's?' Thea asked, after handing her empty plate and bowl to Hettie.

Max nodded. 'Of course.'

Outside, as they walked towards the railway carriage

house, Thea enquired, 'Is your room suitable for your needs? Julia said you'll be working while you're here?'

'Yes, it has everything. I like it. I've met Reuben and he seems very nice,' Max reassured her. 'I'm glad to be here and appreciate you taking me in.'

'If there's anything else you want, please let me know.'

'Thank you, Thea, I will.'

'Did Julia explain to you about the Italian Prisoner of War I'm hoping to have come and work here?'

'She did and she told me you'd like me to translate for you if he can't speak English. I will be happy to do that and assist in any other ways I can.'

Thea nodded. 'Thank you. Your coming here is perfect timing and will make an enormous difference for us and the POW.'

'I'll be glad to help. How soon will he arrive?' Max asked.

'I'm not sure. I've applied to the local representative of the War Agricultural Executive Committee and am waiting to hear from him. If all goes well, I'm hoping the POW could start in the next week or two.'

They reached the steps of Reuben's house and came to a halt. 'Good night then,' said Thea, 'and I hope you sleep well. It will seem quieter here than in London. I remember how silent it seemed when I moved back after living in the city for many years. Even though I'd grown up in the village, it was quite a shock to be without the constant hum of activity all around.'

'I'm sure I'll soon grow used to it here,' Max said. 'It will seem peaceful.'

'It will...' Thea gave a rueful smile, 'until, that is, you hear the owls hooting, foxes barking and Caesar, our cockerel, crowing his alarm to welcome the day! His early morning greetings aren't always so welcome.'

'Then it's lucky I'm an early riser!' laughed Max. 'Good night, Thea.'

'Good night, Max.'

With a small wave, Thea headed back to the main house, glad that despite her unexpected and hectic day the Professor – or Max, as she would now think of him – was here and settled in. Importantly, he seemed to have a very pleasant character and would fit in well with life here at Rookery House. Having new people join them was always a risk in case it upset the harmony, but with Max they were lucky to have been sent an instantly likeable and interesting man.

CHAPTER 6

After spending the morning on duty at The Mother's Day Club in the village hall, Prue was now on her way to this afternoon's task – a visit to the Women's Institute allotment. With spring just around the corner, she needed to check all was in order and think about what they wanted to grow this year, building on the success of the past three years since they'd taken over the allotment. Although back then, 'allotment' was rather an optimistic description of what they'd been given. The tangled thicket of brambles, nettles and docks was nothing like the well-tended plots belonging to other plot-holders. But with hard work, dedication and aching muscles, the volunteers from the village's WI and Mother's Day Club had turned it into a productive plot that they were proud of. The vegetables and fruit they grew there were sold on the WI stall at Wykeham market and proved very popular.

Walking along the road leading out of Great Plumstead, heading to where the allotments were sited, Prue heard engines coming her way. She stepped onto the grassy verge just as a convoy of vehicles rounded the bend behind her.

They must have passed through the centre of the village and, although she was used to seeing military vehicles going this way to the aerodrome, these were clearly different. The jeeps and lorries had white stars on the khaki paintwork of their cab doors and, most strikingly of all, their steering wheels were on the wrong side. The Americans had arrived!

As they went by Prue, each of the drivers gave her a cheery wave and she returned their greeting. As the final lorry passed her, men sitting in the back raised their hands. These were clearly the Americans who'd come to take over the aerodrome. The last of the remaining RAF staff would now leave. It was the end of an era and the beginning of a new one.

Prue set off again towards the allotment, her mind full of questions. Apart from their vehicles, she wondered what other changes the new arrivals would bring.

'Afternoon Missus!'

The man's voice startled Prue. She had been so engrossed in her thoughts that she'd not taken much notice of her surroundings; she had already turned into the allotments.

'Good afternoon, Percy.'

'Is everything all right?' he asked, leaving what he was doing at the far end of his well-tended plot and walking over to her. 'Only you looked miles away when you came in here.'

'I'm fine.' She gave him a reassuring smile. 'But I just saw a convoy of Americans heading to the aerodrome.'

Percy's eyes widened. 'They're here then? I thought I heard something on the road.' He reached into his tweed jacket pocket and took out his pipe, a small tobacco tin and a box of matches and proceeded to fill the pipe's bowl, pressing the flakes of tobacco in with his dirt-smudged thumb. 'Well, we all knew they were coming soon. There's been plenty of RAF lorries heading out these past few days and the planes flew out on Wednesday and haven't come back. It was just a matter of time.' He put the stem of the pipe in his mouth, struck a match and then sucked in smoke, the tobacco glowing orange in the bowl.

'Apparently there will be an official handover from the RAF to the Americans, so I suppose that's happening today,' Prue mused. 'Then the last of the RAF personnel will leave,' she added.

Percy nodded, puffing away on his pipe. 'I'll miss the lads. They were a good bunch who used to come in the Half Moon of an evening.'

Prue had often seen RAF men and Waafs bicycling into the village to go to the pub. 'Perhaps the Americans will visit instead.'

'Maybe. So what are you planning on doing here this afternoon?' Percy asked, throwing a glance over to the WI allotment which stood at the far end of the path, the last plot on the site.

'I want to see how things are doing and have a think about what to grow this year. I've got potatoes chitting at home...'

Percy nodded approvingly.

'...and I have sown some broad beans and peas too, but I'm growing them indoors until they're ready to plant out, otherwise – as we learned the hard way – mice will eat the seeds. What about you?'

'I'm sorting out the old shed and making an outside pen, joining on to it.' Percy gestured towards the wooden building standing at the rear of his plot.

'A pen? What for?' Prue asked curiously, wondering if this was Percy's latest idea for growing something for the Village Show. Percy was never short of a new idea and winning prizes for his vegetables was one of his top priorities.

'It's for a pig!' Percy exclaimed, grinning. 'It'll belong to me, Bert and Wilfred,' he said, referring to his good pals who also had allotments. 'We have been promised a piglet when it's ready from Crossways Farm, so we're making the necessary arrangements. It's all legal and above board and we'll feed it on scraps and foragin's – acorns and such. All being well, we'll have our own home-produced pork and bacon come the wintertime.'

'That sounds wonderful. My sister Thea does the same and it works well.'

Percy looked pleased at the mention of Thea. 'I had a word with your sister a while back when I saw her in the village. Asked her about what she did and how. She gave me plenty of tips – she knows her stuff and was happy to share her knowledge, which isn't always true of some folk around here.' He gave a sour glance towards the allotment directly behind his.

'Thea is always pleased to share her experience. She learned much of what she knows the hard way and if she can help others avoid the mistakes she made, she will.'

'That's the right spirit,' Percy said, smiling again.

'You'll enjoy the meat even more,' Prue told him, 'having produced it yourself.'

'That's the plan.' Percy winked. 'Right, I'd best get back to work.' He touched the brim of his cap, then returned to his pen building.

Prue walked on, wondering if maybe they should have a pig at the WI allotment, but she quickly dismissed the idea. It would be a whole extra lot of work and commitment. Animals needed tending to daily, and more than once. Someone would need to check on it, feed and water it and so on. No, she decided, she would stick with growing fruit and vegetables, and she would continue sending her scraps and leftovers to Thea's for her piglets. Prue was too busy with other things to take care of a pig.

Arriving at the WI plot, she cast her gaze around. The rows of leeks were doing well and would be ready to harvest soon to sell at the market, and the winter spinach was looking good now that it was protected from hungry pigeons under an arch of chicken wire. Prue took her notebook and pen from her handbag and began noting down what needed to be done.

CHAPTER 7

It was Monday morning and Hettie had bicycled into the village to do some shopping at Barker's grocery shop. She had just propped her bike against the shop's wall and was removing her basket from the bike's carrier when a khaki-coloured jeep with a white star on its bonnet came driving along the street and pulled up alongside her. Hettie stared at the jeep, noticing the steering wheel placed oddly on the wrong side and then the driver, who was the first American she'd ever seen in real life.

The young man gave her a wide, beaming smile and launched himself out of the jeep in one swift movement.

'Morning, ma'am,' he said. 'Can I help you with that?' He gestured towards the wicker shopping basket in her hand.

'Good morning,' Hettie said as she took in his smart olive-green tunic, trousers, shirt, tie and forage cap, thinking how stylish it looked. She noticed the three stripes of a sergeant on his upper arm. 'My basket isn't heavy but thank you for the offer,' she told him, already won over by his polite manner.

'Eugene McKenzie.' He removed his forage cap and put out his hand.

'I'm Hettie Brown,' she told him, shaking hands. 'Welcome to Great Plumstead, Eugene.'

'I appreciate your welcome, thank you, ma'am. It's sure good to be here, a real pretty place. So quaint. Let me get the door for you.' He bounded up the three steps leading to the shop door. The bell above it tinkled loudly as he opened it and then stood to one side, holding the door with an outstretched arm to let Hettie pass through.

'Thank you.' She gave him a warm smile as she went in, thinking what lovely manners he had and how his rich voice was straight out of the films she'd seen at the pictures.

Their arrival was greeted by a welcoming, 'Good Morning,' from Grace Barker, who stood behind the long wooden counter at the back of the shop.

Hettie noticed her taking in the American just as she'd done. After Hettie made the introductions, Eugene removed his cap once more and shook Grace's hand.

'How can I help you, Eugene?' Grace asked.

'I think Hettie is first. She arrived before me.' He gestured for her to step forward to the counter.

'I've a lot of things to get.' Hettie took her shopping list out of her handbag and waved it in the air. 'You'd be wiser to go first.'

'Well, if you're sure, thank you. I've come to buy a newspaper. Can you recommend one for me?' He glanced at the piles of different papers on the counter.

'I always have the *Eastern Daily Press*,' Hettie said. 'It's the local paper but has national and international news in as well.'

'I agree,' said Grace, 'the local news will help you get your bearings.'

'In that case, I'll try a copy of that, please, ma'am. How

much is it?' Eugene removed his wallet from his tunic pocket and shook out a handful of coins into his hand.

Grace took a copy of the paper from the pile. 'That's a penny ha'penny, please.'

The American poked at the coins in his palm, pushing them about and squinting at them. 'I'm still not used to the money here. There are so many types, halfpenny, shilling, thruppenny...' He shook his head.

'Here, let me help.' Hettie selected the right money and handed the coins to Grace, who passed him his newspaper.

'Thank you.' He beamed at her. 'I guess I'll get the hang of them but just now everything sure is new.'

'Are you one of the airmen now staying on the aerodrome?' Grace asked. 'We heard the RAF left last week after the Americans arrived.'

'Yes, I'm based at the *aerodrome*,' he said, speaking the last word as if he wasn't familiar with it, 'though we call it an *airbase*. But I'm not an airman. I belong to the Quartermaster Company. It's our job to get the base ready for when the air and ground crews arrive.'

'What does that involve?' Hettie asked.

'First we need to catalogue what's already there and then bring in and organise anything else that's needed, from food and fuel to bed linen. We must be sure that when the crews arrive, they have everything they need to live and work on the base,' he explained.

'Sounds like quite a task,' Grace acknowledged.

He grinned. 'I suppose so, but it's what we do. We're used to it, so it really isn't so bad.'

'How long will it take?' Hettie asked.

'Maybe six to eight weeks, but we'll get it done as fast as we can.'

'Good luck. And I hope you'll enjoy being here in Great Plumstead,' Hettie told him.

'Thank you, ma'am, I'm sure I will. I love the countryside around here – it's so green. I come from California where it's a lot drier and hotter than here.'

'Like in *The Mask of Zorro*!' Hettie blurted out, feeling herself blush. 'I mean the film. It's set in California, so I've been told.'

'You've seen that movie?' he asked, his eyes widening in surprise.

'I have,' Hettie said, 'at the pictures in Wykeham last year. I enjoyed it very much. It was a good story and the setting was so different from here. It whisked me away to another place for a while.' Hettie chuckled. 'And now you've come here from California to a much greener England, you must feel whisked away too!'

'I loved that movie and I love seeing different places as well. It's always interesting to meet new folks like yourselves. I could talk all morning and especially about movies but...' He lifted his sleeve and glanced at his wristwatch. 'Gee, you must excuse me, because I need to get back to work. It's been a real pleasure to meet you both. Have a good day.'

'Hope to see you again,' Grace said.

'Goodbye Eugene,' Hettie added.

'I'll be back, thank you both.' He raised his hand and left, the bell above the door tinkling loudly as he went out.

Moments later, they heard the jeep engine starting up and he drove away.

'Well!' Grace let out a long breath. 'He was a blast of fresh air, wasn't he? Lovely manners and that smile...' Her eyes met Hettie's and they both laughed.

'He'll be setting young women's hearts a'fluttering around here, that's for sure,' Hettie said. 'What a handsome chap, and that uniform is so smart, and his voice... straight out of a film at the pictures. If the others are going to be like him, having Americans here is going to cause quite a stir.'

'It already has!' Grace laughed again. 'And at least we know what's happening at the aerodrome for the time being and that it will be a little while before the planes arrive. Now, what can I get for you today?'

Hettie handed over her list along with Max's ration book.

'This is for the Dutch Professor?' Grace read the name on the front. 'How's he settling in?'

'Very well, he's an amiable man and fits in with everyone. Most of the day he's doing his work in Reuben's home but he comes over to Rookery House for his meals.'

'You've had a lot of different people come and stay there since the start of the war,' Grace said as she gathered the things on Hettie's list and put them on the counter.

'We have, but I like it. If I hadn't taken up Thea's offer to move in with her after I retired, I'd probably be living in a cottage somewhere on my own and feeling quite lonely. It's given me another lease of life and a new family as well.'

CHAPTER 8

A week had passed since Max had arrived at Rookery House and today another new arrival would join them – an Italian Prisoner of War. Thea had quickly finished her breakfast and was now waiting in the gateway by the road, watching out for the lorry that would bring the POW. He would be dropped off here around eight o'clock, so the letter from the local representative of the War Agricultural Executive Committee had informed her.

Pacing up and down to keep warm, Thea wondered if she was doing the right thing employing someone who, in all likelihood, she wouldn't be able to communicate with easily. Max was here to translate for her, but he had his own work to do so would not be around all the time. What if a problem arose when they were out in the field and she couldn't explain what she wanted? How much extra time would it take her to have to show the POW what to do, rather than simply tell him, as she did with Nancy or Flo? Thea was already busy enough – was taking on a POW going to be an added burden on her? She very much hoped not.

'Auntie Thea! Is he here yet?' The sound of George's voice stilled her pacing, and she turned around to see him, Betty and Max heading towards her from the back of the house.

'Not yet.' She opened her arms to catch George as he ran to her and pulled him into a hug, then did the same with Betty, who, not to be outdone by her younger brother, arrived at top speed.

'Is he late?' Betty wondered.

'Not really,' Thea said. 'He'll be here soon.'

'In a lorry?' George asked.

'I think so, maybe the same one that goes past each morning, the one taking the POWs to the farms on the estate. POWs work with Uncle Reuben sometimes,' Thea told him.

The children ventured out of the gateway so they could see further down the road towards the village, watching out for the familiar lorry.

'Another new person is coming and they are excited,' Max observed with a grin. 'I hope it is all right that they came out here with me? Hettie thought you wouldn't mind.'

'It's fine,' Thea reassured him. 'They always like meeting new people.' The children had still been eating their breakfast when she'd come out here to wait. Her own meal had been a small one today, her appetite rather lacking this morning.

'Are you concerned about having a POW coming to work here?' Max asked.

Thea made sure George and Betty couldn't hear them before turning to face him.

'A bit,' she admitted. 'Does it show? I'm just worried that he won't be able to speak enough English.'

'Even if he can't, we will still manage,' he said positively. 'I...'

Betty's shout interrupted him. 'It's coming!'

'I can see it!' George informed them, pointing.

The children returned to her as Thea's stomach lurched. How silly I am to be nervous, she thought. Her fears would quite likely prove groundless and the POW would speak and understand them well enough to get by. And if he didn't have a word of English, well then it was as Max had said. They would still manage. Either way they were employing a POW and she was about to find out what was in store. She was glad at least that the wait was finally over.

The lorry pulled up noisily beside them and the driver wound down his cab window and called to her, 'Miss Thornton? Rookery House?'

'Yes, that's right,' she said, feeling George's hand slip into hers.

The driver looked pleased and switched off his engine. 'We've got a POW for you,' he said cheerily as a second soldier got out of the other side of the cab, went around to the rear of the lorry and unhitched the end board.

Moments later a tall man jumped down from the lorry, waited patiently for the end board to be secured again, then followed the second soldier towards Thea.

'We'll pick him up again at five o'clock or there about,' the second soldier said. 'See you later.' He gave a brisk nod of his head before making his way swiftly back to his side of the cab and climbing in as the driver started the engine. Then the lorry drove off with a blast of exhaust fumes, a group of other Italian POWs looking out of the back at them, smiling and waving and calling out in Italian.

George and Betty waved back at them, beaming at each other.

Thea turned her attention to the POW, who she would guess was in his late thirties, with dark brown hair and friendly brown eyes. 'Welcome to Rookery House, I'm Thea Thorton.' She held out her hand to him.

'Luca Fontana,' he said, shaking hands. 'Good morning.' His English was spoken with a thick accent but she understood him clearly.

'This is Max,' she said, her hopes raised as she gestured to the Professor, who stepped forwards and shook hands with Luca.

'Hello,' Max said, sticking to English for the moment.

Luca looked at George and Betty, his face breaking into a wide smile as he spoke in rapid Italian to them.

The children looked confused.

'Luca says he has two children like you, a son and a daughter,' Max translated for them.

The POW fished in his brown battle-dress tunic pocket. He took out a photograph and held it for them to see, pointing to each person, first the woman, then the boy and girl standing by her side, all the while speaking in rapid Italian.

'His wife Carlotta, son Alfredo and daughter Maria,' Max told them.

Thea's spirits were sinking fast. The POW had spoken only two English words – *good morning*. 'Can you ask Luca if he speaks any more English?' she told Max, who quickly did as she'd asked.

Luca looked at her and gave a regretful shrug before saying slowly, 'Good Morning. Please. Thank you. Goodbye,' counting each word out on his fingers.

'Not much at the moment, but it's a start and we can help him learn more,' Max said encouragingly to Thea. 'What do you want him to do first?'

Thea felt deflated but did her best not to show it. 'Please tell Luca in Italian... welcome to Rookery House.'

Max obliged and Luca nodded enthusiastically in reply. 'Thank you,' he said. 'Thank you.'

'I think the best thing to do,' Thea told Max, 'is show Luca around the garden so he can get a feel for the place. I'll explain what we do here, while you translate for us, please. Then we'll see.'

'Sounds like a good plan,' Max agreed.

While he explained in Italian to Luca, Thea put her arms around George and Betty's shoulders. 'You two need to go in and get ready for school.'

'But...' Betty began before she was silenced by Thea's firm look.

'Today's a school day,' said Thea. 'And that means school is your job for the day. We all have our jobs to do, don't we?'

'Yes,' said Betty and Thea was pleased to see a look of maturity in her expression. 'Come on, George,' she told her younger brother, 'we'll see Luca later. He'll be working here all day and we'll be doing our work at school, won't we?'

'Will Luca still be here when we get home?' George asked, looking from his sister to Thea and back again.

'Yes,' Betty told him.

'Exactly right.' Thea gave the little girl a wink as Betty took her brother's hand and led him away.

'Bye Luca,' George said, before the two children broke into a run back to the house.

After the children had gone back indoors to get ready for school, Thea began the tour of the garden, first showing Luca the animals – the rabbits, chickens, pigs and Primrose their Jersey cow. She pointed out the beehives in the orchard from a distance, then walked around the greenhouse and vegetable beds before ending up in Five Acres field, which was half used for growing fruit and vegetables and half for a hay crop. All the while Max translated what she said in a steady stream of

Italian and Luca made short replies that sounded to Thea like he understood all he was being told.

'Can you ask Luca if he has any experience of growing vegetables?' Thea asked.

'Of course,' Max said and Thea listened as the two of them had a brief conversation, trying not to feel helpless at not being able to understand. She mustn't let her inability to converse with Luca overwhelm her. It was a challenge for both of them – and more so for Luca, who would be surrounded by people most of whom he couldn't talk to. It could be isolating for him and Thea needed to keep aware of that if she was to be a good host and make him feel part of the Rookery House community while he was working here.

Max turned to her. 'Luca grows vegetables at home in Italy and has worked on the estate farms in this area for the past year. He thinks you have a lovely place here and likes it very much, and he is sure he can do the work you need him for.'

Thea nodded at Luca, smiling to put him at ease. 'That's a start,' she said. 'Max, would you ask him, what did he do before the war?'

Again, Max relayed her question to Luca. To her surprise the pair of them were soon involved in an animated conversation which seemed to expand far beyond a simple answer, their hands gesturing and Max smiling openly and eagerly in a way she'd never seen until now.

'My apologies,' Max said, breaking back into English again and smiling sheepishly. 'I got carried away... Luca's family has a hotel on the shores of Lake Como in northern Italy. It is in a place called Varenna and I've been there! It's so very beautiful, Thea, with tiers of houses and guesthouses right down to the lake shore, winding cobbled streets and fishermen's cottages...' Max gave a wistful sigh. 'And the view out across the lake and to the hills beyond is... ah, it is stunning, Thea, truly a miracle of beauty.'

'It sounds heavenly,' Thea agreed, feeling Max's enthusiasm wash over her.

'I would like to return there someday.' He looked thoughtful, the spark in his eyes slowly fading. After a few moments he gathered himself, asking Thea, 'What work would you like Luca to start with this morning?'

Thea considered, thinking through the list of jobs she had planned for today. She would need to divide them up between her, Flo, Nancy and Luca. Barrowing loads of compost from the heaps to where she and Flo would be spreading it over the vegetable beds would be straightforward and perhaps a good first task for Luca. It would free up Nancy to work in the greenhouse, starting some seed sowing.

She explained the job to Max and then Luca nodded while he listened to Max translate.

'Is good,' Luca said finally and Thea was cheered by his use of more English words. Evidently he knew more than he'd counted on his fingers and the more he knew and learned the better it would be for everyone.

Later that morning, Thea took a breather, leaning on her spade as she watched Luca's back as he returned to fetch another load of compost.

'He's keeping us busy,' Flo said from nearby, pausing her compost spreading. 'We can barely keep up with him!' The Land Girl's cheeks were a rosy pink and she'd taken off her jacket.

'I've no complaints about his pace of work,' Thea said. 'And he *sounds* happy...'

They'd been treated to Luca's gentle singing as soon as he'd started loading his first barrow of compost and he hadn't stopped yet. Thea could still just about hear him from the far side of the garden where the compost heaps were. His songs were tuneful and uplifting and, despite not understanding a word, Thea had enjoyed their accompaniment to her otherwise rather monotonous labour.

'If we can't understand and speak to each other, we're not going to waste time chatting...' Flo said, with a wry smile. 'Not like me and Nancy, I mean!'

Thea laughed. 'I suppose that's true. Though don't mind me – you two can talk all you like while you work.'

'You shouldn't encourage us!' Flo said. 'Though I will miss her when she's gone. We've become a good team, Nancy and I. After a shaky start, she really found her feet.'

'I hope the same will happen with Luca,' said Thea. 'We'll need to give him plenty of time to settle in. It's not going to be easy for him with his limited English.'

'I'm sure he'll do well here,' Flo said. 'It looks like he's got the right attitude and that's a good start.'

As she worked, Thea thought through the day so far and considered how she felt about Luca's arrival. Her unease this morning had lightened. Luca was a friendly, hard-working man with a lovely cheery disposition. Thea just needed to be patient and find ways to work around the language barrier, but so far so good – especially as she was lucky to have Max here to translate when needed.

And Luca did already know a few English words. Working here on his own, away from other Italian POWs, there was a greater need for him to improve his English and, given time, Thea believed he would. All in all she was sure that having Luca working here would be a positive thing for everyone – including Luca.

CHAPTER 9

Hettie placed the covered jug of batter she'd just prepared onto the cold marble slab in the pantry. It was Pancake Day and she would make pancakes for pudding tonight. But before then she had another job to do – one of her monthly visits to the Land Girls as part of her role as local Land Army Representative. This afternoon she was going to call in at Crossways Farm to see Iris. The visit would be a brief one because Hettie was running late today but it was important that she checked on each Land Girl regularly. Besides, it would be pleasant to get outside and have a bike ride as it was one of those crisp, bright, late winter days when it felt like spring was just around the corner.

After putting on her coat, scarf, hat and gloves, Hettie fetched her bicycle from the shed. She was wheeling it towards the front of the house when she spotted a familiar figure riding through the gateway. It was her dear friend Ted Ellison, with whom she'd struck up a close companionship after he'd returned to the village nearly two years ago. They'd known each other as children and Ted had been good pals with one of Hettie's brothers before they'd lost touch when Ted moved away for work. Now retired, he'd come back to live with his sister Hilda, and had rekindled his friendship with Hettie. The pair of them enjoyed each other's company and often went out on trips together.

'Afternoon, Hettie. I was just coming to see you,' Ted said, dismounting his bike. 'Are you off out?'

'I'm going over to Crossways Farm to check how Iris is doing. Why don't you come with me?' she suggested. 'It's a lovely afternoon for a bike ride.'

'It certainly is. I'd be happy to accompany you. We can talk as we go.'

'I've missed seeing you. I was worried I might have said something that upset you.' Hettie gave him a searching look. She hadn't seen Ted since the day before Max had arrived, when he'd put in a few hours helping in the garden. That was almost two weeks ago now and it was unusual for him not to call in at least once a week.

Ted looked surprised. 'Of course you haven't! It's just that you've had a lot going on here with both your new arrivals and Hilda said I shouldn't be bothering you when you had a lot extra on your plate!'

Hettie put a hand on his arm. 'Oh Ted,' she chided, 'whatever else might be happening, I'll always have time for you. We're friends and you're important to me so tell Hilda you're welcome here no matter what's going on. Though I know she meant well.'

'She did,' Ted agreed. 'And more often than not, when I'm in need of advice, hers is spot on.' He put his hand over Hettie's. 'I missed seeing you and I'm sorry if I worried you. I didn't mean to. How did you survive without me?'

'I managed,' Hettie replied and they shared a look of amusement, their eyes twinkling. Hettie felt lucky to have a friend in Ted with whom she could be herself. There were no airs and graces with Ted and the easy understanding between them was something she cherished.

'So what brings you back today then? Come to find out what's been happening, have you?' Hettie stepped one leg over the frame of her bicycle, ready to push off.

Ted laughed. 'I'm here mainly to see you, Hettie,' he said. 'Though I have indeed been wondering how you were getting on with the recent additions to Rookery House. I hope it's been all right for you.'

She pushed off and pedalled out of the gate, calling back over her shoulder. 'Keep up, Ted!'

Moments later Ted had caught up with her and the two of them rode along side by side, heading into the village. 'Seriously though, are you managing with the new people? And is Thea and everyone else? I hope it's going well and your POW knows his stuff.'

Hettie threw him a reassuring smile, knowing that Ted cared not only about Rookery House's residents but about the garden as well. He'd invested time and effort in the place, sharing his expertise and experience to help improve things and regularly filling in for Nancy when she'd had days off to look after her unwell children. It was little wonder that he was concerned about the new arrivals, especially the POW who'd be working the land.

'I'm managing fine and so is everyone else at the house. I *was* a bit apprehensive, but both Max and Luca have settled in well. I don't know as much about Luca as I do Max, on account of Luca not being able to speak English, so our conversations have been very limited so far. All he's said to me is *hello*, *goodbye*, *yes please*, *thank you* and *delicious*, mainly speaking when he has his midday meal with us. Mind you, he knows more English than I do Italian, so I'm not criticising. And he's learning a few more words every day.'

'What about in the garden?' Ted asked as they slowed at a junction. 'Is Thea satisfied with his work?'

Hettie checked all was clear and turned right to head past the row of shops before replying. 'She is. I know Thea was worried at first but as each day goes by she's getting more confident about what he can do and with Max around to translate what she wants doing, it's working well. Luca has even learned how to milk Primrose and has taken over the afternoon milking from Thea, which is a big help for her.'

'And Nancy, is she still coping?'

'For the moment. Thea's giving her less physical tasks to do. How much longer she'll carry on I don't know but at least with Luca here it's taken the pressure off. Now Nancy can slowly wind down and Thea no longer has to worry about getting the work done. Luca has been a welcome and timely addition to those working in the Rookery House garden,' Hettie explained.

'And the Dutch Professor?' Ted asked.

'He's settled in well. Max is a quiet, studious man, kind and patient with the children. He's been no trouble at all. Reuben seems happy having him share his home.' Hettie put her hand up to wave to Grace Barker, who was rearranging the display in the window of her grocery shop. Turning her attention back to Ted, she asked, 'Are you happy now? Anything else you want to know?'

Ted chuckled. 'No, that will do for the moment. I'm pleased it's working out well for you all. It can't be easy having strangers come to live and work with you.'

'I suppose not but I try to view it as they are just friends we haven't met yet, and that's worked for me before. Remember, I didn't know Marianne, Flo or Evie before they arrived and they're like family to me now. All it takes is time and patience and a chance to get to know each other. You must come back to Rookery House with me after our visit to Crossways Farm. You can meet Max and Luca then.'

'That's a good way to view things. You're a wise woman, Hettie. And yes, I'd like to meet them later – thank you.'

They were through the village and were now approaching the entrance to the aerodrome when something else crossed Hettie's mind to tell Ted.

'Did you know the Americans call it an *airbase*?' she asked as she pedalled along lightly.

'No, I hadn't heard that. I've seen some of them driving about but haven't spoken to one yet.'

'I have.' Hettie told him about her meeting with Eugene last week in the village shop. 'That's how I know it's called an airbase and what's going on there.'

'Didn't I say you are a wise woman?' Ted said with a wry smile. 'There's not much goes on around here that you don't already know about.'

Hettie chuckled. 'Go on with you! I was in the right place at the right time to find out, that's all.'

As they reached the aerodrome gateway, Hettie turned her head to see what was going on, slowing her pedalling. Ted matched her pace, also looking. The two American servicemen on guard duty waved.

'Good afternoon!' they called, smiling broadly.

Hettie and Ted both returned their greeting.

If she hadn't been pushed for time, Hettie would have stopped and had a word with them. These two seemed as friendly as Eugene had been, and she would have liked to get to know them too and perhaps find out more about the goings-on at the aerodrome and what progress was being made. But that would have to wait for another day. Today she had her duties and a Land Army visit to make.

'Aren't they gorgeous?!' Iris was bursting with pride as she, Thea and Ted leaned on the pigsty wall, looking in at the ten young piglets. Like their mother, who lay on her side in a patch of sunlight, the piglets had the distinctive markings of the saddleback breed. Their skin was black except for a band of pink behind their heads that ran over their shoulders and down, giving them pink front legs.

'They look bright-eyed and healthy,' commented Ted.

'Delilah's such a wonderful mother to them.' Iris bent over the wall to scratch the sow's ear, prompting a gentle grunt of approval.

'You have a way with her,' Hettie remarked.

'I stayed up all night with her while she was farrowing,' Iris explained. 'I didn't want to miss anything and had to be on hand in case something went wrong. Luckily, she handled everything like an expert, which I suppose she is having had two litters before.'

'They are lovely,' Hettie said. 'And look at you!' She put her hand on the young woman's arm, giving it a gentle squeeze. 'Before you joined the Land Army, would you have pictured yourself cooing over a litter of piglets?'

Iris threw back her head and laughed, her blonde curls swaying. 'Never! I hadn't even seen a pig before. But I love living and working here on the farm and don't want to change it.'

'What did you do before coming here?' Ted asked.

'I worked in a factory in Nottingham. I'd lived in the city all my life and had hardly been out into the countryside, but I wanted to do something different and work outside.' Iris grinned. 'And here I am!' She beamed at Hettie, her blue eyes alight with happiness.

'All's going well then?' Hettie said, holding Iris's gaze for a moment, giving the Land Girl the chance to open up to her about any problems she might have.

'It is,' Iris reassured her. 'It couldn't be better.'

Hettie nodded. 'I'm glad to hear it.'

'Beattie's in the kitchen if you'd both like a cuppa,' Iris went on. 'I won't join you as I need to catch up with my other jobs – I've been spending too much time watching these lot!'

'I can understand that,' said Ted, 'they're hard to take your eyes off. Look at those pair!'

Hettie watched two piglets tugging at either end of a sprout stalk. When one let go and the other fell backwards with its prize, she, Ted and Iris all burst out laughing.

'We can't stop for tea, I'm afraid,' Hettie told Iris. 'Like you, I'm behind today but I wanted to drop by and see you were all right.'

'Thank you for caring – I do appreciate it. I was lucky to be sent here – *and* to have you looking out for me.'

'Beattie and Stan are fortunate to have you working for them,' Hettie said. 'The farm was getting into a bit of a state before you arrived. You've made a big difference here.'

Iris's cheeks grew rosy. 'It was hard for Stan managing the place on his own. There's only so many hours in the day and the list of jobs is never-ending.'

'Well, if you need anything at all, you can telephone me at Rookery House, day or night. And I will pop over here again next month – though maybe I'll see you at a WI meeting before then?'

'I hope so,' Iris replied, 'the WI meetings are so much fun and it's a chance to meet friends. Thanks, Hettie. It's good to know you're there for me.' Iris stepped forward and gave Hettie a hug. Then she took a last look at the piglets, who were now suckling from their mother, and sighed. 'I really must get on! Thanks for coming by. I'll see you soon.' With a parting smile to them both, she headed off across the farmyard to tackle her next job.

Hettie lingered by the pigsty for a few moments more, watching the piglets. 'I can understand what Iris means about spending time with them. I'm the same when we have baby rabbits or chicks back at Rookery House. It's lovely to see them playing and exploring their world.' She fell silent for a moment, smiling as some of the now milk-filled piglets snuggled up against their mother's bulk and closed their eyes to have a doze in the sunshine.

'They've got a full belly and now it's time for a sleep,' Ted said. 'Are we going?'

'We are.' Hettie put her arm through Ted's and steered him back to where they had left their bicycles leaning against a barn.

CHAPTER 10

Today was the last Monday in February and Prue was on WVS duty delivering pies for the Rural Pie Scheme. Dressed in her green uniform, with her matching green greatcoat and felt hat, she pushed the borrowed pram packed with baskets of freshly baked pies. The sky was overcast and a stiff, icy-cold wind blew from the north. She hoped the rain would hold off until she was home.

She'd just walked past Great Plumstead station when she saw and heard the train from Norwich leaving, steaming its way under the bridge en route for the next station. The smoke from the engine billowed upwards in loud, rhythmic puffs as it gathered speed.

'Ma!' a man's voice called from behind her.

Prue halted, turned around and her heart leapt at the sight that met her. It was her eldest son, Jack. Like her he was wearing a heavy greatcoat only his was khaki, and he had his kitbag balanced on his shoulder.

'Jack!' Her voice cracked.

'Hello, Ma.' He gave her that beautiful, charming smile of

his as he covered the ground between them in long strides, dropping his kitbag and sweeping her up into his strong arms. 'Good to see you.'

Prue closed her brimming eyes, returning his embrace, her heart bursting with happiness at seeing him. It had been far too long since they were last together – the army was in charge of her son's life now.

When he let her go, she stood back and stared at him, still holding onto his forearms.

'I didn't know you were coming.'

'I wanted to surprise you.' Jack's blue eyes danced with delight.

'You did that all right! It's a wonderful surprise. How long are you home for?'

'I've got a week's leave. I need to return to camp next Monday by 0700 hours so will have to start back on Sunday morning. It's good to be here.' He looked at the pram. 'Where are you off to with that?'

'Delivering pies. I told you in a letter about the pie scheme.'

He nodded. 'Don't suppose you've any going spare, have you? I'm starving.'

Prue laughed – Jack always had a healthy appetite. 'I do, as a matter of fact.' Despite her customers being told they must order and pay for what they wanted the week before, there were often some who didn't get around to it and asked to buy a pie on the day. So she always had a few extra pies with her – and if no one needed them, she bought them herself and she, Nancy and the girls had them for tea.

Jack was already eyeing the baskets of pies.

'What would you like,' she asked him, 'meat and veg or cheese and potato?' She lifted the cloths covering each basket so he could make a choice.

Jack's face lit up. 'Have you enough for me to have one of each?'

She laughed again. 'Luckily for you, I do.' She took a pie from each basket and handed them to Jack.

'Thanks, Ma.' He took a huge bite from one of them and chewed, a look of satisfaction on his face. 'Delicious! Just what I need. How much do I owe you?'

'My treat,' Prue told him. 'I'll be about an hour and a half delivering these. Are you going to go straight home? Remember, you'll have to sleep in your father's old bedroom.'

'That's fine. I'll get some kip until you come home. The trains were packed on the way here and it was hard to find somewhere to sit, let alone get any sleep. Is the spare key in the usual place?'

'It is.' Prue looked at him, still not quite believing he was there. She brushed some pastry crumbs off the lapel of his greatcoat. 'I'll see you later. It's good to have you back for a while.'

'See you soon.' Jack heaved his kitbag onto his shoulder with a swing of one arm and, with his pies in the other hand, he headed off towards their home.

Prue stood watching him go, thinking about how her day had changed in the most delightful way. She couldn't wait to spend more time with him, hear what he'd been doing and catch up with him properly. With him not being the best or most frequent of letter writers, out of all her children she knew the least about what Jack had been up to.

Though before that, she had pies to deliver and hungry customers waiting. Jack might be home, but her work still had to go on.

~

As things turned out, Prue didn't get a chance to have a proper talk with Jack until that evening, after Nancy had taken the girls up to bed. When Prue had returned home after the last of her pie deliveries she'd peeped in Victor's former bedroom and seen Jack was sound asleep. She'd left him sleeping and got on with making a hearty meal for their tea. Knowing her son, she suspected it was the delicious aroma of the stew cooking that finally roused him from his sleep. She heard him moving about upstairs before he appeared in the kitchen doorway in his slightly crumpled battle-dress jacket, his hair tousled, just as she was preparing to serve their meal.

'Is there room for another one?' he'd asked, smiling at Nancy and her girls who were already sat around the table.

'I should think so,' said Nancy, indicating the place set for him. 'Come and sit down. Did you 'ave a good journey 'ere?'

Jack had talked easily for a few minutes about his day's journey and then listened happily to Nancy's tales of the goings-on in the Rookery House garden. When the meal was finished though, Nancy had ushered her girls away promptly, giving Prue a look that said she knew full well how little time Prue would have with Jack. It was the same when Nancy's husband was home on leave. Their time together was never enough and every minute had to be made the most of. Prue mouthed a 'thank you' at Nancy and she and Jack said goodnight to the girls.

Now it was just the two of them. Prue had left the kitchen things until later and they'd relocated to armchairs by the fire in the sitting room. Prue watched her son, overjoyed to see him sitting there and glad to have him all to herself.

'That was the best food I've had in a long while, Ma.' Jack leaned back in his armchair, patting his stomach. 'I'm full up!'

'I'm glad you enjoyed it. Don't they feed you well in the Royal Engineers?' Prue asked.

'They feed us, but how well is debatable. It keeps us going but sometimes it is hard to tell what we're eating... though we still eat it. It's that or go without.' Jack gave a rueful smile. 'It makes me appreciate your meals all the more when I come home.'

'I enjoy cooking for you.' Prue's mind was brimming with questions but she was wary of bombarding her son with too many. Jack had always kept a lot to himself. 'What have you been doing lately?' she asked tactfully.

'Lots of training, preparing.'

'For what?' she probed.

'To do what army engineers do,' Jack said evasively. 'Build things, bridges and so on.'

Prue read the newspapers and listened to the wireless and was aware that at some point the British Army and its Allies must begin an offensive across the other side of the English Channel. They needed to fight and push the enemy back and help the invaded countries regain their independence. The big question was *when* this would happen. With the war now in its fourth year, it couldn't come soon enough and yet... an icy prickle slid down her spine. Jack would be part of that invading force. All of his training and the skills he'd learned would play an important role.

Prue had been grateful that his unit hadn't been posted overseas again. Since his return from Dunkirk, he'd been stationed in Britain, mainly somewhere in the North East. But she feared that his time on home shores was fast running out. She still had nightmares about those dark days after the news had come through about the British soldiers' retreat and their evacuation from Dunkirk. She'd listened to reports on the wireless not knowing where Jack was, if he was alive, injured or worse. The waiting was terrible. She'd been helpless to do anything and could only wait and hope. Thankfully Jack was one of the lucky ones and had been rescued from the beach and brought back to England. She was scared that next time he set foot in France and came up against the enemy, he might not fare so well.

'What's up, Ma?' Jack's voice returned her attention to the present.

'Nothing...' she hesitated. 'Actually, I was thinking about the last time you were in France. Do you know if you will go back there again?'

Jack shrugged. 'That's up to the army.'

'But all the training you do is to prepare for something.'

'Of course, but if you're asking when and where I honestly don't know, Ma. They only tell us that when we need to know. Any plans are top secret. We're all just waiting for a signal to get going, get back in there and do our jobs to win the war.' His eyes lit up as he spoke. 'That's what we've been preparing for.'

Prue nodded. While she was dreading Jack being involved in any attack, he was eager to go and she must support him.

'We're well trained and know what we're doing so we can act without hesitation when the time comes.' Jack looked at her. 'I know you worry and I promise not to take risks.'

Prue managed a smile. 'Worrying goes with the territory of being a mother!' She thought of Jack and his brother as being wholly her children although they were Victor's sons from his first marriage.

'Edwin's been in the thick of things far more than I have since Dunkirk. I know he's driving ambulances but he's still in a war zone. So much for Father's rejection of Edwin for being a conscientious objector. It was disgusting the way Father treated him.' Jack pulled a face. 'Father should have been ashamed of himself but I doubt that thought ever entered his mind in his entire life. He did what *he* wanted and expected everyone else to do the same.'

'He's gone now,' Prue said. 'We're free of his ways and wants and demands.'

'Are you all right, Ma? I mean, still living here and everything.'

'I am. I'm happy and doing things I enjoy and I like having Nancy and the girls in the house. You don't need to worry about me.' She gave him a warm smile. 'Now, what would you like to do while you're at home?'

'Sleep, eat good meals and visit Thea, Reuben and the others at Rookery House. I'm just glad to be back here for a bit, with no one telling me what to do and when.'

'Everyone at Rookery House will be pleased to see you,' Prue said. 'I'll keep you well fed while you're here and you can sleep as much as you want!'

Jack grinned. 'Thanks, Ma – that sounds perfect. It's good to be home.'

'And it's wonderful to have you here,' Prue added. She was going to savour every moment of Jack's leave and enjoy having at least one of her children with her for a while before he had to return to do his duty.

CHAPTER 11

'Afternoon, Thea, I've got a parcel here for the Professor.' The postman held out a brown-paper package wrapped in string.

'Thanks, Henry.' She took it from him.

'Settling in all right, is he?' Henry asked, hovering by the front door of Rookery House and in no hurry to leave.

'He is. Max – that's how he likes to be known – seems to like it here in the countryside very much.' She saw a glint in Henry's eyes as she named the Professor and suppressed a smile. News of a Dutch intellectual coming to stay at Rookery House had already spread rapidly through the Great Plumstead grapevine. Henry, a renowned gossip, would now have the name of 'Max' to share as he went on his round. Though he meant no harm of course – Henry simply liked to know what was going on and his job gave him ample opportunity to pass it on. His gossiping was in effect a service to the community, Thea thought. Everyone knowing other peoples' business was often useful and she'd had no end of people hearing news from Henry and then turning up at Rookery House to offer their assistance, especially in the early days of getting the garden going, when she'd needed all the help she could get.

That said, it was a sight to see when Henry stood motionless and carefully read a postcard before posting it through a house's letter box!

'I'll see that Max gets this straight away,' Thea told him, feeling the corners of her mouth twitching as she chuckled to herself.

'Righto.' Henry, who seemed mightily pleased with this latest snippet of gossip, touched the peak of his postman's cap and turned to go. 'I've got more packages to deliver today. No rest for the wicked!' He waved and went to fetch his bicycle from where he'd left it leaning against the gate.

'Bye Henry.' Thea closed the front door and returned to the kitchen where Flo, Nancy and Luca, who were on their afternoon break, sat together finishing their cups of tea.

'Who's that for?' Flo asked.

'Max.' Thea put the parcel on the table and drank the remains of her own tea. 'I'll drop it in to him and catch up with you in the field. I won't be long.'

She collected her coat from where she'd hung it over a chair and put it on. 'Flo, can you bank up the stove before you go out, please? Hettie will be back from The Mother's Day Club in half an hour and needs it hot for cooking on.'

Flo got up. 'Of course, I'll do it now.'

With a smile of thanks, Thea picked up the parcel and went into the scullery to pull on her boots, then headed outside, where the cool air hit her after the warmth of the kitchen.

As Thea climbed the wooden steps to the front door of

Reuben's house she could faintly hear the tapping of typewriter keys. Max was busy at work.

She knocked on the door before opening it and stepping inside, calling out, 'Max – it's Thea.'

The typing stopped and Max appeared in the doorway of his room.

'Ah, Thea.' He gave her a welcoming smile. 'Do you need me to come and translate for you and Luca?'

'Not at the moment, thanks. The postman's just delivered this while we were in the house having a tea break.'

'Thank you.' Max took the parcel from her, weighing it in his hand. 'More written translation work for me to do,' he guessed.

'Do you enjoy it?' Thea asked.

'Yes, I do. It has its challenges but it helps to keep the languages fresh in my mind. And it means I can spend time here away from London. How about you? Does your work make you happy?'

'It has its difficulties,' Thea admitted. 'It can be quite a responsibility when it's up to me to make the right decisions. Then again, I can't think of anything else I'd rather be doing. I enjoy working outside and I've always liked being my own boss.'

'What did you do before you came here?'

'I had a catering business in London. It was hard work but I had a good team of staff working for me. Selling the business gave me the money to buy Rookery House. I was ready to return to Norfolk after years of living in the city. I missed the countryside,' Thea told him. 'Do you miss Amsterdam?'

'I do, but it was the right thing at the time for me to accept the job in London and now I couldn't go back home even if I wanted to.' Max smiled weakly. 'It's out of my control.'

Thea would have liked to ask more about his decision to

move to London but if Max hadn't volunteered more information then it must be for a reason.

'I hope it won't be long before it's possible for you to go to Amsterdam again,' she said, 'and to travel to far-flung places like Italy.'

'I hope so too.'

'I'll leave you to get on then. See you later.'

As Thea let herself out, she couldn't help wondering what had brought Max to England. Was it just a chance to work at the university in London or was there something else? Everyone has a story in their life, she thought, but not everyone wants to share it. The same was true for many who had found their way to Rookery House. Perhaps in time Max would open up about his past life but whether he did or not was entirely up to him. In the meantime, it was important that she respect his privacy.

Walking into Five Acres field a few minutes later, Thea was met by the sound of singing. Luca's fine voice filled the air as he and Flo continued the hedge trimming that they'd begun this morning. Thea couldn't understand a word of the song as it was in Italian but the tune was upbeat and it made for a jolly accompaniment to a dreary but necessary annual task.

Luca might not have proper conversations with any of them except Max, but he'd already made a significant contribution to Rookery House and not just for his hard work, but for his cheerful manner. He was pleasant to be around and Thea felt a bounce in her step as she headed towards the others to begin work, relieved that she'd made the right decision to have a POW come and join them here.

CHAPTER 12

Hettie felt her heart swell with joy. Gathered around the table in the kitchen at Rookery House were many of the people dearest to her in all the world. None of them were related to her by blood but they were still her family – one built on friendship, respect and love.

It was something Hettie had never imagined having. She'd not married so had no children or grandchildren of her own. Her only close blood relations were her sister Ada, who was now housekeeper at Great Plumstead Hall, and her brothers Sidney and Albert, who had both emigrated to Canada many years ago.

She had expected her retirement to be quiet and lonely, living in a cottage on her own, but Thea had changed all that when she'd offered Hettie the chance to come and live with her at Rookery House. Not for one moment had Hettie regretted her decision to accept.

Now, seated at one end of the table, she gazed happily at everyone who had come together for this special meal. Sitting at the far end was Thea, with George and Betty next to her.

Along one side sat Flo and Marianne with her two girls; across from them were Reuben, Lizzie, Prue and Jack.

Max had excused himself from the gathering, asking if he could have a sandwich instead, as he had work that he needed to get finished today. Hettie also suspected that he felt he might be intruding on what was a family occasion with this being a farewell meal before Jack had to leave tomorrow morning. Hettie had reassured the Professor that he was welcome but he'd been adamant that a simple sandwich would be fine as he could eat it while he worked.

'You look miles away,' Marianne said, leaning towards Hettie so she could be heard above the clatter of cutlery on plates and the chatter of conversations as everyone tucked into the roast meal Hettie had prepared. 'Is everything all right?'

'Yes, I was just enjoying us all being together,' Hettie said. 'We must make the most of occasions like this.'

Marianne nodded, her eyes darting to Jack, who was talking enthusiastically to his uncle and aunts. 'It's so hard when they have to go back,' she said, lowering her voice.

Hettie put her hand on Marianne's arm, aware that the young woman spoke from bitter experience. She'd had to say goodbye to her husband Alex when he returned to his aerodrome and that last parting had been some time ago – more than two years, by Hettie's reckoning. Alex was being held as a Prisoner of War somewhere in Germany. Hettie knew it was difficult for Marianne, not knowing when she would see him again.

'It's going to be hard for Prue,' Hettie said, glancing towards where Prue sat smiling and listening to Jack hold forth. Hettie thought she was looking a little subdued, because she knew the inevitable was coming and Jack would be, once more, taken away from her.

'It never gets any easier to say goodbye,' Marianne said, sympathetically.

'Oops!' Hettie pointed to Bea, who had just dropped a chunk of roast potato on to her lap.

While Marianne attended to her daughter, Hettie turned her attention to her own meal, spearing a piece of carrot and dipping it in gravy before popping it in her mouth. As she chewed, she once again noticed Prue watching her son and sighed to herself. She knew Prue well enough to see the signs of strain on her face that betrayed the turmoil she was feeling inside. It was hard for Prue, with all three of her children off doing their bit she was left worrying about them and only seeing them for short periods while they were on leave.

As if sensing Hettie was looking at her, Prue turned her head and gave Hettie a smile that didn't quite reach her eyes. Her friend was doing her best to keep up appearances, Hettie thought, when inside she was feeling anything but fine. It was important that she keep an eye on Prue over the next few weeks to make sure she was all right. Prue was so busy doing things for other people, it was easy for her own emotional needs to be neglected. Hettie would make sure that didn't happen.

CHAPTER 13

'I've loved having you back at home for a while.' Prue mustered up a smile. Once again, she found herself standing on the platform at Great Plumstead station saying goodbye to one of her children, not knowing when she'd see them again. Each time it was harder. Each time she had to be stronger so as not to let her feelings spill out and spoil their precious last minutes.

'It's been great, thanks, Ma. I forget what it's like to live in a house and be normal. Being in the army and following their routines makes you sort of institutionalised. I have enjoyed just being me.' He looked thoughtful. 'I'll remember this past week. I know I don't write much but I do think of you often.'

'I'm glad to hear that. The important thing is to make sure you look after yourself.' Prue swallowed back the lump that was forming in her throat.

'I will, I promise.' The sound of the approaching train caught Jack's attention. 'Here it comes. You take care, Ma. Keep the home fires burning, as they say.' He wrapped his arms around her and pulled her into a warm embrace.

Prue held on to him, imprinting the feeling of holding him as the train arrived at the station with a blast of steam and a squeaking of brakes. Reluctantly she loosened her grip and, fighting hard to keep her tears at bay, she stood up on tiptoes and kissed his cheek.

'Take care, Jack.'

'I will and you take care too.' He picked up his kitbag that lay on the platform and hoisted it onto his shoulder. 'Bye, Ma.'

She touched his arm before he opened the carriage door and stepped inside, closing it behind him. Jack lowered the window and leaned out.

'Goodbye, Jack,' Prue said as the guard blew his whistle and the train began to move. She walked alongside it for a few yards, but as it picked up speed, she was forced to stop and just watch. Jack returned her wave, leaning out and looking back at her until the train rounded the bend and he was gone. Only then did Prue let her tears fall as a sensation of utter loneliness washed over her. She grabbed a clean handkerchief out of her coat pocket and dabbed at her eyes, taking some slow steadying breaths to calm herself down. She would see her son again, she told herself, because the idea that he might never return was unthinkable.

Straightening her back and composing herself, Prue left the station and, rather than go straight home, she decided to wander. A walk by the river always made her feel better. There was something about the gentle running water – it had a soothing effect on her. And she needed that right now.

Walking through the village, she saw the congregation emerging from St Andrew's church after the morning service and hastened her step, preferring not to stop and talk to anyone.

It didn't take her long to reach the lane that led down to the River Bure, and within a few minutes, she found herself by the water. She stood watching as the river burbled past, diamonds of sunlight glinting off its surface. Weeds caught in the current swayed in a slow, rhythmic dance. Gradually Prue felt her shoulders loosen and her mind drift.

She had no idea how long she'd been there for, staring at the water, when she heard a soft cough. Turning, she saw a figure approaching her on the path that ran beside the river. It was Max Van Gelder, the Dutch Professor.

'Good morning, Prue.' He lifted his hat in acknowledgement before adding with concern, 'Are you all right?'

'Yes, I'm fine, just watching the river. I... find it very soothing,' she admitted, surprising herself by revealing something like that to a person she barely knew. Apart from meeting Max at the station on the day he'd arrived, she'd only seen him briefly on a couple of other occasions when she'd been at Rookery House.

'I understand, Prue. I also like being near the water...' he paused, his face breaking into a soft smile. 'It makes me happy and yes, *soothing*, that is the right word for it. I think growing up next to a canal in Amsterdam has something to do with it. Being by water feels like home – I'm sure that's why I enjoy walking here.'

'What about the sea?' Prue asked, surprising herself again. Talking to Max intrigued her. His eyes were always so filled with enthusiasm while he listened. That must be why she spoke to him so freely, she thought. 'Do you like the sea as well?'

'Oh yes! We had a family holiday by the North Sea every year when I was a child. I loved it. It's been a long time since I last went to the coast though.'

'I love the sea too,' Prue told him. 'The way the land meets the water and how it shifts and changes as the tide goes in and out.'

Max nodded, his eyes bright with memories. 'It's on the edge, constantly changing. The expanse of it makes you feel tiny.' He fell silent for a few moments, watching the river sliding past. 'I haven't seen you here before,' he said. 'I often walk along this path when I've finished some translation work and need to clear my mind.'

'What with one thing and another I don't get to be by the water as often as I would like,' Prue said wistfully. 'But today I *needed* to come here. I didn't want to go straight home after seeing Jack off at the station.'

'Ah yes, Thea told me he was returning to his unit this morning. It is never easy to say goodbye.' Max's voice was sympathetic. 'Was your husband with you to support you?'

His question gave her a moment's pause. Most people she met knew she was a widow. It had been a long time since someone had asked about Victor. Of course, Max wouldn't know, and it was understandable he'd expect her husband to support her through a difficult time.

Never in his life did Victor do that though, she thought, before looking Max in the eye and telling him matter of factly, 'No, he's dead. He was killed in the Norwich Blitz nearly two years ago now.'

'I'm so sorry – I didn't know.' Max put his hand to his forehead. 'Please forgive my blunder.'

Prue looked calmly at him. 'There's nothing to forgive. To be honest, even if Victor had been alive, he wouldn't have gone with me to see Jack off. You see, with it being a Sunday, he'd have been going to Norwich to be with his mistress as he always did.' The words slipped out before she'd had a chance to stop them. The secret that Victor had had a mistress was something few people were privy to. Outside of her sisters and Hettie, Prue had only shared it with her friend, Lady Clemmie Campbell-Gryce. Why she'd just revealed her closest secret to someone she hardly knew, Prue didn't know.

Max opened his mouth to speak but shut it again.

'It was complicated,' Prue said, attempting to put Max at his ease. 'I shouldn't have told you and I'm sorry I've embarrassed you. Please don't tell anyone else about that. I've kept it secret for a good reason. I don't know why I just blurted it out to you. Perhaps it's Jack going away... and me worried he might not...'

She blinked, determined not to cry in front of this near-stranger and make things even worse.

Max put his hand on her shoulder briefly. 'I'm sorry that your husband behaved that way. And I promise you, Prue, your secret is safe with me.'

'Thank you,' Prue said and turned her gaze to the river, watching the water flow by.

'My wife died in childbirth,' she heard Max say quietly, 'along with our daughter. It was eleven years ago now.' She turned to him. His grey eyes were full of sadness. 'That's what made me accept the job in England. I needed to get away from memories at home. I've lived in London ever since.'

'Do you still have family living in Amsterdam?'

'I hope so but I don't know for sure with how it is there now. I know my sister and her family intended to go into hiding if things looked bad for them. Being Jewish in a country occupied by the Nazis makes life very difficult. I haven't heard from them in a long while. I pray they are safe.' He sighed. 'There's nothing I can do to help from here.'

'I'm sorry for your losses, and your worry about your family.'

'Thank you. The war has brought so much pain and hurt

for so many people. That is one reason why...' he gestured towards the river, 'why I come here. It helps.'

They fell into silence once more, both watching the water flow past, with just the sound of the ripples and the March breeze jostling the bare weeping branches of the willow trees growing on the bank. Prue didn't feel the need to speak. There was no awkwardness on her part standing here not talking. She sensed that Max felt the same. With anyone else she would have felt compelled to fill the silence with words. Strangely, with Max she did not. She was comfortable with him just being there.

'I should get back to Rookery House and leave you in peace,' Max said eventually. 'I'm glad to have met you here, Prue. Perhaps we will meet again walking by the river.'

'Or if you'd like to see the sea again, I could show you around Sheringham sometime. There's a direct train from here.' The invitation popped out of Prue's mouth before she knew what she was saying.

'I would like that very much. But maybe we should wait for warmer weather to make the most of it?'

'Well, the offer's there for when you'd like to go – you'd enjoy it.' Prue's cheeks were growing warm. 'The seaside town and beach I mean,' she added clumsily.

'Thank you. Goodbye then.' Max lifted his hat and then headed off towards the village.

Prue stood staring at the river, thinking her mouth had well and truly run away with itself! Why on earth had she offered to accompany him to Sheringham? He was more than capable of going there by himself. It was bad enough that she had revealed Victor's infidelity to someone she hardly knew but then to offer to take him on a trip to the seaside... what had got into her today? Jack's departure must have upset her more than she'd realised. And yet, she'd enjoyed talking to

Max. They shared a mutual love of being by the water and he was so easy to talk to. They'd shared things with each other that usually were kept private and maybe that was a good thing for them both.

Prue lingered for a few more minutes, watching a pair of ducks arrive and begin dabbling by the far shore, their heads down in the water, tails comically in the air. She laughed. Coming here had soothed her as she'd hoped and talking to Max had taken her mind far from her present worries. She'd been reminded that many others had to endure things they were helpless to do anything about. They had to carry on. And that was no problem for her – keeping busy was how she had coped with Victor all those years. She'd got through it then and she would do the same now.

Luckily for her there was always plenty to be done and it was time she got home and made herself useful.

CHAPTER 14

Everyone was back at work at Rookery House after taking Good Friday and Easter Monday off. Even Betty and George, who were still on their Easter school holiday, were helping to plant potatoes in Five Acres field – Thea had teamed Betty up with Flo, while she had George with her.

'Look at this!' The little boy picked a chitted potato from the wooden box they'd been stored in. It had a healthy-looking green shoot sprouting out of it. 'It's already growing.'

'Is very good potato,' Luca said slowly in his thick Italian accent from where he was crouched on the next row. 'Grow well, very well.'

George grinned. 'I hope so.'

Thea was delighted by Luca's expanding vocabulary. She still couldn't have a proper conversation with him and needed Max's help to translate her instructions but, word by word, Luca was making good progress with his English and took great pride in using what he'd learned.

'Plant it for me here, George.' Thea pointed at the hole she'd just dug, and George gently placed it in, with the green shoot facing upwards. 'Perfect,' Thea told him, then used her trowel to cover it over with soil. The two of them moved along the row to repeat the process.

'Do you hear that?' Flo stood up from where she was working with Betty, looking skywards.

Everyone stopped what they were doing and listened alertly.

'Planes. And they're coming this way!' Thea sprang to her feet, her heart beating faster as the rumble of engines grew louder. Were they enemy bombers out in daylight? There'd been no warning, no sound of the air-raid siren going off in Wykeham. Around her, the others stood up too, peering upwards and shielding their eyes with their hands against the bright April sunshine. Thea made sure to take hold of George's hand and saw that Flo had done the same with Betty.

'Look!' Betty pointed at some dark shapes against the blue sky, which were growing bigger by the moment. 'They're over there, over that way, George,' she told her brother.

'What shall we do, Thea?' Flo asked in a concerned voice.

Thea thought quickly. She had to make a choice – the air-raid shelter was by the house, far enough away to make her think twice about making a dash for it and drawing attention to themselves.

She drew in a breath and decided. 'There's been no alarm from Wykeham so I think it must be the Americans' planes arriving.' She hoped she was right. Over the past few days, there'd been lorries passing through the village with more Americans to staff the aerodrome. She'd seen some when she took produce down to Barker's grocery. It made sense that the planes would be arriving – people had been expecting them any day now.

'Is Americano,' agreed Luca and Thea was thankful for his calming words.

The thrumming of engines intensified as the planes circled over the aerodrome, which lay on the far side of the village. Each plane flew at a different height and Thea counted at least twenty of them.

'They're landing!' Flo had to shout to make herself heard.

'What's going on? Is it the American planes?' Thea turned to see Hettie and Marianne hurrying towards them from the direction of the house, worried looks on their faces. Marianne had Bea in her arms, while Hettie was hand in hand with Emily. Max was behind them, one hand shielding his eyes as he watched the planes. Nancy had come out of the greenhouse where she'd been sowing seeds and was staring upwards, hands on her hips.

'The American planes are here!' Betty shouted at the top of her voice. 'They're big and so noisy!'

Hettie caught Thea's eye as she drew near. 'When I heard the engines indoors, I thought for a minute it was...'

'Same here.' Thea gave her friend an understanding look. 'But these are on our side. They've come to help.'

They watched the planes circling and then, one by one, dropping down towards the runways as they came in to land. Even when they were on the ground, their engine noise still filled the air.

'They must be moving to where they'll park,' Thea told the children. 'And yes, Betty, they are very noisy!'

When at last the final engine was turned off, the silence that fell rang in Thea's ears. 'It's been a while since the RAF left,' she said, 'and I think we've forgotten how loud planes can be.'

'I reckon them ones are noisier than the RAFs,' Hettie commented. 'And they looked bigger, chunkier.'

'Did you see them, Max?' George said to the Professor as he joined them. 'Me and Betty did.'

'Yes, I did. Do you know what sort of aeroplanes they are?' Max asked the little boy.

George shook his head.

'B24s,' Max told him. 'And they're also known as Liberators.'

'B24s or Liberators they might be,' Hettie blustered, 'but they're plenty loud enough! Then again, I suppose they've got a job to do and we'll get used to hearing them.'

'I read that each plane has a name,' Max said, 'and sometimes a picture painted on them.'

'Like naming a ship,' Marianne said. 'I like that.'

'I wonder if they'll be flying their missions in the daytime rather than at night like the RAF does,' Flo said. 'If they do, we'll have to look out for them and get to know them.'

'I want to see them,' George said hopefully.

'I expect we'll see some,' said Thea, 'and with their noisy engines we won't miss them coming!'

'They're exciting,' said Betty.

'Them arriving has been enough excitement for me,' said Hettie, 'and I for one am going back to my kitchen. Potatoes won't peel themselves.' With a nod to everyone she turned and headed back towards Rookery House with Marianne and her children, having not let go of Emily's hand the whole time.

'Shall we carry on and get these potatoes planted?' Thea said, with a glance around at her workforce.

Luca, Flo and Betty all nodded and returned happily to their jobs. Thea crouched down, picked up her trowel from where she'd dropped it and dug another hole.

'Right, George,' she said, 'I'm ready when you are.' She watched him carefully to be sure he wasn't overwhelmed by what had just happened and was pleased to see his attention was now firmly back on the box of chitted potatoes. He carefully chose the next one to plant and held it up for her inspection.

Nancy and Max drifted away back to their work, talking briefly, and the world, Thea thought, thankfully returned to normal. As she worked, she couldn't help feeling that the arrival of the American planes marked the beginning of a new phase of the war for the people of Great Plumstead. The aerodrome would soon become operational once more and their days would be punctuated with the sounds of the coming and going of aircraft. It would be a reminder of wartime that would be heard everywhere, even indoors.

'Auntie Thea?' George's voice broke into her thoughts.

She looked at him as he held out a chitted potato to her, an uncertain look on his face. 'Aren't you ready for the next one?'

'I am, thank you.' She gave him a reassuring smile and gestured for him to put it in the hole she'd just dug. Whatever happened in the war, she needed to keep going and protect George and Betty and everyone who lived here as best she could. That wasn't always easy especially with reminders like she'd just had right on their doorstep, but whatever the challenge she faced, she would do her best to respond to it.

CHAPTER 15

Hettie and Ted pedalled their bicycles side by side, up the tree-lined drive leading to Great Plumstead Hall. It was Sunday afternoon and they were on their way to visit Evie and her husband, Ned.

'This must bring back plenty of memories,' Ted said. 'How many times do you reckon you've been along here over the years?'

'A lot! Too many to keep track of.' Hettie threw an amused glance at her friend. 'You know there's a part of me that still feels like I'm heading home when I come this way. Not surprising since I lived here for so long. I started as a kitchen maid after I left school and stayed here until I retired. It was "home" to me for most of my life.'

'Did you ever think of taking a job anywhere else?' Ted asked.

'No, never! Simply because I was happy here. The Campbell-Gryces are decent people to work for. I heard enough tales from visiting ladies' maids and valets who accompanied their Lord and Ladyships' guests to know that we were lucky with our employers. There are plenty of servants who are unhappy, working for people who are lot less considerate than the Campbell-Gryces. Besides, I enjoyed living here in Great Plumstead – it's where I grew up.'

'It's important to be happy *where* you work,' Ted said, 'as well as *what* you work at. That's why I chose to be a gardener; it suited me down to the ground. Literally.' Ted chuckled at his joke. 'Though my mother was keen for me to go into service in a big house, did you know that? She wanted me to be a smart-looking footman. But I couldn't have abided being stuck indoors. I've always like being outside.'

'You wouldn't have been comfortable trussed up in smart livery serving at fancy dinners then?' Hettie asked him in an amused voice.

Ted let out a burst of laughter. 'Can you see me wearing a starch-fronted shirt, bow tie and tails? Give me my comfortable old corduroy trousers, my hands dirty with soil, and I'm happy.'

'I'm glad you had the right job for you.' Hettie gave him a warm smile. 'It made you happy and still does.'

'Very true. Gardening is in my blood. I could no more give it up than give up breathing.'

'I'm the same with cooking.'

'Do you think Ned would show me round the Hall's kitchen garden if I asked him?'

Hettie laughed again. 'Once a gardener, always a gardener! I expect Ned would be delighted to and it will give me and Evie a chance to have a good catch-up by ourselves.'

When they reached the end of the drive their way opened into a wide sweeping arc of gravel. They steered their bikes around to the right, heading for the courtyard at the back of the Hall where Ned and Evie lived in the old grooms' rooms near the stables.

Hettie took care to keep her balance as she rode across the wide cobbled courtyard, braking gently and dismounting by the old stable block. Then she led the way into the stable where the nurses always left their bicycles while they were on duty, leaning her machine against the wall. While Ted did the same, she removed the large round tin from the basket at the front of her bike and together they walked the final few yards to Evie and Ned's home at the far end of the block.

Before Hettie could knock on the door it flew open and Evie stood there, her face lit up with happiness.

'Welcome!' Evie said. 'Do come in.' She stepped back and ushered them into the hallway where they removed coats and hats and hung them from pegs.

'Hello! It's good to see you both,' Ned said, standing in the kitchen doorway. 'We've got the fire lit in the sitting room upstairs.'

'Go right up – it's lovely and cosy up there,' Evie added. 'It won't take me long to make some tea.'

'Let me give you this first.' Hettie handed the tin to the young woman, who opened the lid and let out an appreciative sigh. 'Oh, Hettie, this looks wonderful.' She showed Ned the golden-brown cake nestled inside. 'Thank you so much.'

'I wanted to mark this special day for you both,' Hettie said. 'Your first anniversary needs celebrating, as will all those yet to come.'

Ned put his arm around Evie's waist. 'It's been the best year of my life.' He gave her a kiss on her cheek.

Evie laughed, her face growing pink. 'Ned's such a romantic, though of course I love him for it. You're right, Hettie, it is an important day for us to remember what happened only a short year ago and how lucky we've been. And what better way to begin enjoying the occasion than with a slice of your delicious cake!'

She stepped into the kitchen to put the tin on the table.

'Can I help you with the tea things?' Hettie asked.

'No, it's all ready. I just need to put hot water in the teapot and then I'll bring everything up on a tray. I won't be two ticks. You both go on up with Ned.' Evie nodded towards the staircase that led from the hallway.

Doing as Evie said, they followed Ned upstairs. Having a sitting room on the upper floor was unusual but necessary here since there was only a kitchen and scullery on the ground level. They'd made one of the old grooms' bedrooms into their sitting room and, stepping into it, Hettie murmured her appreciation at how cosy it looked with a fire dancing in the grate, sending out a welcome warmth.

'You've got this all lovely, Ned,' she said admiringly.

'We like it,' Ned replied, 'all the hard work really paid off. It's just how we wanted to start our life together.'

How different it looked from when Evie and Ned were first given the place, Hettie thought. Back then, all the rooms were in a terrible state, festooned with cobwebs, dead flies and layers of dust, having not been used for many years. But with plenty of soap, hot water and elbow grease, followed by a coat of fresh paint, they had been given a new lease of life. Hettie, along with the others from Rookery House, had helped with the initial cleaning and then, with Ned and Evie's labour and a generous gift of furniture, bedding and curtains from the Hall's attics, the place had been transformed into a fine home. Hettie's eyes were drawn to the myriad books that filled the polished bookcase, remembering how Evie was a voracious reader and would always have a book on the go when she'd lived at Rookery House.

'Sit yourself down.' Ned gestured to comfortable armchairs either side of the fireplace.

'Thank you,' Hettie said, taking a seat.

Rather than sitting down himself, Ted was drawn towards the window. 'You've got a fine view here,' he said appreciatively.

'We're very lucky,' Ned agreed as he joined the older man looking out over the Hall's walled kitchen garden. 'And it only gets better as the year goes on and everything grows.'

'Reminds me of where I used to work at the Hall in Suffolk. I miss it sometimes.' Ted's voice was nostalgic.

'Would you like to have a look around after we've had our tea?' Ned asked.

'Thank you very much!' Ted beamed. 'That would be most enjoyable.'

'What would be enjoyable?' Evie queried as she came into the room carrying a tray. She placed it on a side table where there were already cups, spoons and a jug of milk set out.

'Ned's going to show Ted around the garden,' Hettie informed her. 'As Ted had hoped,' she added with a wink.

'Two keen gardeners together – they can compare notes.' Evie smiled. 'But before that, we must have some tea and a slice of your delicious cake.'

The afternoon had turned cold so they all put on their coats and hats before venturing into the garden. Leaving the men to discuss plants and gardening matters in general, Hettie and Evie wandered off on their own, strolling along arm in arm.

'Thank you so much for coming this afternoon,' Evie said. 'I've so enjoyed celebrating with you both and I know Ned has too. I still find it hard to believe that an entire year has passed since we made our promises to each other. I haven't regretted it for a single moment. It was the right thing for us both and we are so wonderfully happy being together.'

'You make a lovely couple. And you deserve to be happy.'

Hettie gave the young woman's arm a gentle squeeze. It was a joy to see Evie so contented and settled, as her life before she'd come to work at Great Plumstead Hall Hospital had been a difficult one. She'd fled an abusive marriage and Rookery House had been both a sanctuary and a new start for her. Ned had been a patient in the hospital and he and Evie had first become good friends. It was only after her husband had been killed that Evie and Ned's relationship had slowly developed into something deeper.

Last year they had made vows to each other in an unconventional way, exchanging promises in a bluebell wood. It wasn't a proper legal marriage because, after what Evie had been through before, she hadn't been able to face another one. However, she and Ned had made a firm commitment to each other. Only a few people knew the truth and they were all trusted friends and family. Everyone else thought they had married on a visit to Evie's mother in Sussex.

Hettie and Evie turned down a path that ran the length of the garden, parallel with the wall on which fruit trees were espaliered.

'I am happy, so very happy.' Evie glanced over to where the men were deep in conversation on the other side of the garden as they peered at some plants. 'Ned has restored my faith in committing to someone. I know we aren't,' she lowered her voice, *'legally* wed, but it doesn't matter. I feel more married to him than I ever did to Douglas. Ned and I share things, household tasks, opinions and thoughts, whereas before it was all one-sided – Douglas's way or no way at all.'

'It's no wonder your marriage to Douglas made you wary of marrying again,' Hettie said. 'One rotten apple can spoil the whole barrel, as they say. And it nearly put you off taking the chance with Ned.'

'It did. And then Douglas would have won and still had

power over me even though he's dead.' Evie frowned. 'That would have been awful. But that's enough talk of the past. Tell me, how are things at Rookery House? Flo's told me that the Italian POW – Luca, isn't it? – has settled in well and works hard.'

'He has and he's learning more English, though Thea still needs Max to translate for her each day. I'm going to need Max's help too because Luca wants to teach me how to make pasta!' Hettie chuckled with glee. 'I'll never be too old to learn new tricks, and I'd like to give pasta-making a try. Luca and Max have explained all about it to me at our mealtimes and I must say it does sound intriguing. And there are things called *pizzas* as well, which sound most tasty. If the pasta-making goes well, perhaps *pizzas* will come next. We'll be eating Italian food at Rookery House – imagine that!'

'Sounds marvellous,' Evie said. 'And highly exotic.'

'If I can master making pasta or pizza and they're as good to eat as Luca says, then you and Ned will have to come and savour them for yourselves.'

'Thank you,' said Evie as they walked on, 'we'd like that very much.'

CHAPTER 16

Thea was just finishing milking Primrose, stripping out the last drops of milk from the cow's udder, when the noise began. The cow started and Thea sprang up from her stool, grabbing the full pail of creamy milk, narrowly avoiding it being kicked over.

After putting the pail down on the far side of the byre, she went to soothe Primrose, stroking the cow's head. 'It's all right, you're safe.'

The throbbing noise outside grew louder — the sound of many aeroplanes over on the aerodrome warming up their engines. They must be going out on their first mission this morning, Thea guessed.

It had been ten days since the American planes had arrived and she'd seen them doing plenty of practice flights, take-offs and landings – *circuits* and *bumps* as the Waafs Marge and Elspeth used to call them, sitting at the table in the kitchen of Rookery House and sharing their news. Thea missed the Waafs a great deal – they'd been moved on when the RAF moved out and now kept in touch by letter from their new posting. It had been all change these past few months and now the Americans were here.

Until this morning only a few of the American aircraft had flown at a time and there hadn't been anything like as much noise. It sounded as if all of them were preparing to fly out, their destination likely to be somewhere over enemy territory.

Deciding it was best to leave Primrose in her byre for longer, rather than leading her straight out to the meadow as she usually would, Thea added some more hay to the rack for the cow to munch on.

'I'll come back and take you outside once the aeroplanes have gone. Hopefully we'll all get used to the noise because it's going to happen a lot.' She patted Primrose's flank, then collected the pail of milk and headed for the house. She'd thought the people – and animals – of Rookery House would be fully accustomed by now to the sound of engines, but the RAF had always flown their missions at night and somehow that had seemed more removed with most people – and animals – safe indoors. The Americans were getting ready to fly a mission in broad daylight and not under the cloak of darkness.

After kicking off her boots in the scullery and giving her hands a thorough wash at the sink, she carried the milk into the kitchen, heading for the pantry.

'Auntie Thea!' Betty called from the table where she and the rest of the children – George, Emily and Bea – were seated with Flo, Marianne and Max, having their breakfast. 'What's that noise?'

Hettie was by the stove. 'Is it what we think it is?' she asked ruefully.

'It's the American planes getting ready to fly,' Thea said. 'I'll be back in a minute, Betty – I just need to deal with the milk first then we can talk.'

'Let me give you a hand.' Hettie followed Thea into the pantry where she steadied the large, clean bowl waiting on the cold marble slab. Thea carefully poured the fresh milk into it. Once the pale-yellow cream had risen to the surface, it would be skimmed off and made into butter. 'Are you all right?' Hettie looked concerned. 'Only you looked a bit strained when you came in.'

'Did I?' Thea gave her friend a reassuring smile. 'I'm fine, really. I suppose hearing the aeroplanes start up together made me...' She paused, searching for the best way to express her feelings. 'Well, it brought the war closer to us this morning. Those men and their planes are going to be heading off into enemy territory from right here in Great Plumstead. Flying into danger. It's a sobering thought. I know the RAF did that too, but under the cover of darkness and we were more distant from it. If we went outside now, we'd be able to see them taking off...'

'Can we go out and see?' a hopeful voice piped up from the pantry doorway.

Thea turned to see George standing there, his eyes wide with excitement. 'I've finished all my porridge and would like to watch them leave and wave at them and wish them luck.'

'I don't...' Thea began but Hettie caught her eye. The older woman gave a slight shake of her head and Thea nodded in understanding. Hettie was right. There was no use denying what was going on right over their heads.

'Please, Auntie Thea,' George pleaded.

'All right,' she replied with a smile.

'Let's *all* go outside and wave them off,' Hettie suggested. 'We're going to be seeing a lot of them so it's as well we get used to it.'

George's face broke into a grin. 'Thank you. I'll tell the

others so they can come out if they want to.' He disappeared back into the kitchen.

Hettie put her hand on Thea's arm. 'You can't hide what's happening on their doorstep from the children; best to be upfront about it so they learn to understand what is going on.'

'You're right,' Thea said. 'My first impulse was to shield George and Betty from this new reality of the war but that wouldn't be right. They are already fully aware of the tough times we're living through. And I daresay the American airmen will be glad of our waves and good wishes – I hope some see us as they fly past.'

Outside in the back garden, little Bea clapped her hands over her ears as the throbbing noise from the aerodrome reached a new intensity. Marianne quickly picked up her youngest daughter and distracted her by pointing to the first plane as it lumbered upwards into the sky.

'It looks like it shouldn't fly, it's so heavy compared with a bird,' Hettie commented.

Thea watched as the next plane took off and followed the first.

'That's two,' George shouted, waving both his arms back and forth over his head.

'Three!' Betty added, doing the same as her brother, along with Emily. 'Can they see us? I can't tell if anyone is waving back.'

'If they can see you then I'm sure they're waving back,' Thea said.

As plane after plane took flight and joined those already airborne, they circled, climbing higher. After the twentieth aircraft took off and gained height, all the planes moved into a formation and headed in a northerly direction. They grew smaller until they were no more than specks in the sky and then vanished. Only the gentle sounds and silences of the countryside filled the air.

'Right, then,' Hettie said. 'Has everyone forgot about school this morning?'

'We could...' Betty began, but Hettie was ready for her resistance.

'Back indoors! Time to get ready!' she said briskly and shooed the children towards the house, following close behind with Marianne and Flo.

'This is the nearest we get to herding sheep,' Flo commented with amusement.

Marianne laughed. 'Too true!'

Thea and Max were both still watching the sky.

'How many will return?' Thea said, speaking her thoughts aloud. 'I hope it's all of them, but...' She left her words hanging in the air, because they both knew that some planes would probably not make it back.

'We must hope for the best, Thea – as they do,' Max said optimistically. 'They are the bravest of men to do as they do.'

'They are,' Thea agreed. 'And I shall be watching for them.' It would be sometime this afternoon, she reckoned, depending on how far they had to go. She'd be working outside and would hear them. How could she not count them in, knowing twenty planes had gone up and hoping with all her heart that the same number came home?

The growl of a lorry stopping outside on the road brought her attention to the here and now.

'That must be Luca arriving,' she said. 'Time to start our working day.'

Thea was hand weeding through radish seedlings when she detected the first faint throbbing of far-off engines. Leaning back on her heels, she shaded her eyes as she looked up into the pearly sky, her heart beating fast – and she spotted them. Five specks growing larger by the moment. The first of the returning planes!

She got to her feet, unable to peel her eyes away as they drew nearer. Then more appeared in the distance, and more. Soon the descending aircraft circled the aerodrome, dropping in to land one by one. Thea counted them in. And as the twentieth plane appeared, drew close and landed, she let out a sigh of relief. Twenty out and twenty home.

Smiling broadly and nearly bursting with happiness that all the planes had made it, she went back to her weeding, plucking out small fat hen plants from between the radishes with gusto. She knew it wouldn't always be like this and that the airmen would be heading out on many more dangerous missions but today's successful return was something to be grateful for.

CHAPTER 17

Prue was in her kitchen, sitting at the table. She'd left the window and back door wide open to let in a breeze of fresh spring air that smelled of sunshine and was accompanied by the busy birdsong of mid-May. She'd rather have been outside enjoying the sunny morning but she needed to read through the latest correspondence from the WI's head office that had arrived in this morning's post.

She was halfway down the second page when she heard a knock on the front door. Nancy was out working at Rookery House, and the girls were at school, so Prue left her reading to go and answer it, expecting it to be one of the women from The Mother's Day Club here to use the sewing room. She opened the door with a smile for whoever it was – and felt it fall from her lips when she saw who was standing on the doorstep.

It was Miriam Roper. The woman who'd been her husband's mistress.

'Hello,' she greeted Prue politely. 'I wonder if you can help me?'

Prue stared at the woman, words failing her. Victor had been with Miriam, in her Norwich home, when he'd been killed in an air raid back in April 1942.

'I hope you don't mind me calling here out of the blue...' Miriam continued, looking apologetic. Then slowly her forehead creased and she appeared puzzled, putting her head on one side before asking curiously, 'Don't I know you from somewhere?'

Prue found her voice with difficulty, though she had no idea what she was going to say. 'I...' she began but was pleased that the woman quickly filled the awkward silence that followed.

'I've got it! Didn't you come and visit me at the hospital after I was hurt in the Norwich Blitz, that's right, isn't it?' Miriam said. 'You were there after they pulled me out of my bombed-out house too. You said you wanted to see how I was after the air raid. That *was* you, wasn't it?'

Should she admit it? Prue hurriedly debated what the wisest course of action might be. Miriam hadn't known who she was then and still didn't now. Prue could continue the deception... though she had always found honesty to be the best path in life.

'Yes, it was me,' Prue heard herself say, her mind racing as she wondered why Miriam was here. How had she found her? And why come now?

'Well, that is a turn-up!' Miriam said jovially, before tilting her head again and saying, 'Though this is a strange coincidence, you being here at his house.'

Miriam pulled a piece of paper out of her pocket and pointed at the address written on it. It was Prue's address. And, of course, it had been Victor's.

'Whose house?' Prue asked, knowing the answer she would receive.

'My Vic's.' Miriam smiled briefly at his memory and Prue saw pain in her eyes. It reminded Prue that Miriam had loved Victor and had suffered his loss in a sudden and tragic way.

Miriam met Prue's gaze. 'The manager at Vic's shop in Wykeham told me that this was where he'd lived in Great Plumstead,' she explained. 'And that Vic is buried here in this village's churchyard. Though I'm confused because Vic always told me that he lived in Wykeham, so I assumed he was buried there. And now you're here at his house – this *is* Vic Wilson's house, isn't it?'

Prue felt herself recovering from the shock of Miriam turning up at her door. She breathed steadily. Two years had passed since Victor's death. Miriam's injuries had prevented her from attending the funeral and, after what she'd just said, she'd clearly never tried to visit his grave before. Her reasons for being here now were understandable. Of course she'd want to see where her 'Vic' had lived and was buried. Perhaps it was time for Prue to set things straight for her at last.

'Why don't you come in and we can talk. This was Victor's house and I'll show you where his grave is afterwards, if you like?' Prue offered.

'Thank you,' Miriam accepted.

Prue opened the door wide and ushered the woman inside, hoping she was doing the right thing.

Once they were settled in the sitting room with a glass of blackberry cordial each, Prue decided to double-check the facts Miriam was aware of before she revealed the whole truth. 'Victor told you he lived in Wykeham then?'

Miriam took a sip of her drink and then put the glass down on the little table by her armchair. 'Yes, that's right. It's where he had his business – Wilson's Seed and Agricultural Merchants. I naturally assumed he'd been buried in the churchyard there. I went earlier this morning to look for his grave but I couldn't find it anywhere. So I asked about it at the shop, and they told me he was buried in Great Plumstead because he'd lived here. I persuaded the manager to give me this address so I could at least see where his house was.'

'You've never tried to visit his grave before?' Prue checked.

'No. I didn't go to the funeral because of my injuries and afterwards...' Miriam glanced down at her hands clasped in her lap before looking up again, her eyes meeting Prue's. 'I just couldn't face it because I was so heartbroken at losing Vic. Our future together was cruelly snuffed out in an instant by that bomb.' Her voice caught and she paused to compose herself before continuing. 'My sister who I went to live with after the bomb destroyed my house – who I'm still living with – advised me to let it go. Least said, soonest mended, and all that. Only now...' She looked down at her left hand and Prue, following her gaze, spotted the ring with a small blue stone that she wore on her fourth finger. 'I'm getting married in a month's time. And I wanted to come and tell Vic. To say goodbye to him.' Miriam bit her bottom lip. 'After he died, I never thought I'd ever love again but I've met a smashing chap.' She smiled through her tear-filled eyes.

'Congratulations,' Prue said, meaning it. 'I'm delighted for you and hope you'll both be very happy.'

'Thank you. We will be. Bill's a lovely man, so kind.'

'It helps me to know that you're happy now and have a good man...' Prue was aware of her heart beating harder. What she was about to say would be a severe shock to this woman. Prue wanted to be doubly sure Miriam was up to hearing it.

Prue took a sip of her drink and tried to calm herself, letting her shoulders relax, though her heart was racing.

'Miriam, if I'm going to explain why I live in Victor's house, then it's going to be difficult for you. Are you *sure* you want to know? I am quite happy for you to leave here none the wiser and go on with your future, happy life.'

Miriam's eyes widened. 'There must be a sensible explanation,' she said falteringly. 'Isn't there? I must know, there's no two ways about it. So please tell me.'

'Very well then.' Prue's mouth felt dry. She took a long drink of her cordial. 'Miriam, what they told you at Victor's business is correct. He did live here. And he is buried in St Andrew's churchyard in the village. As for the reason I live here, well...' Prue paused for a moment, feeling as if she were teetering on the edge of a cliff and painfully aware that she was about to shatter this woman's memories of the man she'd loved. 'I was Victor's wife when he died.'

Miriam gasped, put a hand to her mouth and stared at Prue in horror. 'But you couldn't have been – Vic and I were *engaged*! He asked *me* to marry him!'

Prue gave her a sympathetic look. 'I'm sorry. I know it's a massive shock. But Victor and I had been married since 1921. I was his second wife. His first one died, leaving him with two small boys. They were two and three years old when we married and then Victor and I had our daughter as well. He'd no right to ask you to marry him because he was already married.'

'But he said he was a bachelor and would have stayed that way all his life if he hadn't met me.' Miriam's voice was tight with emotion, her eyes huge in her face. 'He *lied* to me!'

Prue nodded. 'Yes I'm afraid he did. I remember you told me he had a dragon of a housekeeper called Prudence – that referred to me, I suppose. I'm Prue – Victor called me by my full name. I was his wife, not his housekeeper, and I never once behaved like an overbearing dragon.'

Miriam bowed her head in silence while she took in Prue's revelations. When she finally looked up, her cheeks were wet. 'My Vic told me so many lies, didn't he? And I believed every single one of them.'

'You had no reason to doubt him,' Prue said gently. 'He deceived both of us. I found out about you only by pure chance. His Sunday trips to Norwich were supposedly to attend meetings for the various committees he was involved with to help the war effort. I believed him until one of my sisters saw you together in the city. She followed you both to find out where you lived and then told me. That's why I came there after the air raid and saw you, and then Victor, after you were pulled out of the ruins of your house. I'd been on duty with the WVS canteen and had the strangest feeling all day that I couldn't shake off. I needed to come to your house and find out if anything had happened there.'

'But you never said who you were, not even when you came to visit me in the hospital. *Why?* And why did you come to see me?' Miriam pleaded.

Prue leaned back in her chair, thinking back to that morning when she'd woken up at Rookery House. Thea had insisted she stay after they'd returned from Norwich the night before and Prue had been too numb to protest.

Why had Prue then decided to go back into the city and speak to Victor's mistress? It was because she had to know more to satisfy the strange itch that had settled inside her. It had been a crazy idea and she'd ended up finding out far more than she'd bargained for.

'I needed to understand,' Prue explained at last. 'When I was first told Victor was involved with you, I didn't want to know anything, preferring to let him get on with it while I got on with my life. But then when he was gone, my mind was suddenly filled with questions that needed answers.'

'I can relate to that,' Miriam said quietly and Prue wondered if she was of the same mind now, desperate for an explanation of what Victor had put her through. Prue decided she would help Miriam the best she could and tell her whatever she wanted to know.

'In the hospital,' Prue said, 'when you said that Victor was your fiancé, well…' She let out a long sigh. 'It stunned me. I'd never guessed he would go so far with his deceits – and to *both* of us.'

'You could have told me the truth about him then. Why didn't you?' Miriam's eyes bored into Prue's, eager for an answer.

'Because I decided that you'd already suffered enough. You were feeling dreadful. You'd lost your home and the man you were going to marry,' Prue explained. 'What good would it have done to tell you that what you had truly believed was false, nothing but lies?'

Miriam's eyes filled with tears, her expression softening. 'That was a kind and decent thing to do. Many wives in your position would have hated me and wanted to hurt me in return.'

'Perhaps.' Prue waved her hand. 'But I could see that you'd been genuinely deceived by Victor. You didn't know that I or his children even existed.'

'I had no idea, otherwise I would never have become involved with him. I'm not that sort of woman!' Miriam declared adamantly.

'I sensed that,' Prue said. 'You were misled by Victor.'

Miriam took her handkerchief out of her pocket and dabbed at her tear-filled eyes. 'Thank you for the kindness you showed me that day. I'm not sure I would have coped with finding out that he had been lying to me, not after what had just happened. I loved him, dearly I did… and he'd just been cruelly taken from me. And nobody deserves to be killed like that.'

The two women exchanged a look, comforting each other without the need for words.

Miriam sat up straighter in her chair. 'You did the right thing not telling me then, Prue, it was pure kindness and so selfless of you.'

'How are you feeling now?' Prue asked delicately. 'Are you all right?'

Miriam twisted her mouth to the side, sitting silent for a moment before replying. 'Do you know, I *am* all right. I felt so *guilty* to start with about falling in love with Bill. I kept wondering what Vic would say, if he'd be happy for me or if I was letting him down. Now I know he had been stringing me along the whole time…' She put her finger on her chest, pointing to herself. '*I* don't need to feel guilty any more about finding new love and happiness. I am glad I know the truth. It clears the air. Now I'm free to marry Bill, who is evidently a far better man than Vic ever was. I won't be looking backwards any more, I feel sure of that!'

Prue couldn't help smiling. 'Good, I'm glad to hear it. Victor was a man of different guises who lied to best suit himself. He's gone now and we can both live our lives the way we see fit.'

'Are you happy without him?' Miriam asked. Her face flushed and she quickly added, 'I'm sorry, I have no right to ask. There's no need to answer.'

'It's fine and yes, I am happy without him. My life has improved immeasurably,' Prue said. 'Now, do you still want to visit his grave? I wouldn't blame you if you've changed your mind and would rather not, after what I've told you.'

'I still want to. I have things to say to him – not what I'd planned to talk about before I came here, mind you! He might not be able to hear me but I feel I need to tell him a few home truths. Then I'll go home and get on with the rest of my life and enjoy it.'

After Prue had taken Miriam to the churchyard and shown her to Victor's grave, she left her there and waited a discreet distance away to give her privacy. Standing by the War Memorial, Prue scanned down the names of those lost in the Great War, including her own brother, William Thornton. She recalled the faces of the men who hadn't come home, many of whom she'd known from childhood. So many men were lost. That was why she'd ended up marrying Victor, a man who, if the war hadn't happened, she probably never would have seriously considered. But he had given her the chance to be a mother and that was something she did not regret. Three good things had come out of Prue's marriage – Jack, Edwin and Alice.

'I'm done,' Miriam said as she approached Prue. 'I've said my piece, told him exactly what I think of how he treated me *and you.*' She raised her chin. 'I won't be back here to visit his grave again.'

'You can start afresh now,' Prue said sympathetically.

'I will. Thank you for your honesty today, Prue, and for what you did for me when you visited me in the hospital. I hope that you might find another man who would be a much better husband to you. You deserve someone who treats you well, treasures you for the kind and decent person you are.'

'Who knows, perhaps one day,' Prue said. 'But I don't need a husband to be happy.'

Back at home, Prue returned to the work she'd abandoned earlier but she couldn't settle. After reading the same sentence three times, she gave up, pushing the papers away. It was no good; she needed to talk to someone about what had happened. Of the few people, apart from Miriam, who knew the truth about Victor, the person Prue felt she most needed to speak to was Thea – she was not only Prue's closest sister, but her friend and confidante too. Prue would go and see her at Rookery House.

Knowing that Hettie was on duty at The Mother's Day Club this morning and Marianne and her daughters would have gone too, Prue didn't go indoors when she arrived at Rookery House. Instead, she concentrated on finding Thea somewhere outside, luckily spotting her before she bumped into anyone else. She wasn't in the mood for pleasantries and chitchat – she just needed to talk to her sister

'Thea!' Prue called when she saw her at work in one of the vegetable beds.

'Hello! What are you doing here?' Thea leaned on her hoe, then narrowed her eyes, searching Prue's face. 'What's wrong?'

'Can we talk?' Prue asked. 'Somewhere we won't be overheard.'

Thea's eyes filled with concern. 'Of course. Let's go to the orchard; no one will hear us there. Flo and Luca are working up in Five Acres this morning, and Nancy is potting on seedlings in the greenhouse.'

If Prue hadn't been so distracted, she would have reacted with delight at the beautiful pink and white blossom covering the fruit trees in the orchard. The air was fragrant and humming with the sound of bees as they pollinated the flowers. Prue hardly noticed any of it.

'I've had a visitor this morning,' she told Thea.

'Oh no, not Claude again!' Thea grimaced, referring to Victor's unpleasant brother who had been pestering Prue about the business.

Prue shook her head. 'No...' she hesitated, hardly believing what she was about to say herself, despite having experienced it. 'It was Miriam Roper.' Prue lowered her voice even though there was no one else around to hear and added, 'Victor's mistress!'

'What?!' Thea exclaimed. 'Why did she come and see you? How did she find you?'

Prue told her sister what had happened, watching the reactions play across Thea's face.

'Oh Prue.' Thea wrapped her arms around her and hugged her tightly. 'That must have been awful for you. I'm sorry you had to experience that.'

Stepping back from Thea's welcome embrace, Prue raised her chin. 'It's all right. I'm not sorry at all. I admit it was difficult, and it was a risk telling her, but I'm glad I did. It feels as if I've shrugged off a final weight concerning Victor. One I didn't realise I was still carrying. Telling her the truth has freed me. Victor's lies have finally been exposed to those he misled most. Miriam can go on and live her life happily now, with no guilt, no remorse.'

'What about you?' Thea raised an eyebrow. 'Where do you see your future going?'

Prue was taken aback. 'What do you mean?'

'Well, would you like to marry again one day? To a man you love and want to spend the rest of your life with.'

Prue couldn't help laughing. She rolled her eyes. 'Not you

as well! Miriam said something similar, but I told her I'm quite content the way I am. And that's the honest truth, Thea. After years of putting up with Victor, I have no intention of hitching myself up again.'

The corners of Thea's mouth twitched. 'Not all men are like Victor. There are some more agreeable ones out there…'

Prue crossed her arms, smiling. 'I know that, Thea, but I can tell you with certainty that I'm not looking or expecting anyone to come looking for me. I have more than enough going on in my life already, thank you very much!'

'I'm sorry.' Thea gave her an apologetic smile. 'I couldn't help myself. I'll keep my nose out of it, shall I?'

'Indeed,' Prue said, though she was still amused by their conversation. Laughter was just the medicine she needed after her tough and emotional morning. She put her hand on her hip. 'Of course, I could ask the same of you, Thea – would *you* like to get married?'

Thea threw back her head and laughed. 'All right, you got me there! And the answer is, I have more than enough on my plate already.'

'You realise we are behaving the way we did when we were girls, sparring with words and challenging each other?' Prue said, linking her arm through Thea's. 'I'd forgotten how much I used to enjoy it!'

'Me too,' said Thea, grinning.

'Thank you for listening to me. I needed to tell you about Miriam.'

'I'm glad you did. It won't go any further, I promise you. It's been a momentous morning for you.'

Prue nodded. 'Unexpected but important.'

'Come on, it's almost time for our tea break – you're joining us and I won't take "no" for an answer.'

'I'd like that, thank you,' said Prue.

As they walked back to the house, Prue breathed in the sweet smell of the blossom, thinking that this was one of those days when life could turn in a new direction. Where it might take her to next, she didn't know, but being finally free of Victor was truly liberating.

CHAPTER 18

After a few gloriously sunny spring days the weather had changed and now the rain poured down relentlessly from a leaden sky.

Hettie peered out of the kitchen window where raindrops chased each other down the glass pane, then turned to face everyone seated at the wooden table – Thea, Nancy, Flo and Luca. They'd arrived indoors a short while ago for a tea break after spending the morning mostly doing jobs under cover in the greenhouse, byre and barn before dashing through the downpour to get back to the house.

'By the look of it out there, I don't think it's going to clear up any time soon,' Hettie declared.

'There's not much we can do outside in rain this relentless,' Thea said, joining Hettie by the window and peering at the heavy grey clouds. 'And all the indoor jobs that needed doing have been done. We could always give the house a bit of a spring clean instead,' she said doubtfully.

'No need,' Hettie replied quickly. 'The house is shipshape just the way I like it and no trouble for me to keep on top of.

Why not treat the time as a welcome break from all your hard work?'

'I suppose,' Thea pondered thoughtfully, 'but I'm used to working in the day – I like having things to do and getting them done.'

'I know what we can do,' Flo said and they all turned to see a wide smile on the young woman's face and a pink blush blooming on her cheeks. 'How about Luca shows Hettie how to cook pasta?'

At the sound of his name Luca gave Flo a questioning look. 'Pasta?' he queried.

'Yes, pasta!' said Nancy, enthusiastically taking up the idea.

Luca pointed to himself, then Hettie. 'Me, you, pasta, yes?' He grinned, clearly pleased with the idea.

'What do you think, Hettie?' Thea asked. 'Would you like to learn to make pasta with Luca this morning?'

Hettie's eyes twinkled. 'I certainly would! I've been waiting for the chance for Luca to teach me and what better time than a rainy day? The question is, who wants to eat it when it's cooked?'

Nancy led a loud chorus of 'I will!' and they all laughed.

'Right,' said Hettie, smoothing down her apron, 'the first thing to do is get Max. I'll need him to translate for me because if I'm going to do it, then I want to do it properly. I must understand *exactly* what Luca tells me.'

'I'll fetch Max,' Flo offered, standing up and heading into the scullery to put on her oilskins for the quick dash to Reuben's railway carriage house where Max would be doing his written translation work.

'Thanks, Flo!' Hettie called after her.

Thea said, 'When Flo's back we can all take an hour off and maybe the rain will have eased by the time you've finished, Hettie. Do you mind if we watch you make it?'

'Of course not, it's a wonderful opportunity for us all to learn something new. This is going to be most interesting. Luca, come and show me what we'll need.' Hettie beckoned to the POW and he got up from the table and followed her into the pantry.

By the time Flo returned with Max, all the ingredients and equipment they required were lined up on the kitchen table. Hettie and Luca had managed so far just with him pointing out what was needed.

At the sight of the Professor, Luca burst into rapid Italian, gesturing at the table. Max listened, nodded and then replied to the POW.

'Luca is delighted to show you how to make pasta, Hettie,' Max translated, adding, 'I think you're in for a treat. In fact, we all are when we get to eat it. I am very much looking forward to this.'

'I'm feeling nervous now!' Hettie admitted. 'It reminds me of the times when the old Cook at the Hall used to teach me new things. She could be quite demanding, expecting perfection, but she trained me well.'

Thea put a reassuring hand on Hettie's shoulder. 'You'll be fine because you're a natural cook. But if you'd rather not have an audience, we can wait in the sitting room and just leave Max in here.'

Hettie gave her friend a grateful smile. 'No, it's all right, you should all stay because you might want to make it sometime yourselves.'

'If I like it, then I will,' Nancy said. 'Prue would be interested too, I'm sure – I'll be telling her all about it.'

Flo asked Hettie, 'Would you like me to write down the amounts and the recipe?'

'Thank you, dear, that's kind of you.' Hettie passed Flo her kitchen notebook which was filled with her recipes and notes on how to prepare many sundry things and was a record of her whole working life's experience. She was still learning though, and it was fitting that this new recipe was recorded too. She'd no doubt add notes of her own later, so nothing would be forgotten, and she'd be ready to make Luca's pasta again just the way he showed her.

'We'll get started then.' Hettie gestured for Luca to join her at the sink where they both washed their hands. Then Hettie gave him one of her spare aprons to wear, the flowery fabric a striking contrast to his brown battle-dress POW uniform.

With everyone else sitting around the table, Flo with a pencil poised and Max ready to translate, and Thea and Nancy eagerly watching, it was time to begin.

After weighing out flour for each of them, as Luca instructed, Hettie carefully watched him shape his portion into a mound on the large wooden board set out on the table in front of him and make a well in the centre. Then he waited, smiling, for her to do the same.

'Good,' Luca nodded with satisfaction before breaking into Italian.

'Next,' translated Max, 'you need to crack the eggs and add them to the well in the centre.'

Luca demonstrated, breaking eggs into the centre of the flour where their rich yolks stood out like yellow suns.

Luca waited for Hettie to catch up with him then he showed her how to draw the flour into the eggs using his fingers, mixing the two ingredients to create a dough. All the while he talked calmly in Italian and nodded in appreciation of Hettie's work beside him.

'Luca says the dough will become less sticky as you work it.'

'I think mine is,' Hettie said as she concentrated on her task. It was satisfying feeling the flour and eggs come together, forming a soft dough.

'Good!' Luca praised Hettie, then fired off more instructions in rapid Italian.

'Now you need to knead it until it's smooth and elastic. For about five minutes,' Max translated.

'I'm familiar with kneading – I've made enough bread in my time!' she chuckled.

Hettie kneaded the pasta dough, pushing, stretching and folding it.

'Is it different from making bread?' Nancy asked.

'This dough feels firmer and there are no bubbles of air in it from yeast,' Hettie said. 'I'm enjoying it, though; it's good to do something new.'

After they'd worked for a little longer than five minutes, Luca put his hand on Hettie's arm to stop her. He picked up his ball of dough and moved his thumb across the surface, speaking as he did so.

'You can tell when it's ready if you can drag your thumb over it and it doesn't tear,' Max said.

Hettie tested her dough under Luca's watchful gaze. 'It's ready,' she said. She looked at Luca, who nodded his agreement.

Luca's next set of instructions was to put the dough into a covered bowl and leave it on the cold marble slab in the pantry to rest for thirty minutes.

While it was resting, the two cooks got to work making a sauce. Luca had spotted jars of bottled tomatoes from last summer on the pantry shelves, along with dried mushrooms and herbs, and he set to combining them together. Soon the kitchen was filled with a delicious aroma as the sauce simmered on the range.

'My stomach is gurgling!' said Nancy, apologetically.

'Mine too!' Thea laughed.

'Where did you learn to cook like this?' Hettie asked Luca, looking at Max to translate for her.

The Professor relayed her question and listened as the POW answered. 'Luca's grandmother taught him. Working in the family hotel, it was important that he knew how to cook. And he loves it too – being in the kitchen makes him happy.'

'That's a lot different from here,' Hettie mused. 'Not many boys learn to cook – it gets left to the girls and women, which is a shame.'

'You're teaching George how to cook,' Thea said. 'He enjoys helping you.'

'Watching Luca makes me determined to teach George even more,' Hettie said, as Luca added some salt and pepper to the sauce and stirred it in. Taking a clean spoon, he dipped it into the sauce, blew on it to cool, then checked the taste.

'Is very good,' Luca grinned.

Once the pasta dough had rested long enough, everyone gathered with interest around Luca as he showed them the next stage – rolling it into thin sheets, folding it over and repeating the process. After making sure the pasta was thin enough by holding it up a little and checking if he could see his fingers through it, he cut wide ribbons with a sharp knife and lightly coated them in semolina. All the time he kept up a steady commentary of what he was doing and why, which Max translated for them.

'This type of pasta is called *papparelle*,' Max informed them. 'There are lots of different types of pasta in a variety of shapes. Some even have stuffing in them. But all of them are delicious!'

'Hettie, now you...' Luca pointed at the rolling pin.

She rolled out her dough, the POW checking with her

when it was thin enough. Then she cut strips and dusted them.

The next stage was quick, tipping the pasta into a large pot of boiling water with a little salt, waiting hardly a minute for it to float to the surface, then draining it and serving it on plates with a generous helping of the tomato sauce.

'Buon appetito!' Max said as they dug in and the kitchen was silent for a few moments as everyone scooped up forkfuls of the pale pasta and rich red sauce.

Hettie savoured the delicious combination as she chewed. The simple sauce reminded her of warm summer days, of sun-ripened tomatoes and herbs grown for her cooking releasing their fragrance as she picked them. And the pasta complemented it perfectly.

'It's wonderful. Thank you so much, Luca.' Hettie noticed the POW hadn't eaten yet, his meal untouched as he waited for everyone else to sample his recipe.

Luca's face broke into a wide smile. 'Good, good, thank you, Hettie.'

'It's superb,' Thea said, the others echoing her praise. 'You've introduced us to a whole new cuisine, which I think is going to be very popular at Rookery House.' She glanced at Hettie.

'I will make it again very soon,' Hettie said. 'The children will love this and so will Marianne.'

Max relayed their words to Luca and the POW's smile grew even wider and tears shone in his eyes. Then he spoke in rapid Italian, making Max laugh.

'Luca says he would love to teach you how to make more types of pasta – and pizza too. Because he says he is sure Hettie must be Italian, she cooks pasta so well!'

Hettie felt her cheeks grow warm as she laughed with the others.

'Tell Luca it would be a pleasure and an honour to learn more recipes from him. And that I don't think I'm Italian – but I am a good listener!'

She picked up another forkful of food, glad to see that Luca was now tucking into his meal as well.

'If Luca's Italian food all tastes as good as this, then we are in for many more treats,' Hettie said.

'That's something for us all to look forward to,' said Thea.

CHAPTER 19

Prue turned her key in the front door, pushed it open and spotted the envelope lying on the mat. The handwriting on the front sent her heart soaring. It was from her son Edwin. It was always such a pleasure to hear from him, and, unlike his older brother Jack, Edwin was a regular correspondent and always told her as much as he could about what he was up to. She bent down and scooped it up off the doormat along with one for Nancy, which looked like it was from her husband. Both letters had arrived in the afternoon post while Prue was out at the village shops.

Carrying the envelopes and her basket of shopping through to the kitchen, Prue quickly put away the things she'd bought. Once that job was done, she could sit down and read Edwin's news. His letters were a precious link between them, their importance to her increasing with the time he'd been away. It was almost three years since she had last seen him, not long before he'd been sent overseas with the Friends Ambulance Unit to North Africa. Prue sorely missed him.

She poured herself a glass of water and sat down at the

kitchen table. Opening the envelope carefully, she pulled out a folded sheet of paper and read the words that Edwin had written almost three weeks ago.

3rd May 1944

Dear Ma,

Hoping this finds you well and I'm sure as busy as always! I often think of you doing the many things you do, helping others around the village and beyond. It makes home not feel so far away to know you're doing your bit just as I am. I am pleased to tell you that I'm a little closer to Great Plumstead than I was. Although still overseas, I'm further north and very glad to be rid of the sand at last. Being where I am now made me think of Thea's new worker that you told me about – I hope he's proving to be a good help in the garden for her.

Prue let out a sudden laugh as she realised Edwin was telling her he was in Italy. Because of the censoring of letters, he couldn't say his exact location outright but by mentioning Thea's Italian POW, whom she'd told him about in a letter a few months ago, he'd given her a firm clue to his whereabouts. Did Edwin realise what joy it would give Prue to know where he was for once? He probably did, she decided. Edwin had always been attuned to other people's feelings; it was one reason he was such a likeable and level-headed person.

Edwin's ambulance unit must have followed the fighting into Italy after the Allies invaded. *The Eastern Daily Press* was full of reports about the Allies' progress there, battling their way north against the Nazis who still held much of the territory despite the Italian Army's surrender. Now she knew Edwin was part of that – he was nearer to home but still following battles and no doubt transporting the wounded to hospitals. Still in danger.

Prue took a sharp breath, not wanting to think about that for the moment. Concern over Edwin's safety never left her, filling her mind in the early hours when sleep wouldn't come. But right now, she had the rest of his letter to enjoy, she reminded herself. She shouldn't let the worry spoil that.

Taking a sip of water, Prue read on.

The landscape is pretty and it's interesting seeing unfamiliar places.
Are you looking forward to having a new baby in the house? It will be quite a change, I imagine, but a lovely one. I hope Nancy is keeping well.
We're kept busy and I'm enjoying my job. I feel like I am helping while still sticking to my beliefs. The men I work with are a good bunch, and don't worry, Ma, we watch out for each other.
I must keep this short if I want to catch the post.

Look after yourself.

Your loving son,

Edwin

Prue stroked her finger over his signature, wishing he could come home, but the war rumbled on, and while it did Edwin was needed. She just had to go on praying he would be safe and unharmed and get through it.

Edwin had chosen the path of being a conscientious objector but it hadn't stopped him from putting his life at risk. He could have stayed working in Britain but had volunteered for overseas service. It was something Victor had never acknowledged, calling his son a coward when he was nothing of the sort. Edwin's bravery in standing up for his beliefs and then driving ambulances in battle zones proved that. Prue was proud of Edwin – he was a fine young man. Now she would be following the news from Italy closely, knowing that Edwin was somewhere there doing his bit.

CHAPTER 20

Thea was tired after a busy day driving and serving in the WVS canteen. She hadn't been doing one of her regular weekly shifts with Prue but covering for another WVS colleague who was unwell. Thea's planned day of work at Rookery House had had to be reorganised after she'd received a phone call at breakfast time asking if she could step in and drive a canteen. Fortunately she'd been able to say yes because she had a good team working for her; Flo, Nancy and Luca were more than capable of doing what needed to be finished by the day's end.

Now, as she pedalled home from the WVS depot in Wykeham, Thea thought how much she was looking forward to an early night. Even if she didn't go directly to sleep, she could lie in bed and read, allowing her weary body to rest.

The prospect of relaxing and losing herself in a good story was already lulling her mind. She felt her legs slow their pedalling just as a lorry rounded the bend ahead of her, driving on the wrong side of the road and heading straight towards her!

With a start, Thea took evasive action, yanking on the right handle of her bicycle which sent her careering across and then off the road. Her front wheel smacked hard into the verge, halting her bike but throwing her over the handlebars. She landed sprawling in the roadside ditch. Putting out her arm to soften her landing had only rewarded her with a sharp stab of pain as her hand hit the uneven ground.

Thea lay stunned for a few moments, pain radiating from her wrist. She was vaguely aware that the lorry had come to a halt with an urgent squeal of its brakes; the doors of the cab opened and heavy boots hit the road.

'Ma'am, are you okay?'

'You darn idiot!' another voice chimed in. 'You could have killed her! If she hadn't swerved out of the way... let's get down there...'

Thea turned her head to see two young American servicemen clambering down into the ditch.

'Can you move at all, lady?'

Thea cautiously moved her legs and then the arm that wasn't throbbing. All seemed in working order. 'Yes,' she told them, 'but I've hurt my wrist.'

'We'll get you up and out of here.'

Crouching either side of Thea, they carefully helped her to her feet.

'We got you. Now let's get you back up to the road. You took quite a tumble!'

Thea let them lift her from the ditch, trying to ignore the sharp pains shooting from her wrist. She spotted her bicycle lying on the ground, the front wheel bent out of shape. A flare of anger sparked in her.

'You were driving on the *wrong* side!' she told them. 'Look at my bike and...' She winced at another dart of pain and started to shake, realising how close she'd come to being mown down by the large American Air Force lorry.

'I'm so sorry, ma'am,' one of the men said. 'I've not been over here long. Coming around that bend I must've completely forgot you-all drive on the wrong side and switched to driving on the side I'm used to. I am truly mortified by my actions.'

'The *left side* is the correct side of the road in this country!' Thea snapped at him. 'You're not in America any more!'

'I appreciate that, ma'am.' The young man was wringing his hands. 'You need some medical help. Please let us take you to the base to see Doc Summerville. He'll soon fix you up.'

'What about my bicycle?' she said. 'I can't leave it here.'

'We'll put it in the back of the truck,' the other man reassured her.

It seemed like the best option, so a few minutes later, Thea was seated in the lorry's cab between the two Americans, being driven towards the aerodrome. Looking down at her WVS uniform, she noticed the skirt of her dress was torn and had a liberal coating of soil from the ditch. She knew she was in shock. There was a tremor in her fingers and her mind seemed to be waiting for something to happen. She felt sorry for snapping at the young men – anger was never helpful and she'd apologise later.

'You sure are quiet, ma'am. Are you feeling sick at all?'

She shook her head.

'We'll soon be with the Doc,' the man reassured her.

Arriving at the gate to the airbase, the driver stopped and spoke to the guard on duty. 'Can you call ahead to the Sick Quarters, get a message to Doc Summerville, tell him we've got a patient for him?'

'Sure, he'll be waiting for you.' The guard waved them through.

If Thea hadn't been so distracted by throbs of pain she would have taken more interest in the sights she saw as they drove further into the base. She was aware of some B24 planes parked off in the distance around the perimeter of the airfield, and there were plenty of American servicemen going about their duties. It was like a village, with lots of buildings and hangars and people milling about.

'There's the Doc,' the driver said as he slowed the lorry and came to a stop outside a building shaped like a large Nissen hut. A man in his forties – a similar age to Thea – stood waiting. He was dressed in American uniform and looked like any other serviceman.

Doc Summerville opened the cab door and looked in. Thea could see him assessing the situation, noticing her cradling her right arm against her chest.

'Hi there, I'm Walt Summerville, one of the base medics. I'm sorry to hear you've been hurt, Miss…'

'Thornton. Thea Thornton,' she said.

'What happened to you?' he asked.

She explained quickly and noticed the doctor darting several glances at the driver, who remained doggedly silent.

'Okay then, Miss Thornton, we'll get you into the hospital. I can examine you and see what the damage is.'

He helped her climb down from the lorry cab. 'Easy does it,' he told her calmly and she felt his hands gently steadying her.

'You two men stay on base.' His voice was suddenly commanding. 'I'll speak to you later.'

'Sir!' the men replied.

The doctor's calm manner returned immediately as he led Thea into the hospital building, holding the door for her. 'This way to the examination room.' He walked beside her along a short corridor and then guided her through another doorway. 'Please take a seat.' He gestured to the couch bed at the other side of the room and supported her by her good arm as she climbed on to it.

'Thank you,' Thea told him, gritting her teeth against the pain which was getting worse not better.

'I can see you are in some discomfort,' he said sympathetically. 'I will try to keep my questions to a minimum, then I can examine you and work out the best way forward. Though if the pain is getting too much, be sure and tell me.'

'I will,' Thea said, feeling heat high in her cheeks. She really wasn't feeling well at all, but Doctor Summerville would need to do his job properly and she had decided already that she was safe in his hands. 'I'm all right – ask away.'

'Tell me more about what happened when you came off your bike.'

'I put my arm out to break my fall. I didn't think about it, just did it.' Thea demonstrated with her uninjured left hand.

'I understand. You did what anyone would do automatically. I've done the same myself.' He smiled. 'Even though I should know better. Now if I may…' He gestured to her injured arm. 'I'll be as gentle as I can.'

With practised care, he took her hand in both of his. 'I apologise to you for one of our men's carelessness,' he said as he felt along her fingers. 'We take great care to educate them on the many differences here compared with in the States, and in particular to make certain they know to drive on the correct side of the road. Today that didn't check out. I will deal with the driver later and I can assure you he won't do it again.'

'I was rather short with them,' Thea said apologetically, 'after they helped me from the ditch.'

'You had every right to be,' the doctor asserted.

'It is not the way I usually react to things,' Thea explained. 'I'm usually much more measured and...'

He touched gently above her wrist and Thea cried out.

'Forgive me, Miss Thornton,' he apologised, 'I didn't mean to cause you more pain. The way you've reacted to my light touch makes me think your wrist is broken, though I want to X-ray it to be sure. Would that be okay?'

'If you think it best,' she said, the pain now coming in waves. Thea tried to ignore it. Hopefully this would soon be over and she'd be back in the comfort of Rookery House. She eased herself off the couch bed, eager to get a move on. 'Do you have the X-ray machine close by?'

'The pain is worse?'

'Yes.'

'Then follow me.'

As they walked to a room at the far end of a longer corridor, Thea asked, 'How long does a broken wrist take to heal?'

'You'll need to have it in plaster for about six weeks while the bone mends. After that it will need some rehabilitation to increase muscle strength again,' he explained.

'Six weeks and more! That isn't possible – I won't be able to do my work.'

'What do you do?'

'I grow fruit and vegetables, milk our cow, look after animals... all things I need to use *both* hands for.' Her eyes stung with tears, both from the pain and this new frustration. 'This,' she pointed at her injured wrist, 'is going to cause me a lot of problems.'

'I understand,' Doctor Summerville said, 'but let's take

things a step at a time. X-ray first, then we'll know what we're dealing with. Please don't worry – I'm gonna make sure you won't be left in any difficulties because one of our men didn't pay due care and attention to his driving. Whatever you need, the United States Army Air Force will provide, you have my promise on that.'

He gave Thea a dose of painkillers to dull the pain and left her in the hands of his medical assistants to conduct the X-ray. He was back shortly afterwards to tell her the outcome.

'It is broken,' he said, 'but fortunately it was a clean break and will mend fully. A plaster cast will keep it secure and supported while the bone heals.'

While the doctor instructed one of his medical assistants to prepare the equipment ready for plastering Thea's arm, she glanced at the clock on the wall and saw with a jolt of surprise that it was almost half past six. With all that had happened, she hadn't been aware of time. She should have been back at Rookery House well before now. Hettie would be worried.

'I need to telephone home and let them know I'm here,' Thea said as the assistant returned pushing a trolley.

'I'll make the call for you,' Doctor Summerville said.

Thea told him the number and to ask for Hettie. He hurried away leaving his assistant preparing the bandages and returned in a matter of minutes.

'I spoke to Hettie,' Doctor Summerville told Thea as he started to bandage her lower arm down to the base of her fingers in yards of soaked plaster of Paris bandage. 'She said not to worry about anything, all was in hand there and she'll see you soon. I reassured her I'll bring you home myself as soon as possible.'

'Thank you.'

'Hettie sounds like a nice person.' He glanced at Thea for a moment as he wound the bandage around and around.

'She is. We're lucky to have her with us at Rookery House.'

'Is she part of your family?'

'Yes – though we're not actually related. Hettie was a dear friend of my mother's and I've known her all my life. When Hettie retired, I asked her to come and live with me,' Thea explained.

'I like that.' He looked thoughtful. 'Family doesn't just have to be people who are your kin. Friends can be the family you choose. While we're all away from home living here on the base, we're like a family for each other too.'

'I understand what you mean. I drove ambulances in France during the Great War and the women I worked and lived with became my family. We looked out for and supported each other,' Thea told him. 'A shared experience forms strong bonds of friendship.'

His blue eyes met hers. 'That's always been my experience as well.'

Once Thea's wrist had been encased in a cast to the doctor's satisfaction, he tied a sling across her chest to support her arm.

'It looks like you will have a fine set of bruises by tomorrow,' he said, studying Thea's face for a moment and brushing her cheek with his thumb. 'And no doubt you'll be sore and stiff too, so you must take things easy. Rest and, of course, look after your arm. Don't get the plaster cast wet. Make sure you regularly curl your hand lightly into a fist, then spread your fingers and thumb wide apart. And bend and straighten your elbow and lift your shoulder up and down too.' He demonstrated the actions. 'Your wrist might be immobile, but you need to keep your arm and hand mobile. Don't worry though, I'll be checking on how you're getting on. I won't just take you home and abandon you. Your injury is our responsibility and so is your recovery.'

'I feel much better already,' Thea said. Her head was clearer presumably, she thought, because the pain medication was already working. 'Thank you for your care.'

'You're welcome. I'll drive you back to Rookery House as you can't safely ride your bicycle,' he said. 'I wouldn't be happy with you doing so, not after the shock you've had.'

'Even if I could ride my bicycle, it wouldn't be any good – the front wheel is buckled from where it hit the verge,' Thea told him. 'They put my bike in the back of the lorry.'

'Okay, I didn't realise. In that case, I will have it fixed and returned to you as quickly as possible. We've got excellent mechanics here on the base who can turn their hand to just about anything.'

'Thank you.'

'You wait here and I'll fetch a jeep – I won't be long.'

It was almost half past seven when they drove in through the gates of Rookery House. Doctor Summerville cut the engine, leapt out of the jeep and came around to her side to help her out.

'Steady now,' he said, seriously.

'Thank you, but I'm fine.'

'I can see that,' he said, returning her smile. 'And I'm glad of it.'

'Thea!'

She turned to see Hettie rushing out of the front door, her face full of concern. 'Are you all right?' she asked, taking in Thea's plastered arm in its sling.

'Apart from this and some bruises.' Thea nodded towards her broken wrist.

After Thea had introduced them to each other, the doctor

took off his peaked cap and shook Hettie's hand. 'Walt Summerville. Good to meet you, ma'am. Miss Thornton's arm will be fine. It's a clean break and just needs time to heal. She must also rest up over the next few days.'

'I'll make sure she does.' Hettie shook his hand vigorously. 'Thank you for helping her. Will you come in for a cup of tea?'

'That is kind, but I need to get back to the base as I have some things to deal with. Another time perhaps?'

'You'll always be welcome here,' Hettie said.

He turned his attention to Thea. 'Miss Thornton, if you have any problems with your wrist, call me straight away. This is my telephone number at the base hospital.' He took a piece of paper out of a pocket in his tunic and handed it to her.

'Thank you and please call me Thea.'

'And I'm Walt. Take care... Thea,' he replied.

He put his cap on again, returned to the jeep, climbed in and with a wave of his hand drove off.

Thea felt Hettie take hold of her left arm. 'Come on, let's get you indoors. The children are asleep so it's quiet and you can tell me what happened.'

Later, as Thea lay in her bed, she was aware of the heavy weight of the plaster cast on her right wrist. She recalled how she'd been thinking about having an early night as she rode home from Wykeham. That had been moments before the lorry had come around the corner on her side of the road, altering the course of her evening and leaving her with a broken bone. But it could have been a lot worse...

She shuddered and closed her eyes, breathing in and out slowly, hoping to quieten her mind and let herself drift off, but sleep wouldn't come. She found herself getting irritated because, although she was exhausted in mind and body and desperately in need of rest, she was wide awake. Rather than lie there fretting over lack of sleep, she decided to read. Losing herself in a story would distract her. And after a long and eventful day, sleep would come at last.

CHAPTER 21

'Remember, as quiet as mice,' Hettie reminded George and Betty as they quickly got dressed. 'Auntie Thea needs to sleep.'

The pair of them looked up at her, their faces solemn.

She had woken them a short while ago and, naturally, the children had asked where Thea was and why she wasn't waking them as she usually did. Hettie had explained about yesterday's accident. She hadn't told them the full story, thinking there was no need for them to know how near Thea had come to being mown down by a lorry. She'd told them only that Thea had fallen off her bicycle, been helped by some American servicemen and taken to the aerodrome to have her broken wrist put in plaster.

'Ready?' Hettie asked.

They both nodded.

She opened their bedroom door and led the way along the landing past Thea's closed door and down the stairs, each of them treading softly and hardly making a noise.

'Well done,' Hettie whispered as they reached the bottom

step and she ushered them into the kitchen and closed the door.

Marianne and her two daughters were already seated at the table, eating their porridge.

'Morning,' Marianne greeted them, keeping her voice low. 'You were so quiet up there, we couldn't hear you coming.'

George beamed. 'We didn't want to wake Auntie Thea because she's broken her wrist and needs to sleep.'

'Did you see her last night with her arm in a plaster?' Betty asked, sitting down at the table, her eyes wide with curiosity.

'I did,' Marianne replied. 'She's doing really well though and with plenty of rest she'll soon be back to normal. You'll be able to see for yourselves later when you get home from school. I'm going to take you two in, on my way to The Mother's Day Club with Bea and Emily.'

'Here you are.' Hettie served George and Betty their porridge. 'There's some stewed fruit to add to it.' She moved the dish of cinnamon-spiced apple closer to them. 'Help yourselves.'

'Thank you, Auntie Hettie,' the children chorused as the door to the scullery opened and Flo came in carrying a pail of fresh milk, heading for the cold marble slab in the pantry.

'Everything all right with Primrose?' Hettie asked, following her in there.

'She's fine. I led her out to the meadow to graze. Do you think Luca could do the afternoon milking?' Flo asked. 'He enjoys spending time with the animals and has a good rapport with them as we know.'

They both smiled. It was well known Luca sang his gentle Italian songs all the while he cared for the animals.

'Sounds like a good plan to share the milking between you,' Hettie agreed. 'We can run it by Thea later. One thing's for certain, she won't be able to do it herself for a while.' Her eyes filled with tears.

'Hettie, what's wrong?' Flo put her hand on the older woman's shoulder.

'I'm just...' She let out a sharp breath and whispered, 'Thank goodness Thea swerved out of the way; if she hadn't... it doesn't bear thinking about.'

'It doesn't,' repeated Flo, seriously. 'I don't want to think about what the outcome might have been, it's too horrible. We must all be thankful that she has come away with nothing worse than a broken wrist. That's going to be a nuisance for her, but it will heal, and meanwhile we'll all take the best care of her.'

Hettie gave the Land Girl a watery smile. 'You're right. We must look on the bright side. I'm just tired after not sleeping well last night – thoughts of what *could* have happened kept whirling round in my head. Take no notice of me. It was just so unexpected and it makes you realise accidents happen out of the blue like that.'

'They can, but thankfully not very often,' Flo reassured her. 'I hope the American driver who caused this accident sticks to the left side of the road from now on.'

Hettie was kneading bread dough at the table, pushing and folding, stretching it out to make a good smooth texture. The process was a soothing one and just what she needed this morning. When the telephone had rung last night and an American man had introduced himself as a doctor from the aerodrome, telling her Thea was there after an accident, Hettie's stomach had dropped like a stone. Despite his reassurances that Thea was fine apart from a broken wrist,

Hettie hadn't been able to stop worrying until he'd brought her home and she'd seen Thea for herself. The fact was she loved Thea like a daughter and this accident had left Hettie feeling shaken. It had been a very near miss.

Drawing in a deep breath, she reminded herself that she shouldn't dwell on what might have happened but just be grateful it hadn't. She must look on the bright side, like she usually did. Hadn't she learned over the years that worrying about things was a waste of precious time and energy? She needed to remember that now.

With the dough kneaded into a smooth consistency, Hettie placed it in the pale-brown ceramic bowl, covered it with a clean cloth and put it by the range to rise. She'd just washed her hands and was drying them when the telephone rang out in the hall. She rushed to answer it, hoping it hadn't woken Thea.

'Hello, Rookery House,' she said in a low voice into the receiver.

'Hettie! It's Walt Summerville here. I'm calling to see how the patient is this morning?'

'Thea was still sleeping when I last checked on her,' Hettie told him. 'The bruises you warned her about have come out on her face.'

'She'll be achy today and sore. Will you tell her I called and that I've arranged for her bike to be fixed and I'll bring it back as soon as it's ready?'

'I will.'

'And Hettie, if there are any concerns will you please make sure she calls me?'

'Of course I will,' Hettie said firmly. 'I shall insist she does even though Thea won't want to make a fuss.'

Doc Summerville gave a soft laugh. 'That sounds like the Thea I am getting to know,' he said. 'Thank you again, Hettie. I must go but I wanted to check on my patient. I'm pleased to know she's in safe hands and I'll see you folks soon.'

After she'd hung up the receiver, Hettie went upstairs to check on Thea again. Opening the bedroom door a crack, she peeped inside.

'I'm awake,' Thea called out in a croaky voice.

Hettie pushed the door wide open and went in, crossing to the bed and looking down at her friend, whose dark brown curly hair was splayed out on the pillow around her head. Her face was pale where it wasn't bruised. 'How do you feel this morning?'

Thea shuffled up towards the iron headboard and winced. 'Sore. Like I've done a somersault into a ditch.' She touched the bruised side of her face. 'Do I look as if I've been in a boxing ring?'

'Yes, a bit, but it will fade, and no doubt turn purple and yellow before it does.'

'A colourful display then. Is everyone all right, the children…'

'They are fine,' Hettie cut in. 'They went to school with Marianne. Though they would rather have stayed at home to see you. I told them only that you fell off your bike, thinking it best they didn't know the whole story as it might worry them.'

Thea grimaced as she shifted in the bed trying to get more comfortable. 'Good idea. And I hope when they get home from school I'll look and feel better than I do now.'

'Is your wrist sore?'

Thea pulled her plastered arm out from under the covers. 'It's achy but not as painful as it was yesterday. Feels heavy though with the cast on. I suppose I'll get used to it. Who was telephoning?'

'Doctor Summerville. He wanted to check how you were

and tell you he's having your bike fixed. And to remind you to call him if you have any problems.'

'That's kind of him.'

'He seems to be a very thoughtful man,' Hettie said approvingly. 'Now, how about some breakfast? What would you like? I'll bring it up to you.'

'Thank you, but no. I'd rather get up and have something in the kitchen as usual. I've been in bed long enough and I don't want to make a fuss.'

Hettie let out a laugh and Thea gave her a quizzical look.

'Sorry,' said Hettie, still chuckling, 'it's just I knew you'd say that. It tells me you're yourself and therefore already on the mend.'

'I do feel myself again,' said Thea. 'Last night I didn't. Luckily for me I had you to rely on.'

'That's what I'm here for,' said Hettie. 'And if you are sure, I will help get you down to the kitchen. Other than that – I promise not to fuss.'

'Thank you,' said Thea. She threw back the covers and slowly swung her legs around until she was sitting. 'I'm sore and stiff on my right side where I hit the ground. Other than that, I'm fine.'

Hettie put her hand through Thea's left elbow and supported her as she stood up. 'How's that?'

'Well, I won't be rushing about today, that's for sure,' Thea said. 'Can you help me put on my dressing gown, please? I'll come downstairs in my nightclothes to start with and get dressed later.'

'Good idea,' Hettie agreed, thinking she would have suggested that but knowing how independent Thea was, it was best she decided for herself. 'Then we'll go down and I'll make you some breakfast, whatever you fancy. Scrambled eggs, toast, porridge... you tell me what you want.'

'Maybe a slice of toast and some tea. I'm not very hungry.'

Hettie nodded, holding back her advice that Thea should eat. There was something not quite right about her, apart from the bruises and broken bone. Despite her insistence she was fine, Hettie sensed things were not as they should be with Thea.

'Perhaps with some honey on the toast, too?' Hettie suggested.

'I'll see,' Thea replied.

Hettie was pleased to see Thea up and moving about but she seemed fragile and out of sorts. Hettie would keep a close eye on her friend and not hesitate to call for help if necessary.

CHAPTER 22

Prue had just come indoors after hurriedly hanging out some washing and was getting ready to go to the WI allotment to do some weeding when her telephone rang. She dashed into the hall to answer it.

'Prue Wilson here,' she said, slightly breathless.

'Hello Prue.' She recognised Hettie's voice, noticing that she sounded more serious than usual.

'Is anything the matter?' Prue asked quickly.

'It's nothing to worry too much about, but I'm ringing to let you know Thea had an accident yesterday. She…'

'Is she all right?' Prue cut in, her stomach lurching. 'What happened? Where is she now?'

'Thea's here at home with me and she's fine apart from a broken wrist and some bruises,' Hettie told her. 'She was bicycling back from Wykeham and almost got run over by one of the American lorries from the aerodrome. It was driving on the wrong side of the road and Thea ended up in a ditch.'

Prue gasped. 'That's terrible!' She shuddered, imagining a

large lorry bearing down on her sister. The outcome could have been much worse. 'I'm coming straight over to see her.'

'I thought you would as soon as you heard and that's why I didn't ring and tell you last night. I was going to, but Doctor Summerville advised that Thea should rest. She's had a good night's sleep now though and I reckon she's up to a visit from you.'

Prue sensed from the older woman's tone that Hettie was holding back, but she didn't press her. Thea was in good hands with Hettie, who would know when to call for help if she needed to. As she was doing now, Prue began to realise.

Hettie continued, 'Thea was treated by an American doctor from the aerodrome. The driver who nearly ran her over took her back there to get help. Doctor Summerville saw to Thea's arm and brought her home afterwards.'

'I'll be there as soon as I can,' Prue said briskly. 'Tell Thea I'm on my way.'

'I will. She'll be pleased to see you because she's not happy being off work. I'm trying to make sure she takes things easy for a few days before she ventures out to do anything again. When she does, she's going to be limited to what she can do using her left hand.' Hettie paused for a moment before adding, 'I'm hoping Thea will talk to you about it.'

Prue's first instinct was correct, she was sure. There was more to this than Hettie was saying. Rather than waste time with questions now, Prue decided it would be best if she got to Thea as quickly as she could.

'I'm coming now,' she told Hettie and, after saying a brief goodbye, she hung up and got ready to leave. The allotment would have to wait. Her sister had been hurt and clearly needed her and that was her top priority.

∽

The sight of Thea resting in an armchair in the sitting room at Rookery House brought tears to Prue's eyes. Her sister's face was badly bruised on one side and her right arm was held against her chest in a sling, but worse than either of those was the way her strong, independent sister looked so delicate, shrunken even. So vulnerable.

Prue glanced towards Hettie, who stood beside her in the doorway, and a look of understanding passed between them.

'Come to admire my bruises?' Thea asked quietly, giving Prue the ghost of a smile.

'Yes,' said Prue. 'I have. And they're certainly big and purple enough.' Prue fought to keep her voice cheerful but the atmosphere remained an awkward one.

'I'll leave you two alone for a bit,' Hettie broke in. 'Give me a shout when you want some tea.' She went out and closed the door behind her.

Prue hurried across the room and gently put her arms around Thea. Releasing her sister, she crouched down in front of her and asked, 'How are you? And I mean, *really*?'

'I'm...' Thea began, her blue eyes meeting Prue's before they welled up and she looked away. 'I...' Thea's mouth contorted and tears slipped down her cheeks, dripping onto her jumper.

Prue fished in her pocket for a clean handkerchief and handed it to Thea, who wiped at her eyes with it.

'You've had a tremendous shock,' Prue said sympathetically.

'It happened so quickly,' Thea told her. 'I didn't have time to be scared. I just reacted and got out of the way. Then, after they'd extracted me from the ditch, I gave the driver a piece of my mind, though I shouldn't have, and was X-rayed and patched up by a very kind doctor and driven home. I was doing all right... and then it dawned on me late last night... what if I had been just a little further along the road? Or what if the lorry had been going faster? I'd have had no chance to avoid it. I'd have been run over.'

Thea drew in a shuddering breath; her hand reached for Prue's and held it tightly. 'I had some close calls driving ambulances in France, Prue, but they weren't unexpected there and I was ready for them, prepared. But yesterday I was doing something I'd done a hundred times before, cycling down a country lane on my way home to Rookery House... and I was very nearly killed.' She cried softly. 'I'd have left behind my friends, my family... and Betty... and George...'

Prue hugged her while she sobbed.

'Thank goodness you had time to steer clear,' Prue said, her voice husky with emotion. She took hold of the handkerchief that was scrunched up in Thea's hand and gently dabbed at her sister's tears, carefully drying her bruised cheek.

'I don't quite remember that bit,' Thea said thoughtfully, 'whatever I did to get out of the way. Fortunately, I did the right thing in the moment. For which I am grateful, despite all this getting emotional...' She gave Prue a wry grin and then winced as it pulled on the sore side of her face.

'Don't bottle up how you feel,' Prue told her. 'It's best to let it out, the shock and the fear. You can say whatever you need to me.'

Thea nodded. 'It feels better to speak it out loud. I didn't want to upset Hettie so I put on a brave face. Though I think she might have noticed I was putting on an act.'

'Oh, she knows this is about more than a broken wrist and bruises. You can't hide anything from Hettie. She loves you, Thea, and will be glad you're talking about how you feel.'

'I can't stop thinking what would have happened to George and Betty if I'd died,' Thea admitted.

'I understand,' said Prue. 'It's how every parent feels, every guardian. But you know Betty and George would have been looked after, don't you? We're all their family, while they're here with us.'

Thea considered Prue's words and Prue thought she saw the glimmer of a spark returning to her sister's eyes.

'The fact is,' Prue said, 'you survived and the children are safe.'

'Yes,' Thea said, her face brightening some more.

'I suppose they know about the accident?' Prue asked.

'They do but we've played it down. Hettie was adamant we shouldn't say too much to worry them, and of course she's right. I believe Betty insisted she and George should have had a day off school in honour of my condition and all of Rookery House's children are most eager to see my plaster cast.'

'Children can appear to take things pretty well, but they are sensitive to things. Remember how Marie got herself all worked up worrying about how Nancy might get caught in a bomb blast like the one that killed Victor?' Prue reminded her. 'Once she'd talked to us, and we'd explained it to her, she was much better.' She took hold of Thea's uninjured hand and squeezed it. 'And that is why it's good to talk about what's concerning us.'

'Like you do about your worries?' Thea's lips twitched at the corners.

Prue let out a huff. 'You know, I do think you're getting better already, you sound a lot more like your old self.'

Thea smiled as broadly as she could. 'You might be right, sister,' she said. 'Only don't make me laugh yet – my face still hurts!'

The two of them giggled merrily, Thea's eyes sparkling.

'As for me opening up about my problems,' Prue said, 'that's easier said than done sometimes I know, but I think I'm getting better at it. I hid how bad things were getting with Victor, though I think you guessed, didn't you?' Thea nodded. 'Anyway, that's in the past, and it's what we do now that matters.'

'It is,' Thea agreed.

'You need to take it easy for a while. Look after yourself and no rushing back to work.'

'Not that I could do much with this anyway.' Thea moved her plastered arm in its sling. 'I will be careful and have a few days off. Though I'm going to be desperate to do something, even if it is just slowly sowing seeds with my left hand. I enjoy my work. You'd be the same, you know, a broken wrist wouldn't stop you in your tracks.'

'It would not, though I hope I would delegate more things to those who are willing, able and more than happy to help. You've got Flo, Luca and Nancy working here and Hettie told me Ted's offered to come by too.'

'I'm lucky to have them, but I am worried about what's going to happen with the haymaking. It's a big job and…'

'Stop right there!' Prue held up her hand. 'It will get done. Even if we need to bring The Mother's Day Club and WI to our aid.'

Thea let out a soft laugh. 'I give in! I'm going to try to not think about it and just rest and recover. Thank you, Prue, you've been just the person to pull me out of my doldrums.'

The door opened and Hettie came in carrying a tray of tea things. She put it on the small table and stood looking at Thea. 'You've got more colour in your cheeks than you had earlier.'

'We've been talking,' Thea said.

'I'm glad to hear it. It's all too easy to just carry on but sometimes you need to stop and reflect.'

'You sound very philosophical,' Prue said.

Hettie looked thoughtful. 'I don't know about that but I've

seen a lot in my life and lived through many experiences and they all teach you something.'

'If only I could tell my younger self what I know now,' Prue said.

'What would you say?' Thea probed.

Prue waved her hand dismissively. 'Oh, plenty, but I can't go back. None of us can. We can only do our best with what we've learned.'

'Now who's being philosophical?' Hettie raised her eyebrow, watching Prue through her round glasses.

'You two are a tonic!' Thea said, laughing. 'I feel less heavy and forlorn than I did earlier, so thank you. And if I need to talk about it more, I will. I promise.'

'I'm glad to hear that.' Prue's eyes prickled with tears. 'I'm always here for you and so is Hettie. We're family and we care and look out for each other.'

It was early afternoon by the time Prue arrived at the village allotments. She'd joined everyone at Rookery House for the midday meal and was pleased to see her sister was in good form and getting back to her usual self. Prue would keep a close eye on her over the next weeks and months, though, because a shock such as Thea had experienced wasn't to be dismissed lightly.

Bumping her bicycle along the track between allotments, she heard Percy Blake call out to her. Braking, she came to a halt and dismounted.

'Afternoon, Missus.' Percy touched the brim of his hat. 'Come and have a look at Clarabel, if you've got a minute.'

'Clarabel?' Prue queried, leaning her bicycle against the fence at the end of his plot. Percy was known for his prize vegetables and whilst Prue didn't recall him naming them, it wouldn't have surprised her if he did, he held them in such high regard. She looked across to his vegetable patch, asking, 'Is she a marrow?'

Percy gave a great guffaw. 'No, she isn't!' he said, cackling as he mopped his brow with his cap. 'Clarabel is our *piglet*. Fourteen weeks old she is and doing nicely.' He beamed proudly.

Prue followed him down the path running along the middle of his plot between neat rows of carefully tended fruits and vegetables, recalling him telling her he and his friends were getting a pig. At the far end she appraised the rather ramshackle pigsty and adjoining pen he'd been constructing a few months back, wondering if it was built well enough to hold a piglet let alone a grown pig.

'Isn't she a beauty?' Percy said proudly, pointing at the small black and pink saddleback piglet who was rooting through the straw scattered on the floor of her pen. 'She's growing fast and so she should be, considering the amount she eats. It's keeping us busy foraging for her.'

'Oh, she's lovely!' said Prue, clapping her hands in delight. 'And she looks fat and healthy so you're looking after her well.'

'You could keep one on the WI's allotment,' Percy suggested.

'I thought about it but it's too big a commitment.'

'That it is,' he agreed, 'but me, Bert and Wilfred look after Clarabel between us and we're enjoying it.'

'I'm glad.' Prue gave him a warm smile. 'Right, I've got some hoeing to do or the weeds will be taking over.'

Leaving Percy watching the piglet, Prue collected her bike and headed for the WI allotment. After the news and worry of earlier today, she was looking forward to losing herself in the simple task of removing weeds from the rows of vegetables.

She had to admit, though, that seeing cute little Clarabel had already cheered her up immensely. Maybe the WI allotment should get one after all... but no. Piglets were too much work and her life was full enough already to take on anything else, no matter what joy it might bring.

CHAPTER 23

It was Saturday morning and only the second day since Thea's accident. She was playing cards with George in the sitting room, enjoying some quality time with him while his sister Betty accompanied Marianne and her two girls on a trip into the village.

'Snap!' George slapped down his playing card, matching the one Thea had just placed on the table. 'Two penguin cards – I win!' He scooped up all the cards and added them to his growing collection. 'How many have you got left, Auntie Thea?'

The pair of them were side by side on the sofa with a small coffee table beside their knees. She picked up her tiny pile of cards and counted them. 'Four.'

'Do you want some of mine?' George offered. 'You're slower than usual and have hardly won any snaps.'

'That's very kind of you to offer but you won them fair and square.' She gave the eight-year-old a reassuring smile. 'I *am* slow on account of having to use my left hand but even if I was fully functioning I'm no match for you at Snap.'

George laughed. 'I've been practising with Betty. Only she won't play any more because she doesn't like losing.'

Thea chuckled. Competition between the two siblings was amusing to observe. It reminded her of her own rivalry with Prue, when they were a similar age to George and Betty. There was no harm in competitiveness, she believed, so long as it didn't get out of control. Look at how she and Prue had turned out – they were now as close as any sisters could be.

'I'll play you some more at Snap,' she told George. 'I don't mind being the loser. And who knows, I might even start winning...'

George glanced at her plastered right arm in its sling. 'Maybe we should play draughts instead,' he said, 'then it won't matter that you're injured. It would be fairer.'

'All right then, but I don't mind being hampered. Snap is a fun game, win or lose.' Thea put her good arm around George's shoulders and hugged him to her, loving how considerate he was. She was enjoying having more time to spend with him and his sister and they both clearly liked having her around to talk to and play games and read books with. This was one of the few advantages of having a broken wrist, Thea thought. She felt closer to George and Betty than she ever had.

Since her accident Thea had been resting, as Walt Summerville had advised. Hettie was watching over her, making sure Thea took things easy and giving some useful reminders when she was about to do something she shouldn't, like moving coffee tables unaided. Thea hoped that she was being a good patient and she was doing her best to look on the bright side of things. Playing games with George and Betty certainly helped with that.

George was peering at her closely. The bruising on her

face was presenting a dramatic display of colours that must look alarming. 'Does it still hurt?' he asked.

'A bit, but it's not too bad,' she told him. She had been sore and stiff the day before, mainly on the side of her body where she'd landed on the ground, but that was easing; apart from her wrist in plaster, she was feeling well. 'It looks a lot worse than it feels.'

'Good,' George said, giving her a smile.

Thea's only frustration was that she couldn't work. Being one person down, especially at this time of year with so much to do in the garden, was a worry that hadn't gone away.

'Auntie Thea?' George's voice broke into her thoughts. 'Shall we play draughts then?'

'All right, if you'd rather. You get the board and pieces out of the cupboard and I'll gather the Snap cards together.'

They were setting out counters on the black and white chequered board when the sound of an engine caught Thea's attention. She turned to look out of the bay window facing the road and saw a jeep drive in through the gate and come to a halt in front of the house.

'Who's that?' George hurried to the window and peered out.

Thea followed him, watching as Walt Summerville lifted her mended bicycle from the rear of the jeep and leaned it against the side. She waved to him through the window and, spotting her, he grinned.

'It's the kind American doctor who helped me,' Thea told George. 'Remember I told you about how he took an X-ray of my wrist? Let's go and meet him – he's a very pleasant chap.'

Rather than going through the kitchen and out the back way as she normally would, Thea led George along the hall; she opened the stained-glass panelled front door wide and stepped out.

'Hello again,' she said.

'Good Morning, Thea. And this must be…?'

'This is George.' She put her arm around the little boy, who had gone quiet and was standing behind her.

'Hi George, I'm Walt Summerville – you can call me Walt.' He held out his hand to the boy.

George stepped forward and shook it, staring up at the tall American. 'Hello.'

'I see you have my bike,' Thea said.

'Your bicycle is fixed as promised.' Walt gave a flourish of his hand towards it. 'As good as new.'

Thea inspected the front wheel. There were no signs of the damage. 'Thank you, Walt,' she said.

'You're welcome. And if I may, while I'm here I'd like to check on your wrist.'

'Of course.' Turning to George, she asked, 'Would you take my bike and put it away in the shed for me, please? Then go and tell Hettie that Doctor Summerville is here.'

George wheeled her bike away around the side of the house and Thea led Walt through the front door to the sitting room.

'How do your hand and wrist feel?' he asked when they were both seated.

'Fine.'

'Then let me.' He gently took her arm out of the sling.

'I'm doing the exercises you told me to. I don't want my arm seizing up.' Thea formed her hand into a fist and then splayed out her fingers just as he'd shown her.

'Good.' He held her hand, examined her fingers and thumb sticking out of the plaster, then turned her palm over. 'Any numbness or tingling anywhere in your fingers, hand or arm?'

'No.' She shook her head.

'What about pain?'

'The wrist aches a bit but nothing as bad as it was just after I broke it.'

'That all sounds excellent. Keep up the good work, and any problems you let me know, okay?' His eyes met hers.

'I will.'

There was a knock at the door.

'Come in!' Thea called and Hettie did as she was asked, followed by George.

'Doctor Summerville.' Hettie gave him a welcoming smile. 'How's your patient doing?'

'She's healing very well,' he replied. 'And please call me Walt.'

'Walt it is, then. Do you have time for a cup of tea with us this morning?'

'I do, but I'm curious to see more of what you grow here first.' He glanced at Thea. 'I sure would like you to show me around before we have some refreshments.'

'How about we have some tea in, say, half an hour? Would that be all right, Hettie?'

'Of course,' Hettie said. 'And with George's help we'll have a fresh batch of scones to go with it.'

Outside, Thea took Walt on a guided tour, glad it was a sunny day so that Rookery House's garden looked its best. After showing him the orchard where the chickens were scratching about in the tall grass under the trees, Thea took him to the greenhouse where Nancy was working.

'Nancy, this is Walt Summerville from the aerodrome – he's the doctor who fixed my arm,' Thea introduced him as they stood in the greenhouse doorway.

Walt held out his hand. 'Pleased to meet you.'

Nancy wiped her soil-covered fingers on her apron, which ballooned over her swollen belly, before giving Walt's hand a shake. 'Hello,' she said, 'and thank you for looking after Thea.'

'I was glad to.' Walt glanced around the greenhouse. 'What are you working on in here? It's a good temperature for setting things growing, I guess. I'm no gardener, though – I wish I was! It's something I hope to enjoy someday.'

'I'm sowing more lettuce, we do them little and often to keep up a steady crop,' Nancy told him. 'It's always a marvel 'ow the tiny, little seeds become fully grown plants with lovely juicy leaves.'

'That's one of the joys of gardening,' Thea agreed. 'We'll leave you to it, Nancy – I'm giving Walt a tour around so he can see what we do here.'

After they'd left Nancy, Walt commented, 'It looks like you're gonna be a worker down soon. When's the baby due?'

'September,' Thea told him. 'Nancy wants to carry on as long as she can, but I don't think she will be here for more than a few weeks at most. I'm giving her the easiest and least physically demanding jobs to do, like sowing seeds as you've just seen, but even so she gets tired easily and she shouldn't overdo it.'

'That's bad timing with you now out of action,' Walt mused. 'I think we need to figure things out and pretty soon.'

They'd reached the gateway to Five Acres field, which spread out before them. Half of it was used for growing vegetables and fruit bushes and the other half for grass. Flo and Luca were hoeing between broad bean plants over on the far side. Thea waved and they returned her greeting.

'That's our Flo, she's a Land Girl who works for me and lives here. Luca's an Italian Prisoner of War who comes from a POW camp six days a week. He's only been with us for a few months but has settled in well and is a good worker.'

'Does he speak English?' Walt asked.

'Not much, but more than he did when he first arrived. He's learning all the time.'

'You speak Italian then?'

Thea laughed. 'No! We're very lucky to have an interpreter. Max, a Dutch Language Professor who's staying in my brother's house – the one made from an old railway carriage I pointed out to you near the orchard – speaks fluent Italian.'

'That's swell,' Walt said. 'And it sounds like you've got everything worked out.'

'I did have, mostly, only…' Thea glanced at her arm in its plaster cast.

'Only an American truck driving on the wrong side of the road leaves you with a broken wrist and sidelined for weeks!' Walt finished for her, his face serious.

'Quite,' Thea agreed. 'And it was rotten timing with haymaking about to start soon.' Thea pointed to the long grass swaying in the breeze. 'Being a worker down is going to make it a lot harder. It's a massive job getting it dried and stored away. And of course, haymaking comes on top of keeping up with the rest of the work in the garden.' She shook her head. 'I must admit I'm worried about how we're going to manage it all this year. I'm completely out of ideas.'

'Tell me how many you need.'

She turned to him, frowning. 'How many what?'

'Men,' said Walt. 'I can hand-pick those with experience such as farmer's sons, we have plenty of those on the base,' Walt explained. 'I suspect they'll be glad to do these sorts of jobs again.'

'You can do that? And bring them over here to Rookery House?'

'I can and will,' Walt said. 'Consider it done. After what happened to you, we owe you.'

'Thank you very much, Walt,' Thea said. It was exactly the help she needed. 'That would be marvellous. And in answer to your question of how many, I'd say at least three men would be needed as a minimum, if you can spare them.'

'Excellent. I'll come along too if you don't mind. I can follow instructions if you tell me what to do and I'm eager to learn.'

'You'd be very welcome,' Thea said. 'Especially with the haymaking, which is always a race against time to get it inside the barn before the weather breaks. The grass has grown well this year so it's going to be a big crop. The more helpers we have, the better.'

Thea was buoyed up by Walt's offer. For the first time since being run off the road she felt like she was back to her old self. 'Let's go and have some tea,' she told Walt. 'Hettie worked as Cook at Great Plumstead Hall for many years and you'll not taste finer scones.'

'In that case, lead the way!' said Walt, his eyes lighting up. 'My mother was English-born, and she often made scones for us – I loved them. I'm sure Hettie's are a treat not to be missed.'

'They are,' said Thea.

As they walked back to the house, Thea felt as if a weight had lifted from her shoulders. She chatted easily with Walt and enjoyed simply being in the Rookery House garden which, of all the places she'd known, was the most soothing to her heart.

CHAPTER 24

'If I fold this bit here,' Betty said, concentrating hard as she made a sharp crease in a piece of blue paper that had been saved from a sugar bag, using her thumbnail to score down it, 'it will make a nice pleat in the skirt. See?' She held it up for Thea to inspect.

'That looks good, I can tell you've learned a lot from Marianne.' Thea was in the dining room, seated at the table beside Betty who was making paper dolls and the clothes to go on them. Thea was helping as much as she could with one of her hands out of action, but this was more about spending quality time with ten-year-old Betty. It was rare for Thea to have precious moments like this with Betty, but as George had gone with Flo, Marianne, Emily and Bea to visit Evie and Ned for Sunday afternoon tea, it was the perfect opportunity. 'You enjoy doing this sort of thing, don't you Betty? Do you think you might like to sew proper clothes for people when you're older?'

Betty's eyes widened. 'Yes!' she said without hesitating. 'I'd love to do dressmaking and make my own designs like

Marianne does. This is practising, and because it's paper it doesn't matter if I get it wrong. Let's check how it looks on our model.' She placed the skirt against the doll shape she'd cut out of cardboard from a box oats came in. 'It needs another matching pleat on the other side,' Betty said.

Thea watched as Betty made a second pleat in the blue paper and tested it against the cut-out doll. 'That's just right, but I need to shorten the length next,' Betty said. 'It should be not too short and not too long.'

It was impressive, Thea thought, how well the little girl applied herself to working things out, experimenting with different shapes and styles until she had what she wanted. Betty's interest in clothes and making them herself had been sparked and then developed thanks to her watching Marianne working. Betty had sometimes been given simple sewing tasks to do by Marianne, and she helped Hettie at the clothing depot in the village, often coming home with a new item she'd chosen for herself to wear.

Betty looked up at Thea. 'Hettie told me about how when she was a girl, the women wore floor-length skirts all the time.'

'That's right, and they did when I was little too. If a woman had worn trousers or dungarees back then like Flo and I do, people would have been horrified!' Thea laughed. 'What we wear now is so much more practical and comfortable, especially for working outside.'

'I haven't got any trousers,' Betty said. 'I would like some though.'

'Maybe we should see about making you a pair. Shall we ask Marianne if she would help?'

Betty beamed and nodded. 'I'll make some for the paper doll first.'

She began by placing her paper doll on a fresh piece of

blue sugar-bag paper and drawing around the lower half with her pencil. Then, putting the doll to the side, she sketched the shape of the trousers around the outline of the legs. 'There,' she said, then frowned. 'Do you think that will work?'

'I do,' Thea replied. 'Why not try it and see?'

Betty cut out the trousers she'd drawn, then fitted them against the doll. She clapped her hands. 'They're perfect, Auntie Thea!' Leaning into Thea, she gave her a hug, holding her tightly. Thea's eyes misted; it was rare for Betty to make such a spontaneous show of affection. Thea took the opportunity to return her hug, the two holding each other silently.

Spending time with just Betty, as Thea had done with George the day before, was something she cherished and she was determined to do more of it. Breaking her wrist had been shocking, painful and frustrating but it had also been a lesson to her. She should slow down and spend time with her two young charges whenever the chance came along.

'Next I will make...' Betty began but stopped as her attention was caught by movement outside the bay window that faced the road at the front of the house. 'Auntie Thea!' she said excitedly, ending their embrace as she twisted around to see better.

Thea followed her gaze and watched six men on bicycles riding in through the gate. Each of them was dressed in American Air Force overalls. She recognised the one in the lead and could hear his voice through the open window issuing instructions to dismount and wheel their bicycles around to the back garden.

'It's Walt!' Betty had met him yesterday after she'd returned home with Marianne, Bea and Emily.

'It is – and I wasn't expecting him and his men so soon and

on a Sunday!' Thea carefully stood up. 'I must go and meet them. Do you want to come with me?'

Betty thought for a moment, her eyes sliding over the paper doll and the different outfits she'd created for it so far this afternoon. 'Can I stay here? I want to think about a top to fit with the trousers and then maybe a coat.'

Thea smiled at her. 'Of course you can; you're enjoying yourself, so carry on.' She put her good arm around Betty's shoulders and gave her a sideways squeeze. 'I'll look forward to seeing what else you design later.'

Leaving Betty to create more clothes for the paper doll, Thea hurried along the hall and into the kitchen where she saw Walt standing at the open back door talking to Hettie. On seeing her, his face lit up.

'Good afternoon, Thea! I've brought you a team of workers. Five young men eager to get their hands in the soil again.'

'That's perfect,' Thea said as she crossed the kitchen to him. 'I never expected you to organise them so quickly. You only suggested the idea yesterday.'

'If a job needs doing, then I don't like to hang around,' Walt replied. 'What do you want us to do?'

Thea pondered for a moment. 'If there are six of you including yourself, then a job that would be really helpful to get done is earthing up the potatoes in Five Acres.'

Walt seemed puzzled. 'I'm sorry Thea but I'm not sure what you mean by that. I've got a lot to learn, remember?'

'It's a simple job,' Thea explained, 'just drawing up soil around and over the growing potato plants to produce a rounded ridge. We need to do it to stop the tubers from turning green and poisonous in the light. It's easy, just time consuming as we grow a lot of potatoes.'

Walt still seemed unsure of the task. 'Well okay, we can do

that if you show us how and I expect some of my men have done it before,' he said. 'Come and meet them.' Walt led the way and Thea and Hettie followed him outside.

Thea noticed that the five waiting American servicemen stood up straighter as they approached.

'Let me introduce Chuck here, this is Vinnie, then Hudson, Gil and Earl.' Walt gestured towards each man as he named them and they responded with hellos and friendly smiles. 'Men, this is Thea and Hettie, who we're here to help in any way we can.'

'Welcome to Rookery House,' Hettie said.

'Thank you all for coming; we appreciate you giving up your free time to help us,' Thea said, thinking that none these young men could be older than twenty.

'We're sure glad to come and help, ma'am,' Chuck responded. 'It will remind us of home, working on the land again. What job do you have for us first?'

'We'll start you off with earthing up potatoes,' Thea said.

Chuck glanced down the line at the other men who, from the looks on their faces, knew exactly what she was talking about.

'Sure, we can do that no problem,' Vinnie told her.

'Let's get to it,' Walt said and the men responded with an obedient, 'Sir!'

'I'll go in and get some baking done,' Hettie said. 'I daresay you'll work up a good appetite this afternoon and be ready for something to eat come tea break. You can all look forward to some Norfolk shortcakes – one of our local recipes.'

'I love the sound of those,' Walt said. 'Thank you, Hettie.'

Thea gave her friend a grateful smile then turned to Walt's men. 'Let's get you some tools and then I'll show you where to start.'

Hettie put the last of the Norfolk shortcakes she'd just taken out of the oven onto the wire cooling rack and stepped back to survey her baking with a critical eye. Each cake looked good and there were plenty of them to keep the workers going.

She'd used chopped-up dried plums instead of currants or sultanas, which were now hard to come by, and found they were an excellent substitute and were delicious. With several plum trees growing in the orchard, she had a plentiful supply of fruit to dry and store for use in her recipes throughout the year.

'How soon can we eat them?' Betty asked, the smell of baking having lured her from the dining room and into the kitchen.

'Not yet, unless you want a burnt mouth,' Hettie warned her. 'We'll start on the washing up and by the time that's done, they'll be cool enough to eat.'

'Can I wash?' Betty asked.

'If you like,' Hettie said, pleased with the offer. 'And while you do it you can tell me how you're getting on with your clothes designing.'

'All right,' said Betty, as Hettie put an apron on her and tied it around the back.

They'd almost finished washing and drying up when Thea came in the back door, sniffing appreciatively.

'That lovely smell is wafting out into the garden – I couldn't help following the trail back to here!'

'The shortbreads are cooling and nearly ready,' Hettie said. 'How are the workers doing?'

'They've done the work of a dozen of us in half the time!' Thea said. 'They'll easily finish earthing up the potatoes this afternoon. I'm so pleased because it's a job that would have taken several days for Flo and Luca to do, having to fit it around other daily tasks. If there's time, some hoeing and weeding could get done as well today.'

'What about Walt?'

'He's managing okay, as the Americans like to say.' Thea smiled wryly, shaking her head. 'I *did* warn him to watch out for getting blisters on his hands…'

Hettie sighed. 'Well at least he'll know how to treat them.'

'Shall we have the shortcakes and drinks in the garden since it's a lovely day?' Thea suggested.

'Good idea.' Hettie agreed. 'We will bring them out when you tell everyone it's ready.'

'Out of this world, ma'am!' Chuck said after his first mouthful of a Norfolk shortcake. 'You sure are a whizz in the kitchen.' He quickly took another bite.

'I'm glad you like it.' Hettie chuckled. Thea, Walt and his men were sat at the wooden table in the garden where she and Betty had just laid out the shortcakes on a large plate and brought jugs of blackberry cordial for everyone to slake their thirst. 'Did you grow up on a farm?' she asked him.

Chuck's eyes widened, his mouth full of shortcake. 'Pardon me,' he said, after he'd swallowed and taken a sip of his drink. 'I must work on my manners. I was raised on a farm, in Washington State. My pa grows a lot of raspberries and all kinds of vegetables. It's a beautiful part of the world and I miss it.' He looked wistful for a moment before adding, 'I sure am glad to be here at Rookery House today and to be able to work the land. It's a welcome change from my usual job.'

'What do you do?' Hettie asked.

'I'm a grease monkey!' Chuck waited, smiling, for the question he clearly knew would be coming.

'What's a grease monkey?' Betty and Hettie both said together, then laughed.

'It's what we call the mechanics on the airbase,' Chuck explained. 'I repair damaged aircraft. Fix them up so they can fly again.'

'Do you enjoy it?' Hettie asked.

'Most of the time. It's a challenge and we always have a lot to do – we work long hours.'

'Are you all mechanics?' Hettie gestured towards the other Americans, who were talking to Thea and Walt.

'No. Hudson there, he's in air traffic control. Earl is in the weather office, Vinnie's ground crew and Gil's a medical technician who works in the hospital with Doc Summerville. All of us are from farmer stock though, born with the dirt between our toes as we say. When the Doc asked for volunteers to come here, we jumped at the chance.'

'We're very grateful for your help.' Hettie patted his arm. 'It's a busy time of year and with haymaking around the corner it will get even busier.'

'We all plan to come along whenever we can and sure will enjoy helping with the haymaking.'

Hettie noticed he'd finished his shortcake. 'Would you like another one?' She held the plate out to him.

Chuck grinned and took one. 'I sure would, thank you, ma'am.'

CHAPTER 25

Prue had unlocked the door of the village hall, ready to go in and set up for this morning's Mother's Day Club, when she heard the loud, urgent ringing of a bicycle bell behind her. She turned to see Hettie arriving on her bike, her cheeks flushed and her eyes wide.

'Did you hear the news?' Hettie said in an excited voice as she dismounted.

'What's happened?' Prue stared at her.

'The liberation of Europe has begun! It was on the eight o'clock bulletin on the wireless.'

Prue gasped, putting a hand to her mouth, her thoughts flying to her son Jack. 'I hadn't heard. What did they say on the bulletin?'

'Apparently the Allies gave advance warning of aerial attacks and bombing in coastal areas,' Hettie said, leaning her bike against the wall and removing her basket from its carrier on the back. 'They've told civilians in towns to evacuate. Get out into the open countryside. Leaflets were dropped from Allied planes telling people what was coming and what to do.'

'Did it say where?' Prue asked.

'No, not yet. I expect we'll hear more later. I know you're worried about Jack. We all are.' Hettie rested her hand on Prue's arm. 'Jack's a sensible lad.'

'He is, but that doesn't mean he won't get hurt.' Tears stung at the back of Prue's eyes; she quickly blinked them away. 'Come on,' she told Hettie, 'we need to get ready for The Mother's Day Club. Whatever might be going on across the English Channel today, we still must carry on here.'

'Yes, and all the while we will keep our hearts and minds with our brave servicemen,' Hettie said as she followed Prue into the hall.

Anyone who hadn't heard the news soon learned of it after arriving at The Mother's Day Club. There was little talk of anything else while they attended to a batch of sewing.

'It 'ad to 'appen if this war is ever to come to an end,' Gloria declared. 'But even so, it ain't easy thinking about what's going on over there.'

'It must 'ave been carefully planned and everyone will 'ave trained 'ard and be prepared for it,' Annie said positively, threading a new length of cotton through her needle. 'I wish every single one of them well.'

''ear, 'ear,' Gloria said. 'And they've managed to keep it secret till now so as not to let the enemy know they were coming.'

'Despite that, they'll still be up against the might of the German army.' Prue let out a sigh and gave up on her sewing, abandoning it on the table in front of her. 'The enemy will have strong defences and be ready for an attack. They knew it would come at some point. It was just a question of when.'

'When and *where*,' Gloria added. 'It's a long coastline along the Channel. It will be 'ard to defend every bit all the time. Our men'll do their job, you mark my words.'

Prue listened as the conversation went back and forth, speculating on where and what might be happening. Until news came through of what was going on, they couldn't know for sure, but at least talking about it kept her mind from fretting. There was nothing she could do to help Jack now; if the time came when he needed her, she would be ready to do her utmost in whatever way she could.

Prue had hurried straight home after this morning's session of The Mother's Day Club and now sat at her kitchen table. *Workers' Playtime* on the Home Service was filling the room with music. It felt odd listening to the lively tune, all the while knowing what was going on across the Channel today. She watched the clock on the wall, urging the minute hand around faster so it would be one o'clock and time for the news.

Prue knew she wouldn't be the only person in Great Plumstead listening and waiting right now – the other women from The Mother's Day Club would be doing the same, as would people in cities, towns and villages across the length and breadth of the entire country. Great Britain waited with bated breath.

Workers' Playtime finally ended, and Prue's heart picked up speed as the BBC Home Service announcer introduced a special bulletin.

'D-Day has come. Early this morning, the Allies began the assault on the north-western face of Hitler's European fortress...'

At last, Prue had the answer to her question of where the attack was – on the northern coast of France. She listened alertly, sitting tense and forward in her chair as the radio voice told of army groups of British, Canadian and American forces under the command of General Montgomery. It was, however, the message from the Commander-in-chief General Eisenhower to the men attacking that sent an icy finger of fear trickling down Prue's back.

'Your task will not be an easy one. Your enemy is well-trained, well-equipped and battle-hardened. He will fight savagely.'

Those words were a stark warning of what the sons, husbands and brothers from families here in Britain and in Canada and America were facing.

Prue didn't know if Jack had landed on a French beach this morning. There was no possibility of her finding out right now. It was hard not knowing. It made her feel so helpless.

She listened to the rest of the bulletin, which, after more detail about the landings in Normandy, went on to talk briefly about the fighting in Italy. Edwin was there somewhere. Now both her sons were in danger and all she could do was wait and hope they would survive.

At the end of the announcement, Prue switched off the wireless. A heavy silence filled the room. She didn't fight the wave of sadness, worry and helplessness that flooded through her. She let her tears fall, her shoulders shaking as she sobbed.

CHAPTER 26

Members of the Great Plumstead singing group were giving voice to the last tune of the evening – *There'll Be Bluebirds Over the White Cliffs of Dover* – filling the village hall to its rafters with uplifting music. Hettie, standing between Prue and Flo, felt her heart soar like the bluebirds in the song.

It was such a beautiful sound, Hettie thought. Singing along with the other women was powerful – there was something magical and otherworldly about how their voices combined as they each lost themselves in the song. Whatever else was going on in their lives could be left at the door for two hours while they sang. And even though everyone had to return to real life afterwards, somehow things always felt a bit easier after spending time singing together.

Gloria, who was their founding member and an experienced performer, stood in front of everyone, her bobbing hand guiding them through the higher or lower notes while she accompanied them with her beautiful, clear voice.

As the song drew to a close, they fell into a hush for a few moments, everyone clearly affected emotionally by the music.

Hettie watched Gloria wait, not wanting to break the peaceful silence, her eyes shining.

'That was bloomin' marvellous!' Gloria declared finally. 'It caught me right 'ere.' She placed her hand on her chest, over the scarlet fabric of her dress.

'And me,' Hettie agreed.

Calls and nods of agreement by the other women echoed the sentiment.

'See you all at the same time again next week then.' Gloria beamed. 'And carry that song 'ome with you in your 'eart.'

'Thank you, Gloria, it's been a lovely session,' Prue said. 'I always look forward to it.'

'There ain't nothing like singing together in a group. It fills our 'earts and souls,' Gloria said.

Outside Hettie and Flo fetched their bicycles from where they'd left them at the side of the village hall and were about to set off home to Rookery House when Hettie heard her name called.

'Just a minute, Flo,' Hettie said. 'Somebody wants me.'

She looked around to see Iris from Crossways Farm. The Land Girl was walking towards them hand in hand with an American serviceman looking smart in his uniform.

'Evening, Iris,' Hettie greeted her warmly. 'It's good to see you. You look lovely in that dress.' It was good to see the young woman wearing something different from her Land Army uniform, Hettie thought.

'Thank you. Hettie, there's someone I'd like you to meet – this is Frank. Remember I told you about him? Frank, this is Hettie, the wonderful woman who keeps an eye out on behalf of the Land Army and makes sure I'm happy and being well looked after at the farm.'

'Good evening, ma'am,' Frank said, holding out his hand.

Hettie shook it. 'Hello Frank. I'm pleased to meet you. Iris has told me all about you.' On Hettie's last few visits to the farm, Iris had been full of chatter about the American airman she was stepping out with.

'And this is Flo – she's a fellow Land Girl,' Iris explained.

Frank and Flo shook hands.

'Where are you off to?' Hettie asked Iris.

'The Half Moon.' Iris nodded towards the pub on the far side of the village green, which was popular with the Americans, many of them cycling into the village to spend evenings there. 'We're going to celebrate... Hettie, we're engaged!' She held out her left hand for them to see the ring set with a ruby stone on the fourth finger. 'Frank asked me last week.' Iris gave her fiancé a loving look. 'He's been waiting for the engagement ring to arrive from America. It was his grandmother's and his mother sent it over for him to give to me. It arrived this morning. Now we're properly engaged to be married!'

'Congratulations to you both!' Hettie gave them a warm smile.

'It's wonderful news!' Flo added. 'Have you set a date yet?'

'It's going to take a little while to get things arranged,' Frank said. 'Even though we're keen to marry as soon as we can, there are procedures we must deal with first. There's a lot of paperwork to be completed.'

'I've got to have an interview with the aerodrome's commanding officer or chaplain to check that we're serious and being sensible,' Iris added. 'I know we haven't known each other that long but we love each other so much and want to spend the rest of our lives together.' Iris smiled at her fiancé. 'We want to grow old together.'

'We certainly do.' Frank put his arm around her shoulders.

'Once we get permission to marry, we'll have to wait sixty days before the wedding ceremony can take place,' Iris explained. 'We're hoping we can get married in late August.'

'That will give you time to plan your wedding,' Hettie said. 'Decide what you'll wear and so on.'

'I'm hoping to hire one of the wedding dresses sent over from America for women in the Land Army or forces to use,' Iris said. 'I'd rather not get married in my uniform.'

'Our Land Army uniform is more practical than pretty,' Flo said, looking down at her own corduroy breeches and green woollen jumper. 'It's fine for our work, but…'

'If you can't get a proper wedding dress, then we'll have to make you one!' Hettie said. 'Keep me informed of how things are going. I'm always here to help when you need me.'

'Thank you,' Iris said, giving Hettie a hug.

'Would you care to join us at the Half Moon?' Frank asked.

'It's a very kind offer,' Hettie told him, 'but I'm heading home where I've got things to sort out for the morning. You could go, Flo?' Hettie suggested.

'I think it's your special time to enjoy together,' Flo told Iris. 'I'll join you another time though.'

Frank nodded. 'Another night, then.'

'Good to see you both.' Iris linked her arm through Frank's and they headed off towards the pub.

Hettie and Flo mounted their bicycles and pedalled through the village towards Rookery House.

'That was a surprise,' Hettie said as they rode alongside each other. 'Iris has only been stepping out with Frank for a couple of months at the most. He seems a nice young man though.'

'Courtship gets speeded up in times like this,' Flo said. 'People don't wait so long to get married, especially couples with one or both of them in the forces.'

'Well I hope it works out for them. Iris is a lovely girl and I'd hate to see her regret her decision.' Hettie was concerned about the speed of their engagement but, as Flo had reminded her, things were different now. At least there would be a sixty-day wait once they were given permission to marry. That would give them longer to get to know one another before they were legally bound together. Marrying Frank would probably mean Iris moving to America after the war, leaving behind her family, friends and all she was familiar with. She'd be starting a whole new life in a strange place and that was a huge step to take, especially with someone she had only known for a matter of weeks.

CHAPTER 27

It was two and a half weeks since Thea had broken her wrist after narrowly avoiding being mown down by an American Air Force lorry. During that time, she'd learned to be patient with the limited things she could do while her right arm was in plaster and accept that there was still plenty she couldn't manage. Using only her left hand she could still feed the chickens, collect eggs, pick peas, sow seeds and do some weeding, all at a slower pace than she normally worked. But at least she could do something.

Now with haymaking in full swing, it had been frustrating to have to stand back and watch while the others worked. After Reuben had borrowed a team of horses and a mower to do the cutting, the grass needed turning twice a day with pitchforks until it was dry. With Thea's injury, there was nothing she could do to help. She'd tried but it had been useless. The motion needed to lift and flip the grass over required both hands and Thea had been forced to admit defeat.

Today, the hay was almost ready to bring into the barn to

store for the winter months. One last turn would complete the drying in the warm June sunshine. Thea watched the team of workers spread out across the rows of hay in Five Acres field. Flo, Luca, Max, Ted, Prue and Marianne were steadily working their way along, deftly flicking hay over with their pitchforks, filling the air with the sweet, heady scent of dry grass and wildflowers. Max had insisted on helping as he was feeling much fitter, his recovery aided, he said, by the clean air and good food at Rookery House.

Over the past few days, the young American servicemen from the aerodrome had also been here to turn the hay and they were coming again later to help bring it in. That task was long and heavy and sometimes a race against the weather; the hay had to be safely under cover before rain arrived.

Since their first visit to Rookery House, the young Americans had become frequent visitors, bicycling over from the aerodrome whenever they had time off. Walt Summerville had come too when he could. Their assistance had been a significant boost and, after the hay was gathered in, Thea planned to throw a party to thank them along with everyone else who'd worked so hard over the past few days and weeks.

'Thea, can I 'ave a word?'

She turned to see Nancy approaching, noticing that her friend's walk had more of a waddling gait now.

'Of course, are you all right?'

'Yes, apart from feeling 'eavier by the day. I'll be glad when this one is safely 'ere.' She stroked her belly. 'I'm sorry, Thea, but I am going to 'ave to stop work at the end of the week. It's getting much 'arder with the tiredness. I know you give me easy jobs to do and I appreciate that, but the time 'as come like we knew it would.'

'It's fine, Nancy, don't worry. You've done a marvellous job carrying on for so long. We'll all miss you.' Thea put her arms around her friend and embraced her.

'I've loved working 'ere,' Nancy said. 'Given 'alf a chance, I'll be back some day.'

'And you'll be most welcome,' Thea said, releasing her at last. 'You know, I've an idea. We'll have a party at the weekend to celebrate the end of haymaking. How about we make it a farewell for you too? That way we can all thank you properly for everything you've done for us. What do you think?'

'It's a smashing idea.' Nancy grinned. 'It will be fun and a lovely way to end my time working at Rookery 'ouse! Everyone loves a party, don't they?!'

CHAPTER 28

'Thank you, everyone...' Thea smiled around at her family and friends gathered in the back garden at Rookery House. Hettie, Flo, Marianne and her two daughters, along with George and Betty, occupied the chairs they'd brought out from the kitchen. Reuben, Max, Luca and Ted stood together where they'd been deep in conversation. Prue, Nancy and her girls Marie and Joan were amidst the five young American servicemen, Chuck, Earl, Vinnie, Hudson and Gil, their eyes bright with mirth at some joke or other. Slightly apart from the crowd, Walt was standing with his arms folded, his cap pushed back on his head, looking relaxed and very much at home.

'For all your hard work with the haymaking,' Thea continued, 'whatever role you played it made a difference. Together we were a wonderful team and brought in a magnificent crop to last our animals through the winter months. Your help means a great deal to me.'

Chuck let out a whoop of delight and clapped loudly and everyone else joined in.

Thea laughed. 'Without further ado, let's start our celebrations! Flo, would you organise the music, please?'

'I'd be delighted to,' Flo said. 'Let's get the dancing started. I hope you'll be joining in too.'

Thea looked down at her arm encased in plaster. 'I'm not sure...'

'Walt?' Flo called over to him. 'Would dancing be allowed with a broken wrist?'

'Of course.' Walt came over to them.

'There you go, Thea,' Flo said, 'it's Doctor's Orders. Dancing is excellent exercise and fun too, isn't that right, Doc?'

'I agree, and...' The American looked at Thea. 'I'd be happy to dance with you, if you're willing?'

Thea's cheeks grew warm. 'In that case, thank you. I accept your offer.'

Flo grinned. 'Excellent! I'll get the music started...' She headed over to the table that stood by the open French doors, where a gramophone had been set up beside a pile of records. 'I must thank Lady Campbell-Gryce for lending us these,' she called back to Thea, 'and Prue for asking her!'

'It's lovely 'aving a party 'ere,' Nancy said, coming over to Thea and Walt. 'And a perfect way to end my time working at Rookery 'ouse.'

'You know you are always welcome to visit whenever you want,' Thea reminded her. 'You'll be able to push the baby here in its pram.'

'I will. Only I've got to get through the birth yet. It's worrying me,' Nancy admitted.

'You've done it before,' Thea reassured her.

'It ain't that bit,' Nancy explained, 'it's because I'm supposed to be going away into the maternity 'ome. *That's* the problem. Marie and Joan were both born in my own 'ome.

This one…' Nancy placed her hand on her swollen belly, 'well I wish it could be the same and I didn't 'ave to leave the girls and give Prue even more to do looking after them while I'm stuck away for a couple of weeks.'

'Why can't you have your baby at home?' Walt asked curiously, after listening to the conversation. 'If it's what you'd prefer.'

'All expectant mothers in this area are encouraged to 'ave them in the maternity 'ome now. They've got the staff ready in case there's 'elp needed,' Nancy said. 'There's no guarantee a midwife could get to me if I gave birth at 'ome.'

'Heavy snow stopped Marianne from getting to the maternity home when Emily was born,' Thea told them. 'She gave birth here with the help of Gloria, who has experience of helping with deliveries and can always be called on. The midwife didn't get through until afterwards.'

'Snow won't be a problem in September though, will it?' Nancy said worriedly.

'Not at all,' said Thea, 'but it's good to know Gloria is here in the village should she be needed.'

'I used to attend births in my practice back home,' Walt said. 'It was a privilege to deliver the babies.' He smiled at the memory. 'I miss that kind of medical work – there's not much call for it on the airbase.' He laughed, then his expression changed to one Thea recognised from when she'd first met him, when he was her doctor and was assessing the damage to her wrist. He had an air of kindness and professionalism, Thea thought, and she guessed correctly what he was about to offer.

'How would you feel about me delivering your baby?' Walt asked Nancy. 'It would mean you could stay at your home here in the village.'

'Really?' Nancy's eyes widened.

'I'd have to clear it with my superiors first and make sure my fellow doctor could cover duty on the base when you went into labour, but I expect that could be arranged easily enough. I would very much enjoy doing some regular physician work again, just as I do daily back home at my practice in Maine.'

Nancy blinked as she considered it. 'Yes, please,' she said, beaming. 'I'd be very 'appy for you to deliver my baby at 'ome for me, if you're allowed to. It would be so much better for me and my girls and Prue.' Nancy spoke rapidly, the words flying out of her mouth. 'Thank you ever so – you've taken a weight off my mind.'

'It's not a given yet, but I will do my best,' Walt said. 'I will let you know as soon as possible.'

'I'll keep me fingers crossed. I must go and tell Prue.' Nancy rushed off to where Prue was talking to Hudson and Gil.

'That was generous of you,' Thea said.

'I miss practising family medicine. I…' He halted as the music finally started and the partygoers cheered. Bowing slightly, Walt held out his hand. 'May I have this dance? I promise to take it easy. No jitterbugging.'

'That's good,' said Thea, 'because I have no idea how!'

Taking Walt's hand, Thea stepped with him onto the impromptu dance floor on the short grass lawn behind Rookery House where Prue was dancing with Gil and Nancy with Hudson. Hettie arrived with Ted, and then Marianne with Luca. Shortly afterwards Chuck began teaching Flo some energetic moves; they kept to one side, the children watching them and imitating their actions, Betty the only one brave enough to join in. Reuben and Max stood over by the gramophone, examining the records and talking animatedly. It was a delight to see everyone having fun.

'Is your arm okay?' Walt asked as they moved slowly around in a waltz.

'It's fine if we stick to this. If we tried emulating Flo and Chuck I might end up breaking the other one.'

They both turned their heads to see Chuck twirling Flo over his head and down again. Flo, in a pretty summer dress, landed on her feet and continued moving without missing a beat. Thea had never seen Flo enjoying herself so much and it warmed her heart to see her like this after all she'd been through.

'If you're sure?' Walt raised an eyebrow questioningly.

'I am,' Thea assured him firmly. 'No twirling me in the air.'

'Don't worry, then, I'll keep you safe.' Walt returned her smile. 'There'll be no new broken bones on my watch.'

Prue thanked Gil for the dance and headed across to where her brother and Max hovered over the gramophone.

'Tired out already?' Reuben asked her with a cheeky grin as he removed a record from its protective cardboard sleeve and placed it on the turntable.

'Not at all,' she retorted. 'I merely wondered if either of you would like to dance with me? I saw you both tapping your feet...'

Reuben vehemently shook his head. 'You know as well as I do, dear sister, that I've got two left feet. For the sake of your toes, I'd best just keep doing what I'm doing.'

'Max?' Prue asked.

'I would be delighted.'

Leading her to the dance floor, Max took her hand and, as the music started, he steered her confidently around and amongst the other dancing couples.

'You dance well,' Prue commented.

'Thank you, as do you, Prue. My mother taught my sister and I. She believed it an important skill to have and I'm grateful for her persistence with my fumbling efforts. I eventually got the hang of it. It's been a long time since I last had the opportunity.'

'I bet you never thought you'd be dancing to celebrate a successful hay harvest.'

Max laughed. 'No, never. But life is full of surprises, isn't it?' He looked down at her for a moment, their eyes meeting.

'It is,' she said, not looking away.

They fell into silence, moving to the music. Prue was very aware of her hand in his and the gentle pressure of his other hand at her waist as he led her around. It felt different from dancing with Gil and she considered why that was... it just felt *right* with Max. That was the only way she could express it.

'You're frowning – I didn't stand on your foot, did I?' Max's voice broke into her thoughts.

'No, I was just thinking, I'm sorry.'

'Don't be sorry. Just tell me what you were thinking about, or perhaps that is none of my business...' Max apologised.

'I was thinking how lovely it is dancing with you.' The words slipped out before Prue could stop them. She felt a sudden emotion burning behind her eyes but didn't let herself flinch or be embarrassed. She didn't regret what she'd said – why should she?

Max's eyes creased into a smile and then he said in a soft voice, 'I'm enjoying dancing with you too. Very much.'

'One more dance and then I really must go in and get the last-minute food preparations sorted out,' Hettie said.

Ted laughed as he spun her around, keeping up to the lively beat of the music. 'You said that two songs ago.'

Hettie chuckled. 'I know – but it's so lovely to be out here dancing away the afternoon under the blue sky with friends. Don't you think?'

'I agree. It's not often we get to dance, maybe we should start going to the ones in the village hall.' He let go of her waist and held his arm up high for Hettie to go under and around, coming together again seamlessly and then continuing as before. 'We could show the young ones that us old folk know a move or two.'

They both glanced over at Flo and Chuck, who were jitterbugging, the other dancers giving them space for their exuberant moves.

'If we tried that, I don't think I'd be able to get out of bed the next morning,' Hettie said. The pair of them burst into peals of laughter.

'Best stick to what we know then,' Ted said. 'Although I'm quite partial to a quickstep, if you're up to it? We could ask Reuben to put on a tune that would suit it?'

'Go on then,' Hettie encouraged him and Ted steered her towards Reuben, ready to make their request when the music finished. The food could wait a little while longer. At least with all the dancing going on, everyone would have worked up a good appetite. And if there was one thing she'd learned in life, it was to enjoy opportunities to the full when they came along. Dancing with Ted in the Rookery House garden was certainly something to make the most of.

CHAPTER 29

On such a warm June day, Thea felt in need of a cool drink of water after returning from the village. She'd been there to deliver this morning's order of fruit and vegetables to Barker's grocers using Marianne's pram as transport. With the good weather, things were growing well, and Grace had commented favourably on the high quality of the peas, carrots, radishes and spinach Thea had brought her.

Thea returned the pram to where it was kept in the corner of the scullery. Pushing it was easy enough, even with her wrist in plaster. It was a lot slower than using her bike for deliveries as she normally would but needs must. She was determined to carry on doing her regular jobs where possible, despite any drawbacks.

She headed into the kitchen, where Hettie was busy churning butter.

'There's a letter for you.' The older woman gestured towards the pile of post on the dresser.

'Thanks, Hettie.' Thea poured herself a glass of water at the sink and took a long drink. 'I needed that; it's warm out there.'

She collected the envelope addressed to her, recognising the handwriting on the front.

'That from Violet?' Hettie asked, her cheeks flushed from the effort of turning the butter churn. 'I noticed the London postmark.'

'Yes, it is.' Thea sat down at the table and opened the letter.

'It would be lovely to have her stay here again,' Hettie said.

'I agree. But getting Violet to take a holiday is far easier said than done. I keep asking her to come again, encouraging her to have a break from her ambulance station for a while, but I haven't been able to persuade her.' Thea unfolded the single sheet of paper and began to read.

18th June 1944

Dear Thea,

I hope all is well with you and everyone at your wonderful Rookery House.
I often think of you all there and it's like a delightful oasis that I can escape to in my mind for a few moments. I've needed that these past few days more than ever. Have you heard about the latest weapon that the enemy is throwing at us? These ghastly pilotless V1 rockets – or doodlebugs as they're now calling them – are launched from across the English Channel. They fly until their engines cut out, then dive to the ground and explode.
It's a different tactic from the bomber air raids we'd grown used to dealing with and it's been harder than ever to keep on top of things. We've had so many more call-outs to incidents since the doodlebugs started that I fear it's taking its toll on my crews. It's not just the increased workload but the

psychological worry of where and when they might fall next. Nobody feels safe. Though my crews are magnificent – true Angels as they're sometimes referred to – and I have every faith in them. They soldiered on through the darkest days of the Blitz so I know they will carry on now.

Oh, Thea, these rockets are casting a new fear over everyone in London. Whenever I hear one, my heart plummets as I listen and hope the engine keeps on going. It's a horrible sound – like a noisy motorbike without a silencer. At night you can see a flame burning out of its tail against the darkness.

'Are you all right? Only you've gone pale.'

Thea tore her attention away from the letter. Hettie's face was full of concern.

'Violet's written about the doodlebug rockets we read about in the paper at the weekend. They're the latest weapon being used to attack London and they are causing a lot of damage, and fear as well.'

'Hang on, I'm sure we've still got that paper.' Hettie went over to the pile of old newspapers she kept on a shelf near the range and rummaged through them. 'Here it is. On the front of Saturday's *Eastern Daily Press*.'

Hettie spread it out on the table and sat down, pointing at the headline as she read out, 'Germany Launches Secret Weapon,' followed by, 'Pilotless Planes Over Southern England.'

Scanning through the article, Hettie said, 'They're much smaller than a Spitfire but look like one. "Midget planes" it says. At night they have a yellow glow at the rear. Is Violet scared? I know I would be.'

'I think she is struggling,' Thea said. 'She's upbeat about her crew though. Knowing Violet, she'll guide them through, keep them going.' Thea let out a sigh. 'It brings a whole new type of warfare to our capital city. This war keeps on inventing more hideous things. When will it ever end?'

Hettie took hold of Thea's hand and gave it a gentle squeeze. 'You're right but try not to let it get you down. We're doing our best. The Allied armies are making inroads into France. It *will* end sometime and the sooner the better.'

Thea nodded and smiled her thanks. 'I'm worried about Violet though.'

'Your friend is a strong woman. She won't let this new threat stop her from doing her job.'

'Violet will carry on regardless,' Thea agreed, with a wry smile.

Hettie gave Thea's hand a last squeeze and let go. 'I must get on with the churning. That cream won't turn itself into butter.' She got up from the table and Thea returned her attention to Violet's letter.

Yesterday I had to send a crew to where a doodlebug had landed in Aldwych. It's out of our usual catchment area but there were so many casualties they needed extra help. The rocket gouged a deep hole in the road and the blast scythed down the street, destroying everything in its path, even ripping apart double-decker buses. It hit in the daytime so there were many people about.

Thea knew London well and could easily picture the place where the doodlebug had exploded. The semi-circular road, which was near the BBC's Bush House, would have been busy with people when the rocket struck – the attack coming with little warning. It wasn't like during the Blitz, when the bombers had come under the cover of darkness and Londoners had sought shelter in the underground or in Andersons. These doodlebugs arrived at any time. They were a new and terrifying threat hanging over the city. She read on.

My crews did their jobs with courage and care and I'm so proud of them and the work they do. I think of what we did driving our ambulances in France, how we kept going and didn't give up. Now another generation is doing the same, but on home soil this time.
Thank you for reading this and listening. It helps to write to you, more than I can express. Holding the reins at Station 75 is a job I love, but the responsibility of it sometimes weighs heavily on my shoulders. And with this new weapon, this is one of those times.
I'm confident we will endure and survive and come out even stronger than before. Once this war is over, I look forward to coming to Rookery House again. That delightful thought helps keep me going.
Until then, be well and send my good wishes to all.

Your friend,

Violet

Thea took another drink of water and sat back in her chair. She needed a moment to steady her nerves and knew Hettie understood and was giving her time to digest what she'd read.

'Violet is doing the right thing writing to me,' she said at last. 'She needs to put what she's experiencing into words, to give what she's thinking an airing, not hold it in. I'm here to support her, though what she describes almost takes my breath away. They show such bravery, her crews – and Violet herself.'

'What else does she say?' Hettie asked sombrely.

'That she'd like to come and stay here when all this is over,' Thea said, deciding not to tell Hettie about the Aldwych doodlebug. It was enough that she knew about the rockets, there was no need to give her more graphic details.

'Violet will be most welcome and I look forward to it,' Hettie said as she turned the handle of the churn. 'She looked a different person by the end of her holiday here, relaxed and restored.'

'I remember.' Thea folded the letter, returned it to its envelope and put it in her dungarees pocket. 'I'd better get back to work.' She drank the rest of her water and stood up. 'I'll see you later.'

As Thea headed into the garden to do some hand weeding, thoughts of her treasured friend filled her mind. It was unusual for Violet to voice her fears so candidly in her letters and it was a sign of the stress she was under. Thea imagined how she herself would be feeling if they were living under such constant threat at Rookery House. It would be unbearable, she decided. She would write back to Violet that evening and do her best to support her dear friend who needed her now more than ever.

CHAPTER 30

Hettie had not long come indoors after collecting the eggs and was at the scullery sink washing her hands when the telephone rang in the hall. Hurriedly drying her hands on a towel, she went through to answer it hoping it wouldn't stop ringing before she got there.

Snatching up the receiver, she said, 'Hello, Rookery House.'

'Hettie, is that you?' a woman's voice came down the line. 'It's Beattie Southgate, from Crossways Farm.'

Hettie stiffened, her sixth sense telling her something was wrong. Beattie had never rung here before; they didn't have a phone at the farm so she must have gone to a telephone box to make the call and that meant it was important. 'Beattie, are you all right?' Hettie inquired.

'Not really. It's Frank, Iris's fiancé. His plane went down yesterday with no survivors. Hettie – he's dead!' Beattie's voice cracked.

Hettie gasped. 'Oh! I'm so sorry. Poor Iris – how is she?'

'She's devastated. Could you come, please? We're doing our

best to console her but if she could talk to you, it might help. She thinks the world of you, Hettie.'

'Of course I will come. I'll be there as soon as I can.'

'Thank you. I didn't know who else to turn to.' Beattie's voice was choked with tears. 'We all thought the world of Frank. He was a lovely young man and he made Iris so happy. I was worried something like this would happen with him flying daytime missions into enemy territory.'

'Those men risk their lives every single time they go up,' Hettie said soberly.

'But they still go,' Beattie said. 'They must. Oh that this war was over.'

After they'd finished the call, Hettie put the receiver back in its cradle and then slumped down to sit on the stairs for a moment, needing to take in the news. The future that Iris had been looking forward to, with the man she was going to marry, was gone, snuffed out in an instant. No wonder she was devastated, Hettie thought. Having only met Frank once, none the less she could tell he was a decent man, and he had met with the approval of Beattie and Stan Southgate as well. She thought of Frank's family back in America finding out their son had been killed far away, doing his duty, and felt her eyes fill with tears.

Hettie let out a deep sigh. Iris wasn't alone in her grief nor in losing the man she loved to this war. There were many women like her whose fiancé or husband or son had been killed and until this war was over even more men would be lost. Hettie couldn't help them all but she could support Iris. Hettie would show the young Land Girl that she wasn't alone, that she had people who cared for her and supported her. That would be a start.

'She's in her bedroom,' Beattie said, leading Hettie into the kitchen at Crossways Farm. 'She's been crying her eyes out ever since she heard the news this morning. One of Frank's friends came from the aerodrome to see her. He'd promised Frank he would, if anything happened to him. The friend was flying in another plane and saw Frank's explode and go down in flames. There were no parachutes, no survivors.' Beattie swallowed hard. 'He had no chance of getting out, none of them did.'

Hettie put a hand on Beattie's shoulder. 'It's hard to take in.'

Beattie pulled a handkerchief out of her cardigan pocket and dabbed at her cheeks. 'I can't believe we'll never see him again. That he won't come riding down the lane on his bike the way he did, or we'll never hear him and Iris laughing together.'

'You were fond of him too,' Hettie said.

'Yes, and Stan was. Frank fitted in so well. He helped us about the place and didn't mind getting his hands dirty. He was a perfect match for Iris. They made such a lovely couple. Only now...'

'Make yourself a cup of sweet tea; it will help,' Hettie said sympathetically. 'I'll go up and see Iris.'

'Shall I bring some for you and Iris?'

'Not yet.'

Beattie caught hold of Hettie's sleeve as she was leaving. 'Thank you for helping her.'

'I will do my best.'

'Iris's bedroom is the second door on the right.'

Hettie went out of the kitchen into the hall and then climbed the stairs. Reaching Iris's door, Hettie paused before knocking, bracing herself. It would not be easy because however much she supported and comforted Iris, the stark truth was that the young woman's fiancé was dead. That couldn't be fixed, only accepted.

With nerves jangling suddenly in her stomach, Hettie tapped on the door. 'Iris. It's Hettie. Can I come in?'

There was a muffled reply from within, which Hettie took for consent, and she opened the door and peeped inside. Iris lay on her bed, curled up like a wounded animal. Hettie's heart went out to her. She crossed the room in a few strides, sat down on the side of the bed and pulled the young woman into her arms. Iris didn't protest but clung tightly to Hettie, bursting into sobs that shook her body.

Hettie made a soft soothing sound, gently rocking Iris and rubbing her back. She couldn't tell how long she held her for, but gradually Iris's sobs subsided — her body softened, her head a weight against Hettie's shoulder.

'I'm so sorry, Iris. So very sorry. I wish there was something I could do to make everything all right again for you, but...'

'You can't, no one can.' Iris's voice was hoarse. She pulled away from Hettie and looked at her through puffy red eyes, her cheeks blotchy. 'Frank is dead! I can't believe I won't ever see him again.' Saying those words aloud brought a fresh flood of tears coursing down Iris's face and she did nothing to wipe them away. 'We were getting married in eight weeks. Why did his plane go down? Why? Frank only had five more missions to do, then he was going to volunteer to stay and work as ground crew so he wouldn't have to go back to America. He didn't want to be away from me and wait until the war was over before we could be together again.'

'Frank loved you very much,' Hettie said. 'I could see that when I met him.'

'I loved him too!' Iris said. 'And always will. Nothing will change that.'

'Of course not, love carries on.' Hettie fell silent for a moment before saying, 'If it would help, you could go home to Nottingham for a while. Take some time off for compassionate leave.'

'No!' Iris pulled her knees up to her chest and wrapped her arms around them. 'I won't do that.'

'Perhaps your mother could come here and see you then,' Hettie suggested.

Iris grimaced. 'Definitely not! She was dead against my marrying Frank because he was an American. She told me in a letter that I was making a big mistake and if I went ahead with the wedding, then she never wanted to see me again. She will be pleased Frank's gone.'

'Not that he's dead, surely?' Hettie said.

Iris's eyes met Hettie's. 'You don't know my mother. If that's what it took to stop me marrying him, then she'd be glad of it. You see why I can't go back there?'

Hettie pursed her lips. There was no point pursuing that path. A caring mother might have been a great help to her but clearly their relationship had broken down. 'I understand, Iris,' she said. 'You can have time off here instead. That will allow you to rest.'

Iris gave a sad shrug. 'Maybe a few days. But it will give me too much time to think and to...' her voice tailed off. 'I might just carry on with my work. What else is there now anyway?'

Hettie held Iris's hand. 'Whatever you decide, you have my support, and Beattie's and Stan's. We all care about you and want to help you through this however we can. You are not alone.'

Iris managed the faintest ghost of a smile. 'Thank you. I just don't know what to do now. It's too soon to decide.'

'Best take things one day at a time,' Hettie advised. 'Or one hour or even a single minute. Be kind and patient with yourself. Frank would want you to heal,' Hettie said gently. She squeezed Iris's hand. 'How about coming down for some sweet tea? Get you out of here for a bit?'

Iris's face fell and she shook her head. 'Not yet.'

'That's fine. I'll go down and get you some. Have you had anything to eat today?'

'No. I don't want anything.'

'In that case, I will put extra sugar in yours.' Hettie stood up. 'I won't be long.'

Glancing back at Iris as she left, she saw the young woman still sitting in the same position but now hanging her head and she was crying again. It would take her time to recover from losing Frank. Grief had its own path and however long it was, Iris ought not to be hurried. At least Iris wouldn't be facing it on her own. She had friends and a wider community to help her.

CHAPTER 31

It was a little after nine o'clock in the morning and Prue's house was quiet. Marie and Joan were at school and Nancy had gone shopping to get some groceries. Now she'd finished working at Rookery House, Nancy insisted on doing more household tasks. Prue was keeping an eye on her friend, making sure she didn't overdo things, and was glad to see she was being sensible and taking an afternoon nap each day.

Prue folded up todays's copy of *The Eastern Daily Press* that she'd been glancing through for the latest news from the battle fronts in France and Italy. She checked the news each day to gain some understanding of what Jack and Edwin might be doing as she worried about them. Prue was grateful that at least Alice was safely in Lincolnshire serving as a Waaf, her daughter's weekly letters and occasional phone calls were always most welcome.

Leaving the newspaper on the kitchen dresser, Prue took in a deep breath. There was nothing she could do to help any of her children, but she did have an important job that needed doing today. One which could prove to be rather difficult. In her role as local billeting officer, she was tasked with finding billets for a new batch of evacuees who were due to arrive from London in the next couple of weeks. She'd been told they would receive children and hoped that would turn out to be the case. Although going by past experience, when expectant mothers had been sent *instead* of children, Prue wouldn't believe it until the evacuees were here.

Whoever came to Great Plumstead would need a place to live. The problem was, with this being the third lot of evacuees coming to the village, spare rooms were now much more limited than they had been at the start of the war. Not even Thea could help Prue this time as the last possible space at Rookery House had been filled by Max when he'd arrived back in February. Although he was now fully recovered, he had no plans to leave soon, so her sister had told Prue. Max was enjoying life in the countryside and not in a hurry to return to London.

Prue finished some light and unnecessary tidying up in the kitchen before heading purposefully for the hallway. The sooner she started, the better. She collected her list of homes in the village, along with the notes she'd made showing those that already had evacuees and no room for any more. Then, determined to do the job to the best of her abilities, she put on her hat and jacket and left.

After an exhausting morning, in which Prue had had to use her powers of persuasion – and the weight of the law – to encourage several householders to agree to give a home to evacuees, she was finally bicycling to a place that had never taken an evacuee before. That wasn't because the householder had been unwilling but simply that they were already fully occupied. Joan Palmer had brought up four daughters. Now each of them, like Prue's own daughter Alice, had left home to work in various roles for the war effort. Prue was hopeful Joan might accept evacuees in their place.

Taking a turning off the main drive leading to Great Plumstead Hall, Prue pedalled towards Keeper's Cottage, which was set on its own on the edge of the estate's Great Wood. It was an isolated spot, but beautiful and would be a sharp contrast to the city life of potential evacuees.

She spotted Joan hanging out washing. Joan was a little older than Prue and a widow. Her husband had been the estate gamekeeper but had been killed in an accident several years ago, after which the Campbell-Gryces had allowed her to stay living in the cottage.

'Hello!' Prue called, catching her attention.

Joan shielded her eyes against the sun to see who it was, then waved back enthusiastically. 'Hello, Prue, what brings you out here?' she asked.

'I need to ask for your help.' Prue braked and dismounted from her bicycle, leaning it against the brick-and-flint wall that surrounded the Keeper's Cottage garden. 'We're being sent evacuees from London on account of these new V1 doodlebug rockets.'

Joan's face clouded. 'Those poor Londoners,' she said, 'taking the brunt of yet another attack on our country. Let's go in, Prue – we can talk about it over a cool drink.' Joan picked up the empty wicker washing basket and peg bag.

Inside the cottage felt cooler after the warmth of the July day.

'Are you working later?' Prue asked as Joan filled glasses with cordial. Prue knew Joan was a part-time housekeeper at the Grange in the village; they often crossed paths in Barker's grocers and Prue found Joan to be likeable and understanding.

'No, I'm there again tomorrow. I work Tuesdays and Fridays.' Joan passed a glass to Prue and motioned for her to take a seat at the kitchen table before sitting down herself. 'So tell me about these evacuees.'

'I've been *assured* they're sending us children but, as you know, what they say and who arrives isn't always the same. Though of course it worked out brilliantly with the expectant mothers and has been a huge benefit for the village.'

The two women smiled. Prue was thinking of the difference evacuees like Gloria and Marianne had made.

'Life wouldn't be the same here without them,' Joan agreed.

'The thing is, Great Plumstead is bursting at the seams when it comes to places for people to be homed, after two earlier waves of evacuees plus those moving into the village who were displaced by building the aerodrome. I was hoping that, with your daughters away, you would take some in?'

'Of course I will.'

Prue felt a huge sense of relief. 'Thank you, Joan.'

'It's my duty,' Joan said, 'but I'd be glad to anyway as it feels so quiet here with my girls gone. To be honest, I've been quite lonely. So whether it's children or adults or both I have room for four. There are two empty bedrooms, with two beds in each of them. When any of my girls come home to visit, they can share my room.'

Prue beamed at Joan. 'I wish everyone was as welcoming as you are.'

'Will you have enough rooms for all the evacuees now?'

'I hope so. I've got a few more calls to make yet but I'm getting there.'

'You'll get it done, Prue,' Joan said, admirably.

Prue gave a soft laugh. 'I'm trying. So as soon as I know when the evacuees are arriving, I'll let you know. They'll be met at the station and taken to the village hall for refreshments first. Then hosts like yourself can come and collect them from there.'

'It must be hard for mothers to send their children away.' Joan looked thoughtful. 'I'm not sure I'd have been able to.'

'Me neither, but I suppose if it was a choice between your children living or getting killed by a bomb or rocket...' Prue lifted her hands. 'It's life or death.'

'Whoever comes to live with me, I'll make sure their families know they're safe and keep in touch with them.'

'They will appreciate that.' Prue drank the rest of her cordial. 'I must get on.'

'Good luck,' Joan said.

'Thank you.' Prue stood up. 'I'll need it.'

CHAPTER 32

Thea was out in the WVS canteen with Prue and they were at their last stop of the day before heading back to the depot.

'Have you decided yet?' Thea asked with her hands plunged in a bowl of hot soapy water as she washed up a mug, taking care not to bare any weight on her right hand, which had only recently been freed of its plaster cast.

'I can't make up my mind,' Prue replied as she wiped the clean mug she was drying.

They'd been discussing the call for WVS members to go to London for a week. They were needed to provide relief cover for the overstretched local members living and working in the capital, giving those women the chance to have a break or at least a lighter workload.

'I'd like to go,' Prue explained, 'but I have so much to do here. We've got evacuees coming soon, who'll need organising, and all my other regular jobs are ongoing as well. People rely on me.'

'You don't need to tell me that,' Thea said with a smile. 'Though it is only for a week. The evacuees will be settled in their new homes in the village by the time you leave for London. And as for your other jobs, I'm sure you can find someone to take your place. Gloria might be happy to help at The Mother's Day Club and another member of the WVS will cover your shift on the canteen with me.'

'I'll have to think about it,' Prue said.

Thea stopped washing the mug she was holding and looked at her sister. 'Are you willing to be in the city while it's being targeted with doodlebugs?'

Prue frowned. 'Nowhere is safe while we're at war. And I'd like to do my bit.'

'In that case it would be a good experience for you to work in London. I know it won't be any kind of holiday as you'll be busy doing WVS work but it would be a change – and worthwhile. You'd see how they operate there. You said yourself you enjoyed finding out about how the WVS do things in York when you went there last year, and you brought back plenty of new ideas.'

Prue nodded her agreement. 'I did. My trip to York was interesting in so many ways.'

Prue's cheeks grew warm, and she decided to quickly change the topic. She had never told Thea the whole story of her journey to York with Lady Campbell-Gryce – she had been asked to keep Her Ladyship's secret, and she would honour her promise even if she did feel guilty about not confiding in her sister.

'I think I *will* volunteer to go to London,' Prue said, making her decision. 'Though if I'm accepted I'll have to arrange lodgings.'

'Leave that to me. I'll write to Violet and ask if you can stay with her at her flat. I'm sure she'd be happy to have you. You know each other and get on well.' Thea gave her sister a cheeky smile. 'Looks like you're all set then – if you're accepted.'

'You could volunteer too and come with me,' Prue suggested, putting the clean, dry mugs into one of the small compartments in a drawer which held them securely while the canteen was moving.

'It's simply impossible for me to go. It's our busiest time of year at Rookery House and I've only been out of plaster for a week. I must be careful with my wrist until it gets its full strength back again. Walt was very clear about that when he took the plaster cast off.'

'Fair enough. Though I'll be glad when you can take the reins of this canteen again.' Prue rubbed the muscles on her arms.

'Hopefully I will be back in the driver's seat in a few weeks' time, once my wrist is strong enough.' Thea cast her gaze around the inside of the canteen which was packed with all the things they needed to serve drinks and meals wherever they turned up. 'She is a heavy old girl though,' she admitted, 'and she needs a lot of hauling on the steering wheel to manoeuvre her about.'

'I much prefer driving my little Austin 7,' Prue said fondly of her car, which she only occasionally had the opportunity to use these days.

They settled into the driver and passenger seats and got ready to take the canteen back to the depot in Wykeham.

'Walt's right to tell you to take care,' Prue said as they set off. 'He's doing a good job looking after you and clearly takes his responsibility seriously.'

'He has been very kind,' Thea agreed. 'And it's been fortuitous getting to know him. I'm not sure how we'd have coped at Rookery House this summer without the help he organised for us. I would have preferred not to have been nearly run over and in plaster for six weeks but there has been a positive outcome.'

As they journeyed through the countryside, Thea half-wished that she could go with Prue to the city. It would be a good opportunity to see for herself how Violet was really coping. Needs must, however. Thea had to be here. She'd just have to keep corresponding with her friend by letter and hope things worked out for the best.

CHAPTER 33

Hettie was on her way to Crossways Farm to see Iris, pedalling past the aerodrome from where planes had flown off on a mission just a couple of hours earlier. It had been almost two weeks since Iris's fiancé Frank had left from there on his last flight and never come home, breaking her heart.

Arriving at the farmyard, Hettie left her bicycle leaning against the wall of a barn and headed for the kitchen to ask Beattie where she might find Iris.

'She's in the dairy.' Beattie paused in her kneading of bread dough on the scrubbed wooden table.

'How is she today?'

Beattie pressed her lips together. 'About the same. Sad, so sad. She's doing her work as well as she always did but there's a cloud of despair hanging over her. I'm worried for her, Hettie, I really am. Iris has lost her spark.'

'It's no wonder, Beattie,' Hettie said. 'She's had a terrible shock after being so happy and excited about marrying Frank and seeing a bright future ahead of her. Now that's all gone she's bound to be downhearted.' Hettie let out a sigh, shaking her head. 'It will take a long time for her to recover and, even then, she won't be quite the same as she was before. No one ever is after they've lost someone close to them. They must accept a new life without that person in it. That's hard to do and Iris is only young. I'll go and see her now and have a chat – talking usually helps.'

'There'll be a cup of tea here for you when you're ready,' Beattie said.

'Iris,' Hettie called as she went into the whitewashed interior of the dairy.

The young woman was at the sink, scrubbing one of the metal milking pails with hot water and soap. It was just as Beattie had described; Iris had an air of sadness about her. Her slim body looked heavy and tired and her face was gaunt; her eyes that used to twinkle with amusement and happiness seemed empty of life.

'Hello. Have you come to check up on me?' Iris stopped her work for a moment, and her mouth managed a forlorn smile that was like an arrow to Hettie's heart.

'I have,' Hettie said honestly, gathering herself. She had to be in control of her own emotions if she was going to be able to help Iris. 'I take my responsibilities as Land Army Local Representative seriously, you know that. I look out for you girls in good times and bad.'

'We're all lucky to have you,' Iris said and returned to her scrubbing, going over the same bit again and again, Hettie noticed.

'I was hoping you might have felt up to coming to the WI meeting last night.'

Iris shook her head. 'Just couldn't face it. I have no energy for being around other people right now.'

'I understand. Though I hope you'll come back when you feel ready.'

Iris gave a noncommittal shrug. 'I can't think about the future. I'm doing what you said, taking it day by day, minute by minute even. The thought of never seeing Frank again is just so...' Iris's voice choked. She bowed her head, her tears dripping onto the front of her brown Land Army dungarees, leaving dark splashes on the fabric.

Hettie quickly crossed the room and laid a hand on Iris's shoulder. 'From my experience, when the love for someone runs deep, then the grief will too. There's no easy fix for it. You just need to work your way through it little by little.'

Iris nodded. 'I had a letter from Frank's mother yesterday. She said he wrote about me a lot in his letters and she was glad I'd made him so happy and that his last weeks alive were such joyful ones.'

'It was kind of her to let you know that.'

'Frank made *me* happy too. I was the happiest I have ever been. Now I'm the saddest.' She raised her head and looked at Hettie, her eyes swimming with tears. 'How will I go on without him?'

Hettie put her arms around the Land Girl and hugged her tightly, wishing she could take her pain away, make it as if this horrible situation had never happened. But she couldn't. No one could, no matter how much they might want to.

'You will go on,' Hettie assured her. 'It may not feel like it right now but it will slowly get easier.' Hettie loosened her arms and took a step backwards to look at Iris. 'Frank wouldn't want you to give up, he loved you and would wish for you to carry on, be happy again.'

'He used to say that to me in case...,' Iris's mouth twisted with the pain of what she was saying, 'in case he never came back. Frank *knew* he might not make it. Every time he went on a mission he was taking a risk.' Iris swallowed hard. 'We hoped and hoped he would be one of the lucky ones that made it through – but we were wrong.'

'Frank was a brave man,' Hettie said. 'He had so much courage.'

Iris nodded. 'He volunteered for flying. He could have had a role on the ground, been safer.'

'Frank did what he felt was right for him. And it brought him here, where he found you.'

'I am so glad he did. We had a wonderful time together. Frank filled me with such love and joy. I will never forget him.' Iris's chin trembled. 'But it hurts so much now he's gone.'

Hettie pulled the young woman into her arms again and held her as she sobbed, struggling to keep her own emotions in check. This war brought people together but also cruelly tore them apart, leaving broken hearts and shattered futures. The sooner it was over, the better.

CHAPTER 34

Thea glanced up from the book she was reading aloud and saw Betty's eyes flickering open and shut, the little girl fighting to stay awake. Lying in bed beside her, George had already fallen asleep. Thea read on to the bottom of the page, and when she looked up again, Betty had drifted off to sleep. Closing the book, Thea put it on the chest of drawers then stood up and kissed each child on their forehead before tiptoeing out of the room, quietly shutting the bedroom door behind her.

She'd just reached the top of the stairs when the sound of a vehicle coming through the gate caught her attention and she looked out of the landing window. It was a jeep. Hurrying downstairs, she headed through the kitchen to the back door and, as she opened it, Walt appeared around the side of the house; spotting her, his face broke into a smile.

'Good evening, Thea. I've come to see how you are and check out your wrist.'

'It's doing well, I think. Come on in.' She led the way inside. 'Would you like something to drink?'

'No, not tonight, but thank you. I'm on my way to the Half Moon and thought I'd call in. Would you like to come to the pub with me after I've had a look at your wrist? There'll be a group of men there from the base, including Chuck and Vinnie who you already know.'

Thea considered for a moment. It had been ages since she'd had a night out. She decided to go for it, knowing Hettie and Marianne were at home and would take care of George and Betty for her. 'Yes, I would like that, thank you Walt.'

'Great. Okay, now let's see how your injury is healing.'

Thea let Walt take her arm; he felt along it gently, manipulating her wrist and fingers. 'The muscle tone is much improved from when the cast came off and you have good movement. Is there any pain at all?'

'No, it's achy sometimes but I'm being careful not to overdo things. No heavy lifting.'

'You're doing great,' he said, giving her another smile. 'Just keep on doing what you're doing.'

The door to the hall opened and Hettie came in. 'Hello, Walt! I thought I heard voices. How's our patient?'

'Healing nicely, I'm pleased to say. She's even agreed to a night out.'

Hettie's gaze turned to Thea. 'Oh, that's a good idea. Where are you two heading?'

Thea's cheeks grew warm. 'We're going to join Chuck and Vinnie and some others from the base at the Half Moon pub,' she explained quickly. 'Would you like to come?'

'I appreciate the offer,' Hettie said, 'but I'll stay home and put my feet up. It's been a busy day.'

'What about Marianne and Flo?' Walt asked.

'Flo's gone to see Evie and Marianne's having a bath,' Thea told him.

'Okay, it's just you and me then, if you're still willing?' Walt turned to Thea, one eyebrow raised.

She laughed. 'I am.'

Stepping from the warm July evening into the cosy interior of the Half Moon, Thea felt herself instantly relax. A night out was just what she needed. The pub was busy with American servicemen, Land Girls and village locals and a pleasant, welcoming hubbub of chatter and laughter filled the air.

'What would you like to drink?' Walt asked, leaning towards her so he could make himself heard.

'Half a pint of beer please, Walt,' she said.

'Coming right up.' As Walt made his way over to the bar, Thea noticed Percy Blake was perched on a stool at a small table near the bar, alongside several of his pals from the allotments. He raised his pint glass to her in greeting.

Just then a loud cheer drew everyone's attention to a rowdy game of darts going on at the far end of the room. It looked to Thea like a team of American servicemen, playing against some locals, had just lost. There was plenty of good-natured backslapping going on and Thea was pleased to see how well everyone was getting along.

One of the American servicemen noticed her. 'Thea!'

Chuck headed over, an empty glass in his hand. 'Great to see you. Can I get you a drink? I need to drown my sorrows – our team are losers yet again. We yanks will get the hang of throwing tiny arrows at a target one of these days though!'

'I've got one coming, thank you – Walt's getting it.' Thea gestured towards where Walt was now bending down, listening to Percy; the older man was waving his arms about dramatically to illustrate whatever tale he was telling.

'Looks like the Doc's hearing the unfortunate story of Percy's pig.' Chuck grinned. 'We've all heard it and more than once – I reckon if Hollywood hears about it, we'll be watching it on the big screen sometime soon!'

'What's happened to it?' Thea asked. 'I know how keen a pig keeper Percy is – he asked me for advice earlier this year.'

'I'll let the Doc explain.' Chuck tilted his head towards Walt, who was heading their way carrying two glasses of beer. 'Hope to catch you later!' Chuck said, and with a nod to Walt he went to get a refill.

'Chuck was just telling me something about Percy's pig. Is everything all right?'

Walt handed her one of the glasses, his eyes twinkling with amusement. 'He's told me all about it. Come on, let's sit outside and I'll tell you the sorry episode. We'll have to shout to be heard if we stay in here.'

Thea followed him out through the back door of the pub into the garden, where there were benches set out. They sat down by one of the apple trees.

'Spill the beans then,' Thea said. 'What's got Percy so worked up?'

'I guess you know he's keeping a pig on his allotment, raising it for meat?'

'Yes. Has something happened to it?'

'You could say that. You see...' Walt's mouth twitched and suddenly he threw back his head and roared, slapping his thigh. 'I'm sorry, I...' and he was off again, unable to control himself. The sound of Walt's laughter and his inability to stop had Thea laughing too.

'This Percy story had better be a good one!' she said, wiping a tear from the corner of her eye.

Walt nodded and took a few deep, steadying breaths.

'I think it's the funniest thing I've heard in a long while,' Walt told her. 'And it's made my day.'

'Then I'd better hear it,' Thea told him.

Walt bowed his head, as if to prepare himself, then looked her in the eye. 'The pig, her name is Clarabel.'

'Really?' Thea said, while Walt took several seconds to control himself again, his face twisting with the effort.

'And Percy,' Walt explained, 'has spent every waking hour taking care of her. He's given her fine treats and the choicest leftovers. He's stayed up with her, past his bedtime, and talked to her. All in all, Percy has been determined to make Clarabel the happiest – and so the *tastiest* – pig in the entire county. Nay even the world.'

'Did Percy say all that?' Thea asked.

'Words to that effect,' Walt said.

'I'm pleased to hear she's been so well cared for but I'm not sure why that's so funny.'

'I'm getting to that. I suppose you also know Percy grows prize-winning marrows every year?'

'Yes, I do. I've never known anyone so competitive when it comes to marrows. It wouldn't surprise me if he stayed up talking to them too!'

'Well,' Walt went on, 'Percy, claims to have been growing the largest marrow anyone would have ever known. It was going to be a marvel of international importance that would have drawn interest in this country and beyond. In short, Percy's life's ambition, not to mention his skills as a gardener, was about to be realised at long last. And it was all because of Clarabel.'

'Because?' Thea asked, though she thought she knew the answer.

'Clarabel's *manure* was like Clarabel herself – perfect in every way. For growing marrows.'

'I noticed you said he claims to *have been* growing it and that this marrow was *going to be* a marvel... what happened to it?'

'Clarabel ate it.' Walt roared with laughter and would have fallen from his seat if Thea hadn't steadied him; Thea herself had aching ribs by the time she composed herself.

She took a drink of her beer; Walt did the same, eyeing her.

'Good story?' Walt said.

'Very,' she conceded.

'The rest of it is about how she got out of her pen – I think one of Percy's pals gets the blame there, for leaving a latch open. Whatever the cause, Clarabel got out. She ran amok around his allotment, eating her way through his vegetables and Percy found the dear pig sprawled out amongst his strawberry plants dozing in the sunshine.'

'I know it's not good to lose plants and produce,' said Thea, 'but since Percy's always going on about how marvellous his allotment is, how amazing he is at growing things and how wonderful his pig is, it is a little bit ironic how it's all ended.'

Walt sighed happily. 'I can picture his pig stuffing itself and then taking a snooze in the strawberry bed afterward. It's priceless!'

Thea imagined it herself. She knew how proud Percy was of his plot and how dismissive he'd been when Prue and the other women had taken over an abandoned allotment for the WI. Pride came before a fall, they said – and sometimes it was true.

'What's happened to the pig?' she asked.

'It's back in its pen with added security. It won't stand a chance of getting out now.' Walt took a sip of his beer. 'Chuck and the others who helped you at Rookery House have offered to help Percy get his allotment back in shape again. He agreed, though only after they told him about working for you. He holds you in the highest esteem, Thea.'

'Percy can be kind and generous,' Thea said. 'I'll take him along some spare seedlings, to help him get re-established.'

'I'm sure he'd appreciate that.' Walt looked thoughtful. 'You know, I haven't laughed like that for a while; it felt good. I think it will amuse a lot of people when the news spreads across the airbase. There's few who haven't met Percy and heard about his precious pig and amazing vegetables.'

'It will spread around the village as well.' Thea took a long drink of her beer, savouring the taste of hops and barley. 'Do you and your men come here to the Half Moon a lot?'

'I only come now and again, usually when I want to have a change from the base. It's popular with a lot of our men.' Walt looked around to where other American servicemen were seated or standing in groups, all looking relaxed. 'It's a place for them to let off steam, forget their jobs for a while.'

'Is it the same for you?' Thea asked.

'Maybe.' He thought about it. 'Yes, sometimes,' he admitted, 'but I come here also because it's somewhere that the men can talk to me if they need to. Some find it easier here than on the base if they've got a problem they need to discuss.'

'What about you? Where do you go to talk about a problem?'

Walt gave a shrug.

Thea understood the strains and tensions of serving in wartime from her time in France. Bottling things up inside wasn't a good idea as sooner or later it would burst out. 'You can always talk to me. I'm a good listener.'

He looked at her. 'Thank you, I appreciate that. I would happily do the same for you too. I remember you telling me about being in France and knowing what it's like to develop that family away from home. You know how it feels for us to be here, such a long way from home in wartime.'

'I do, although I never went as far as you have. Do you find it hard to be away?'

'I guess... but I enjoy being in England. Remember, my mom was English. She came from Yorkshire and made sure that I knew about how things are done here.'

'How does she feel about you being in England now?' Thea asked.

'She died five years ago.'

'I'm sorry. Do you have other family waiting for you?'

'Not really, just some cousins on my Pa's side. He died a couple of years before my mom. I don't have a wife or children. I only came close to marrying once but she decided I was already married to my job and called it off.' He took a drink of his beer. 'How about you?'

'You've met Prue and Reuben. I've a younger sister Lizzie, who lives in Norwich. Our parents died a long time ago. I was engaged once but my fiancé was killed in France.'

'That's tough, I'm sorry.'

'I wasn't the only one to lose someone then. The sad thing is, it's happening again. Hettie's worried about Iris, one of the Land Girls she looks out for. Her fiancé Frank died when his plane went down a couple of weeks ago.'

'I knew Frank. He was a good man.' Walt let out a sigh. 'Every time a plane goes down, we lose another ten men.'

'That must be hard to bear.'

He nodded slowly. 'It is, but we have to keep on going.' He glanced around at the American servicemen. 'That's why coming to places like this is so important for the men. They're making the most of their free time, out enjoying themselves just in case...' He was about to say more but stopped as Chuck came striding out of the back door of the pub and headed towards them.

'Hey Doc, Thea, we're starting a game of darts against Percy and his pals, wanna join our team?'

Thea glanced at Walt. 'I'm willing if you are. I must warn you though, I'm a terrible aim.'

'You'll fit right in with us then,' Chuck laughed, 'but we don't let that stop us.'

Thea and Walt stood up and followed Chuck inside. Just before they went in, Walt put a hand on Thea's arm. 'Thanks for listening.'

'Any time.' She smiled at him.

'Same goes for you,' he replied. 'It's good to talk to someone who knows how it is.'

CHAPTER 35

Prue gazed around the village hall, checking that each of the evacuee children, and the volunteer adults who'd accompanied them from London, had something to eat and drink. They were seated at tables, tucking into fish paste sandwiches and rock cakes, along with cups of tea or cordial. Satisfied that all was well, Prue's thoughts drifted back to when they'd arrived at Great Plumstead station half an hour ago on the one o'clock train. The moment she'd spotted children peering from the carriages had been such a relief – they were the young evacuees she had been told to expect and there had been no mix-up this time.

'You're looking thoughtful. You all right?'

Gloria's voice brought Prue's attention to the present.

She gave her friend a reassuring smile. 'Yes, I'm fine and I'm glad to see our new arrivals tucking in, although the food on offer today isn't as good a spread as we put on when you came at the start of the war. Food rationing hadn't started then.'

'I remember,' Gloria said. 'What a nice selection there was, lovely cakes and sandwiches. Still, these children ain't turned anything down; they're accustomed to living with rationing and are pleased to 'ave something decent to eat after their long journey.'

'You can see the effect of years of war on them though – their clothes are patched and worn.'

'None of us are looking as smart as we used to,' Gloria sighed, gesturing at the fuchsia-pink dress she was wearing. 'I've 'ad to mend this a few times and there's no chance of replacing it. It's got to last me till the end of the war.'

'I hope it does – you brighten up the place no end.' Prue loved the way her friend dressed; she was like a colourful bird of paradise.

'I never was one for 'iding myself!' Gloria let out a throaty laugh. 'What time are the 'osts coming to collect their evacuees?'

'Any time now.' Prue lowered her voice. 'I'm hoping they all turn up and I don't need to take children around the village and remind the missing hosts of their legal obligation to provide a home if they have space. It's better for the children's sake if they don't have to go through that; it's hard enough for them leaving their family and home as it is.'

'If it comes to that, I could stay 'ere in the 'all with the children while you fetch the missing 'osts. That would save the poor dears from witnessing any unpleasantness,' Gloria offered.

'Thank you, that's a good idea.' Prue patted Gloria's arm. 'I'd best go out and see who's turned up.'

Armed with her list of expected hosts, Prue went outside into the July afternoon sunshine and was delighted to see that Joan Palmer was already waiting, and others were making their way along the road.

'Hello, Joan,' Prue said. 'You're keen!'

'I am!' Joan's face lit up. 'Everything's prepared at home, and I can't wait to meet the evacuees. Did they send children this time?'

'Yes, they did. They're all having some refreshments and then they will be ready to go to their new homes. I'm glad you're first here as we've got three children from the same family whose mother is adamant that they should stay together. Two girls and a boy. I think they'd do very well living with you at Keeper's Cottage.'

'How old are they?'

Prue checked her list. 'The girls are ten and eleven and their brother is six.'

'That sounds perfect.'

'Good, I hoped you'd agree. Go on in and ask Gloria to introduce you to the three children. Then, whenever you're ready, you can take them home.'

'I'm feeling nervous!' Joan admitted.

'You'll be fine. The children are lucky to be going to live with you. You've brought up four girls of your own and know what to do.'

Joan took a deep breath. 'Here I go then.'

As Prue watched Joan head into the village hall, she hoped that the other hosts would be as eager and understanding of their role. Making a good home for young evacuees wasn't always convenient or easy but it was a duty. Everyone had to do their bit, and Prue was ready to put that point across strongly if she needed to.

CHAPTER 36

Thea walked through the Rookery House garden towards Reuben's, enjoying the early morning sun on her bare arms and face. It was going to be a warm day working in the fields but that was something she enjoyed, and many times over the winter months she'd harken back to July days like these.

Max was sitting on one of a pair of chairs on the veranda which ran around Reuben's railway carriage house; he was making notes with a pencil on a pad of paper. Spotting her approach, he got to his feet.

'Hello, Thea!'

'I'm sorry to disturb your work but I want to ask you something.'

'Of course, please join me.' Thea climbed the steps and they both settled down on a chair. 'How can I help you?'

'You said last night at teatime that you need to visit London soon.'

'That's right.'

'Do you know *when* you're going?'

'I'm not sure – sometime this month.'

'Oh, I see.' Thea's idea wouldn't work. 'I'd hoped it might be a little bit later. It's no problem though, I'll let you get back to your translating.' She began to stand up.

'Wait! Do you mind if I ask why? Is there something I can do for you?' Max enquired.

Thea sat down again. 'Prue is going to London,' she explained. 'She found out yesterday that she's been accepted to help relieve WVS workers for a week. She'll be leaving here on the first of August, and I've arranged for her to stay with my best friend Violet in Holborn. The thing is, Prue doesn't know the city well. She won't want me interfering at all, and she's quite capable of not getting lost, but I've been thinking about it and wondered if by chance you were going down on the same day...'

'Then we could travel together?' Max finished for her.

'And you could have taken her to Violet's to drop her off,' Thea said. 'Prue visited me several times when I lived in London but I always met her at the station and guided her around.'

Max considered for a moment. 'I can be flexible when I travel and I *could* go on the first of August. It would be a pleasure to share the journey with Prue and ease your concern. I know Holborn well.'

Thea smiled. 'That would be wonderful, Max! Thank you.'

'Does Prue know about your idea for us to travel together?'

'No.' Thea shifted in her seat. 'And she's bound to think I'm sticking my nose in where it's not wanted.'

Max raised his eyebrows, his eyes twinkling with amusement. 'I don't want to cause a disagreement between you,' he said, delicately.

They sat in silence for a moment.

'I may have an answer,' Max said. 'I will simply ask Prue whether she'd like to share the journey with me. If she's already looking forward to going alone, she can simply tell me so.'

'And if she asks you whether the idea came from her busybody older sister?'

'I must tell her the truth, Thea,' Max said, smiling. 'Though perhaps she will not mind too much.'

'Perhaps,' Thea said dubiously, 'but I am prepared to suffer the consequences. I'm happy Prue will have the offer of your help.' She stood up. 'Thank you, Max.'

'You're welcome. I'll let you know if Prue agrees to our travelling together.'

'She will be at The Mother's Day Club this morning,' Thea informed him. 'I'll cross my fingers for a good result. See you later, Max.'

Heading off to join Flo and Luca planting out broccoli plants, Thea was pleased and relieved. Although it was up to her sister whether she accepted Max's offer, if she did it would hopefully make for a smooth and pleasant journey.

CHAPTER 37

Prue took the toy cars out of the box and put them on the blanket spread out on the floor. She was setting up the children's play area in one corner of the village hall, ready for this morning's Mother's Day Club. It was something she always enjoyed, the toys reminding her of days when her own children were small and she'd spent many happy hours with them making up stories and games.

At the sound of the outside door opening, she glanced around, thinking it must be one of the mothers arriving early. She was therefore surprised to see who was standing in the doorway.

'Max!' She stood up from her kneeling position, wondering what had brought him here.

'Good Morning, Prue.' Max took off his hat as he advanced into the hall towards her. 'Thea told me I would find you here.'

Prue's mind jumped to the conclusion that something must be wrong for him to come here so unexpectedly. 'Is everything all right at Rookery House?'

'All is well,' Max reassured her. 'I have merely come to ask you something.'

'Ask away then,' Prue said, smiling.

'I was talking to Thea this morning,' Max explained, 'and she mentioned that you are going to London next Tuesday?'

'Yes, that's right. I'll be volunteering with the London WVS for a week.' Prue frowned, curious as to why he was asking about her trip.

'I need to go to London as well, for my work,' Max went on, 'and I wondered if you would care to travel there together with me and share the journey? Please don't feel any obligation to say yes if you'd prefer not to. My plans are flexible and I can go another day.'

Max regarded her calmly while she gazed at him. His offer had come out of the blue and her mind needed to catch up with it. She was about to give herself time to think it through by asking him which part of the city he would be travelling to, when she heard entirely different words slipping out of her mouth. 'Yes, I'd like that very much, Max,' she said. 'It would be a pleasure.'

Max's face lit up. 'I'd enjoy it too. What time are you leaving?'

'I'm planning on catching the half past nine train to Norwich. Then walk across the city to Thorpe station to get the London-bound train.'

'In that case I'll meet you at Great Plumstead station next Tuesday morning. I look forward to seeing you then.' Max put his hat on and, after a slight bow of his head, left the hall, closing the door quietly behind him.

Prue stood staring after him. Suddenly she laughed softly, both at the unexpected offer and her quick acceptance of it. It wasn't like her; she was noticing changes in her behaviour, especially with Max but around other people too. She was being more decisive – and that wasn't a bad thing at all. Her big sister would be proud of her.

Was this the new Prue? she wondered. If it was, then she liked her!

Smiling to herself, she returned to her task of setting out the toys. She would enjoy the journey with Max as he was always good company. Now her trip to London had an extra element to it, one that lifted her heart in a most delightful way.

CHAPTER 38

Pedalling slowly along the drive from Great Plumstead Hall, Hettie was grateful for the cool shade cast by the towering beech trees. She'd been to see her sister Ada, who worked as Housekeeper there, and they'd had a good chat over a cup of tea, catching up with each other's news.

Movement off to the side in the woods caught Hettie's eye and she coasted to a halt as three children and a woman emerged onto the drive ahead of her.

'Afternoon, Hettie,' Joan Palmer called, walking towards her. She was holding the hand of a little boy.

'Hello!' Hettie climbed off her bicycle and wheeled it towards them, delighted to see that these new evacuees looked happy and well – as did Joan herself, Hettie noted. 'How are you getting on?'

'Very well. This is Susan, Pamela and Sid.' Joan introduced the children who stood beside her; all three were clearly related and regarded Hettie with the same intelligent green eyes.

'Pleased to meet you. My name's Hettie Brown. How old are you all?'

'I'm eleven.' Susan spoke with a strong cockney accent. 'Pamela's ten, an' Sid 'ere 'e's six.' She gestured towards each of them.

'What do you think of living at Keeper's Cottage?' Hettie asked.

'It ain't like where we lived in London,' Pamela piped up. 'There's lots of green 'ere.' She looked up at the trees, then back to Hettie. 'But I like it.'

'We all do,' said Susan, putting a hand on Sid's shoulder. He looked at his older sister thankfully, clearly nervous of meeting new people. And missing home too, most likely, Hettie thought.

'We're out getting some air and exercise,' Joan told Hettie. 'We've been having races.' She turned to address the children. 'How about you three run to the end of the drive and back again? Only don't go right up to the building – remember it's a hospital where patients need peace and quiet to get better. Just touch the last tree –' she pointed, '– and see who gets back to me first. Ready? Set? Go!'

The children took off, their feet crunching along the gritty drive. Hettie saw the two girls get in front, leaving Sid following on behind.

Joan smiled fondly as she watched them. 'I'd forgotten how much energy youngsters have. They seem to enjoy having plenty of open space to charge around in. I know it's only been a week since they arrived, but they've settled in so well and we get along nicely. I love having them with me and the house feels lived in again.'

'That's wonderful to hear,' said Hettie. 'I'm pleased for you all. We're lucky to have George and Betty living with us at Rookery House – it keeps us young having them about the place. It will be a terrible wrench when they eventually go home, once it's safe for them to do so.'

'I already know I'll miss these three terribly!' Joan admitted. 'Hopefully they'll always keep in touch, maybe even come back to Norfolk for holidays.'

'Have you heard from the children's mother?'

'Yes, we had a letter back yesterday. I wrote the day after they arrived to let her know where her children were and to tell her about the house, the village and myself, and I included letters from Susan, Pamela and Sid.'

'That was thoughtful of you,' said Hettie, approvingly.

'It's what *I* would have wanted to know, had the tables been turned and my girls evacuated away, to be taken care of by a stranger in a place I didn't know. I want the mother – her name is Ellen – to feel like she's still very much involved in their lives, as much as she can. I've asked her to come and visit. She must miss them.' Joan fell silent for a moment. 'I miss my girls,' she said and Hettie saw her eyes had misted over, 'and they're all grown up!'

'I hope Ellen can visit and see what good care you're taking of her children,' Hettie said. 'George and Betty's mother comes to see them twice a year at Rookery House, sometimes at Christmas, otherwise it's during the summer holidays. She must fit it in around her work but it always does her – and Betty and George – the world of good. It's important for them all to see each other, even if it's not very often.'

'I agree. The only thing I'm worried about with the children is keeping them in clothes. They didn't bring much with them and children grow so fast.'

'No need to worry about that,' Hettie reassured her. 'We've got a clothing depot in the village hall where you can borrow from. They make a lot of garments for it at the workroom in Prue's house, using fabrics Lady Campbell-Gryce donated.

The next opening is this coming Saturday at ten o'clock. We open once a month, although anyone who needs something urgently can get in touch with either me or Prue and we'll open it just for them.'

'That's so helpful, thank you, Hettie. And it's a weight off my mind – my own sewing skills are limited to repairs, not whole new outfits! I'll bring the children along on Saturday morning. Here they come now.'

Hettie turned to see the children racing back towards them, wide grins on their faces. Sid, who had clearly turned around and run back before reaching the last tree, was out in front, but he was being caught by Pamela, who was a talented runner, her skinny legs a blur.

The three children passed the two women like a whirlwind, with Pamela loudly proclaiming her victory.

'I think I'll stick to pedalling!' Hettie said to Joan, with a chuckle. 'I'll see you soon at the clothing depot.' She climbed onto her bicycle and pushed off. 'Bye then!'

'Goodbye, Hettie,' Joan called after her.

'Bye!' came a call from the children.

Hettie smiled. It was heartening to see how well the latest wave of evacuees were settling in. In Joan's case, it looked like their arrival was helping her as much as it was the children.

CHAPTER 39

It was the first day of August and Prue was on a London-bound train with Max, the pair of them sitting in a compartment on their own after several passengers had disembarked at Ipswich.

'Cream cheese with either herbs or beetroot — which would you like?' Prue held out the two packets of sandwiches she'd taken from the basket of food that Hettie had sent with Max this morning. Each was labelled in pencil on the outside paper wrapping.

'I don't mind; what would you prefer?' Max replied from his seat opposite. 'I like both, so either is fine with me.'

'All right, in that case, I'll have the cream cheese and herbs.' Prue handed Max the other. 'It was kind of Hettie to send us off with all this.' She gestured towards the wicker basket sitting on the seat beside her which was packed not only with food for their journey – sun-ripened tomatoes from Rookery House's garden, buttered scones and bottles of diluted cordial – but also cheese, eggs, butter and a selection of fresh vegetables and fruit for Violet, who would be hosting Prue for the week.

'Hettie was most insistent that we were well provisioned for our trip,' Max said. 'She wanted to be sure we didn't go hungry if there wasn't a buffet car on the train, and she was pleased with the opportunity to send some things for Violet to supplement her rationing.' Max unwrapped his sandwich. 'Hettie likes to keep us well fed – and with her baking skills, we are thoroughly spoiled. This looks delicious!'

'Then let's tuck in...' Prue bit into her sandwich and chewed on the delicious combination of fresh homemade bread, butter, cream cheese and herbs. It was far superior to anything they could have bought from a train buffet car.

As she ate, Prue looked out of the window at the passing countryside and was suddenly enchanted as the wide vista of the Stour estuary came into sight. It was stunning. Under a blue summer sky dotted with small puffy clouds, diamonds of light sparkled on the water. The tide was partly out, revealing muddy banks where birds were probing their beaks into the soft ooze.

'It's so beautiful,' she commented. 'Such a glorious view.'

'Being near water is always a delight. I know we both agree on that.'

'We do indeed.' Prue looked at Max, remembering when they'd talked of such things by the riverside back in Great Plumstead. Their eyes met and held for a few seconds before she returned her gaze to the scenery outside.

Taking another bite of sandwich, Prue recalled her and Max's unexpected encounter by the river. It was on the day Jack returned to his regiment. She'd been upset and talking to Max had helped. They'd discovered a shared love of being by the water. That was the first time she'd talked to Max in a more personal way.

'This place reminds me of the day I came to England.' Max's voice broke into Prue's thoughts as they came to a halt at Manningtree station. 'I arrived at Harwich harbour and changed here to catch the London train. It was the beginning of a new life for me, a chance to start again.'

'It must have been difficult in an unfamiliar country,' Prue said.

'Yes and no. Of course, it was challenging being in a place I didn't know, with a new job too, but it also freed me from sad memories. Even a year after my wife and newborn daughter died, it was hard living in our apartment in Amsterdam. Every room I went into held memories – it became too painful to remain. When the opportunity arose to work at the university in London, I took it.'

'Did you intend to stay for so long in England?' She remembered Max had told her he'd been here for over ten years.

'I didn't have a plan. But events and growing problems in Germany, which spread to the Netherlands, dictated what I should do. I encouraged my sister to come here with her family as things grew worse for Jewish people in Germany. I feared it was only a matter of time before another war broke out and if the Nazis invaded the Netherlands and brought their hideous beliefs with them then...' he sighed, shaking his head. 'But my sister wanted to stay, believing it would be all right. Now I do not know where she is or even if she's still alive.'

Prue reached across and took hold of his hand. 'I hope she is safe.'

Max nodded and managed a smile. 'Hope is important; that's what I cling to.' He looked down at their joined hands for a moment. 'Thank you for listening to me, Prue. I appreciate it. But...' He pressed her fingers and then let them go. 'I will not dampen the spirits of our trip any more. Tell me what made you volunteer to work in London with the WVS there?'

Prue leaned back against the springy train seat, considering his question. 'I did it for a challenge,' she said, 'and to see other ways of doing WVS work. I know I'm probably going to see sights that will shock me and that I might find difficult. I haven't had much experience of a big city, especially one ravaged by war, and it will be very different from my normal life in a Norfolk village. However, I'm ready for it, and for some hard work helping those in need.'

'I hope you'll still be able to enjoy some of the city – London can be quite the marvel.'

'That would be nice,' Prue said.

'Seeing other places, doing other things – these broaden and enrich us. I always loved travelling and hope when the war is over, I can go again.'

'I'd love to travel abroad,' Prue mused, hardly able to imagine it. Where would she go? she thought. 'I've never been anywhere really.'

'Then one day you must change that,' Max said. 'You would love Italy and you would not tire of the Swiss Alps. I love being in the mountains. Maybe because they are such a complete contrast to the flat landscape of the Netherlands!'

Prue laughed lightly. 'They sound so exotic and colourful and far away. Come on, we'd better eat up. Hettie would be disappointed if we don't finish her picnic before we get to London.'

As the train steamed into Liverpool Street station and drew to a stop under the high arching roof, Prue gathered her things.

'Let me get your case.' Max reached up and took her small brown suitcase from the overhead netted luggage rack above her seat before retrieving his own.

'I'd be happy to take you to Violet's home if you wish,' he offered. 'I know the area well as it's not that far from my flat.'

'Thank you, that would be most kind,' Prue accepted. 'I'm sure I'd be able to find my way there eventually, but it would be a lot easier if you guided me there. And being with you will help ease me into the bustle of the city. I'm not used to the buses or underground and what goes where.'

'Then it will be my pleasure.'

Disembarking, they joined the throng of passengers heading to the station's main concourse, from where there were several exits – Prue let Max lead the way.

Outside the station, most of the people around them were dressed in uniforms of the different services. London already looked like a different place from when she'd last come here, on a visit to see Thea before her sister moved back to Great Plumstead. That was before the war started, over five years ago. So much had happened to her and her family since then.

As well the people in uniform, there were plenty of other signs of wartime on London's streets, from constructions of sandbags to windows criss-crossed with paper. They were reminders of why she was here, Prue thought. There was work to be done.

Meanwhile she was glad Max had offered to lead her to Violet's flat to begin with. It would be a good start to a week which would most likely prove extremely challenging. Prue was ready and as prepared as she'd ever be.

CHAPTER 40

Rookery House, Norfolk

Thea was walking back through the orchard after checking on the beehives, still wearing her beekeeping veil, when she spotted George running towards her.

'Auntie Thea, I've got a letter for you!' he called, waving it in the air. 'It just arrived in the afternoon post and was in the envelope with mine and Betty's letter from our mam,' George added as he reached her; he held out the folded sheet of paper.

Thea took it and saw her name written on the blank side. 'What does your mum say?'

'I don't know – we haven't read it because it's addressed to you,' George said. 'It's not right to read other people's letters.'

Thea put her arm around the boy's shoulders, squeezing him to her, loving how honest he was. 'I'd best see what it's about then.'

She opened and read the short note.

31st July 1944

Dear Thea,

Hoping all is well with you and everyone at Rookery House. I'm writing to ask if it would be convenient for me to visit from Saturday 5th to Wednesday 9th of August? Now that George and Betty are on their summer holiday from school, I could spend plenty of time with them. It feels a long while since Christmas, when I last saw them.
Please let me know if it would be all right for me to come on these dates.
I look forward to hearing from you and hopefully seeing you all soon.

With best wishes

Jess

'Why has mam written to you?' George asked.

'To tell me she's coming to see you.'

Thea watched as George's face broke into a wide smile. 'When?' he said eagerly. 'And for how long?'

'She'll arrive on Saturday and leave next Wednesday.'

'Can we meet her at the station when she arrives?'

'Of course. Your mum would like that very much.'

'Thank you for letting her come and stay, Auntie Thea.' He flung his arms around her and hugged her. 'I must tell Betty.'

Thea smiled to herself as he raced off, running as fast as he could to break the news to his older sister. Betty would be as excited as George about spending time with their mother. The three of them – George, Betty and Jess – always got on so well together and, despite their long separations, they were a close-knit family when they were together.

Thea loved looking after George and Betty but she'd been careful to never forget that they weren't her own. They were under her care while it was too dangerous for them to live with their parents in London. They'd be returning home again as soon as it was safe to do so.

One day Thea would have to let them go. There was no two ways about it.

Pushing to the back of her mind the grief she knew she'd feel when that time came, Thea quickened her pace back to Rookery House. She had things to do and a letter to write. She would tell Jess she was most welcome any time and that everyone would be looking forward to her visit in the coming week.

CHAPTER 41

Violet's Flat, London

'Here's a spare set of keys. The smaller brass one's for the flat and the larger is for the building's front door – that can stick a bit so you might need to wiggle it about before it will turn.'

'Thank you,' Prue said, slipping the keys into the pocket of the green WVS dress she was wearing.

It was eight o'clock and her host Violet was about to leave for her shift at the ambulance station. They were sitting at the table in the kitchen and had just eaten breakfast together. Prue had enjoyed their conversation, as she'd done over their meal the previous evening after Max had dropped her off and gone on to his own flat.

'You've got your map of where to go?' Violet's eyes were alert behind her owlish horn-rimmed glasses.

'I do.' Prue tapped her bag, which was on the chair beside her. 'It's safely stowed in here and it will be a great help, I'm sure. I'm going to try my best to get my bearings but, as soon as I'm lost, I'll fish it out!' She grinned. Violet had drawn her a map of the local area, showing the best route for Prue to take to the WVS depot she needed to report to. With that as a back-up, she felt a lot more confident about navigating her way through the big city.

'I don't think there's anything else you need to know but you can always ring me at Station 75. I've left the number by my telephone.'

'Thank you.'

'I'll be home again tomorrow morning about half past nine,' Violet said. 'You'll have left by then, so I will see you tomorrow night when you get back. I'm sorry to be here so sporadically but the twenty-four-hour shift patterns we do are rather awkward.'

'It's no trouble,' Prue assured her.

'Depending on what sort of shift I've had – and they've been rather busy lately – I probably need to catch up on sleep once I get back.'

'It must be hard to fit your home life around your work,' Prue said with sympathy.

'It is,' Violet replied, 'though we must do what's necessary.' She gave Prue a warm smile. 'Good luck today. I look forward to hearing how you get on.'

Prue followed Violet out into the flat's hallway. She saw the note written for her, left on the small table by the telephone, with the number for Station 75 written clearly.

Violet took her black uniform tunic, with its LAAS flashes on the shoulders, off the coat stand and put it on over her white shirt, black neck tie and skirt. Then she added her ambulance service hat to complete the outfit.

'Your uniform is very smart,' Prue said, admiring it.

'Thank you. We were delighted to get one, though we had to wait until 1942 until they finally arrived. Before that we wore our own clothes for work, which was rather a nuisance, especially once clothes rationing came in.' Violet glanced at her watch. 'I must go so I'll see you tomorrow. I hope all goes well for you.'

'And you,' Prue said, seeing Violet out and then closing the flat's door behind her.

Left on her own, Prue cleared away and washed up the breakfast things and then prepared to leave. She was due at the WVS depot at nine o'clock and wanted to give herself plenty of time to walk to it, just in case she really did get lost. Once there, she was all set to start the relief work she'd come to London to do – whatever that might be.

'Anyone here with canteen experience?'

Prue was sitting in a sparse room with the other relief volunteers, having arrived in good time and without mishap. The group of around fifteen women was waiting quietly to be assigned jobs for the day, and Prue felt her nerves tingling like it was her first day at school. She'd do anything that was needed, of course, but if it was something she had experience of that would be a safe way to start.

She put her hand up. 'I've worked in a canteen.'

'What's your name?' asked the WVS woman in charge, who'd introduced herself to everyone as Mrs Carmichael.

'I'm Prue.'

'Right, Prue, you can go with Peggy here.' Mrs Carmichael gestured towards one of her colleagues, who stood over by the doorway. 'You'll be taking a canteen to Paddington Station.' Without waiting for an answer, Mrs Carmichael checked her clipboard ready to assign more jobs.

Peggy stepped forward and smiled down at Prue. 'Good to

have you on board. If you'd like to follow me... where have you come from?'

'Great Plumstead, that's a village in Norfolk,' Prue said, standing up and quickly falling into step beside Peggy who led her briskly outside to where three canteens were parked.

'It must be quite a change but we're very grateful that you and the others are here to help us.' She stopped at the nearest canteen. 'This delightful old girl is prepared and ready to go. I'll explain more about what we'll be doing on the way. Do hop in.'

Prue climbed in the passenger seat of the canteen, which was unlike the converted delivery van that she and Thea worked in. This one had the front half of a car, with a van-type box added on the chassis at the back. It was rather odd but functional-looking, Prue thought.

After Peggy had skilfully manoeuvred the canteen out of the yard and onto the road, slipping into the traffic, she spoke more about their task ahead. 'This morning we'll be providing refreshments for the evacuee organisers at Paddington Station. There are more children due to leave from there today. After keeping track of all those youngsters, making sure to herd them to the correct train, a cup of tea and a biscuit is always much appreciated.' Peggy braked, coming to a stop while a red double-decker bus pulled over to pick up passengers.

'We've been on the receiving end of the evacuations,' Prue told Peggy. 'We had our third lot of evacuees arrive a couple of weeks ago.'

Peggy glanced at her. 'How's that going? Have they all stayed?'

'So far. We received children recently, but we've had expectant mothers and, another time, mothers and their children. A few of the mothers returned to London, some taking their children though others thankfully opted to leave them in the village,' Prue explained. 'It's hard moving to such a different place. Living in the countryside is not at all like the city and being away from family and friends and all you're familiar with isn't easy.'

Peggy let out a huff. 'I hear what you're saying, but honestly, Prue, after some of the dreadful things I've seen doing this job, I just wish the evacuees would all stay put in the countryside until it's safe to come home again. They're jolly lucky to escape from the bombing. Sometimes in life you must put up with things, especially if it will protect your children, or even just yourself.'

'Let's hope the evacuees going today stay where they're sent,' Prue said, thinking that Peggy's words showed how much tougher life was for the WVS members here in London. It wasn't surprising, with the city having been under attack for so long.

After they'd arrived at Paddington Station they parked by one of the entrances and quickly set up the canteen. Prue was pleased to find things were organised the way she was already used to. Cups were packed in drawers in their own compartments to prevent them breaking while in transit and everything else she needed was close to hand.

As Peggy opened the hatch ready to start serving, Prue spotted lines of children arriving, with organisers keeping them together and calling out instructions. A few children held small suitcases while others carried their belongings in pillowcases or even wrapped up in paper parcels tied with string. Younger children clutched the hands of older brothers and sisters. Most of them looked unsure and some were downright scared and the sight of them tugged at Prue's heart.

'You all right?' Peggy asked.

Prue swallowed. 'It's not easy to see them like this, at the beginning of their journey, going off to the unknown. I'm glad we make such an effort to welcome them and help them settle when they get to us.'

'Let's hope it won't be too long before it's safe for them to return,' Peggy said, putting plates of biscuits on the counter.

'I hope so too,' Prue agreed.

By the time Prue arrived back at Violet's flat a little after half past five she was worn out. After a morning serving in the canteen with Peggy, she'd gone to work at a large WVS clothing depot where she and other relief volunteers had helped sort through and fold piles of donated garments that had been sent from Canada. The donations needed dividing into type and size, ready to be distributed to families who'd been bombed out of their homes. Prue was proud of the clothing depot they'd built up in Great Plumstead but it was tiny compared with the one she'd worked at today.

After washing and changing into her own clothes, Prue made herself a sandwich for her tea, having had a main meal at a British Restaurant in the middle of the day. She'd not long finished eating when the doorbell rang. She looked out of the sitting-room window down to the street, two flights below, and was surprised and delighted to see who was standing waiting on the steps leading up to the front door. It was Max.

Prue hurried downstairs to meet him, opening the door with a wide smile.

'Max! What a lovely surprise. Come in.'

'I was wondering how you were getting on and wanted to check everything was all right for you,' he said, stepping into the hall.

'I'm fine.' Prue closed the front door behind him. 'I had a good day. It was tiring, but I enjoyed it. Come on up and I'll tell you about it.'

Settled in Violet's sitting room with cups of tea, Prue told Max about her day's work.

'It's been an education already and I've only done one day so far,' Prue commented. 'Some of the WVS members are quite... battle hardened, though that might not be quite the right phrase to use. Their wartime experience has been a lot tougher than for us WVS women out in the countryside.'

'You said you wanted a challenge,' Max said and raised a questioning eyebrow. 'It sounds like you're getting one.'

Prue let out a laugh. 'I did say that, didn't I? And it's true – I wanted one and I'm getting one. How about you – what have you been doing today?'

'I've been at the university, having meetings and being given more translation work to do.'

'And how is your flat – are your friends looking after it well?' Max had told Prue on their journey down that he'd let some Dutch refugee friends live in his flat while he was at Rookery House.

'They are and I'm enjoying seeing them again. Is all well with Violet?'

'Yes. She's at work now and won't be back until the morning – they have a twenty-four-hour shift system. Violet has offered me the chance to visit Ambulance Station 75 while I'm here and I'd like to go. I've heard lots about it from Thea and would love to see how they go about things.'

'A volunteer ambulance station sounds fascinating,' Max said.

'Would you like to go there with me?' Prue offered.

'I'd like that, thank you.' Max looked thoughtful for a few moments. 'Prue, I wondered if you'd care to go out some evenings while you're here. We could attend the theatre or go dancing?' He smiled. 'I enjoyed our dances at Thea's haymaking party.'

'So did I.' Prue's cheeks grew warm as she remembered how much she'd liked dancing with Max. 'Yes, I'd love to do all those things, or as much as we can manage in the short time we have.'

CHAPTER 42

Great Plumstead, Norfolk

Hettie was on duty at The Mother's Day Club this morning and had just collected the empty cups from the tea break, wheeling them on the trolley into the kitchen. As she tipped out the tea dregs, she could hear the women chattering in the hall as they resumed their work – some sewing, others unravelling old jumpers so the yarn could be reused and knitted into new garments. Hettie loved the air of industriousness and companionship the women created and looked forward to joining in with them again as soon as she'd finished the washing up.

Humming to herself, her hands deep in the sink full of hot, soapy water, Hettie was unaware that anyone had come into the room until she heard her name called.

'Hettie. You've got a visitor.'

'Oh, you made me jump!' Hettie exclaimed, turning around to find Gloria standing behind her and Iris lingering outside the doorway, the Land Girl looking down at her feet and twisting her hands together nervously. Curiously, she was dressed in normal clothing, not her usual Land Army uniform.

Hettie caught Gloria's eye and saw her look of concern. 'She looks like she could do with some 'elp.' Gloria spoke softly so that only Hettie could hear.

'Yes,' Hettie replied, quickly drying her hands on her apron and crossing the kitchen.

From up close, she saw that Iris's face was pale and drawn. She was a shadow of the cheerful soul she'd been until two months ago. The sight of her touched Hettie's heart.

'Hello, Iris. Come on in and sit down.' Hettie pulled out a chair from the large table in the centre of the kitchen for her.

Iris did as she was asked, not making eye contact and keeping her gaze downwards.

Gloria gave Hettie a questioning look and Hettie considered asking her to stay. Gloria was an immensely kind and considerate person and a wise one too. She might well be a good person to help Iris. However the young woman was looking so delicate, Hettie decided she should talk to Iris alone – and go very gently with her.

'Thanks for bringing Iris in.' She and Gloria shared another silent look.

'You're most welcome,' Gloria said cheerfully. 'I'll leave you both to talk and get back to unravelling some wool. I'll be just outside if you need me,' she added and patted Hettie's arm reassuringly as she left.

Hettie shut the door behind Gloria. 'Can I get you a drink, Iris? Tea?'

'Just some water, please,' she said without looking up.

As Hettie fetched a clean glass from one of the cupboards and filled it at the sink, she wondered what was going on with

Iris. Why was she here? Had she left Crossways Farm? Given up being a Land Girl?

'There you go.' Hettie put the glass of water down on the table in front of Iris, then moved another chair from under the table and sat next to her, turning slightly so that she faced the young woman.

'Thank you.' Iris had a sip of water. She regarded her hands, which were twisted in her lap.

'What's wrong?' Hettie asked her gently.

Iris waited several long seconds before she said in a voice that was almost inaudible, 'I'm expecting.' Then she dissolved into sobs.

Hettie gathered Iris in her arms and held her. No wonder the young woman looked so wan and anxious. It wasn't only due to losing her fiancé, but to being pregnant as well!

Hettie's thoughts whirled about her head. Pregnancy was going to have an enormous impact on Iris's life. She'd probably have to leave the Land Army... leave Crossways Farm... find somewhere new to live. She would be an unmarried mother with an illegitimate baby and would face the stigma that brought with it. Iris's problems had become far more complicated and this was all on top of a terrible grief.

'How long have you known?' Hettie asked, letting go of Iris as her tears subsided.

'Only since this morning for sure.' Iris dried her face with a handkerchief she'd fished out of her pocket. 'I've been to see the doctor and he confirmed it. I'd thought maybe I had missed my monthlies because of being so upset over Frank, but it wasn't that – I'm having a baby.'

'Does Beattie suspect?' Hettie asked.

Iris shook her head. 'I don't think so. I haven't been sick or anything, just more tired than usual. I put that down to not sleeping well these days and Beattie probably does too.'

Not for the first time, Hettie wished with all her heart that Frank's plane hadn't gone down. If he were still alive, then Iris's pregnancy wouldn't have mattered; they would have got married and the baby would have been born to legally wedded parents. They wouldn't have been the first couple to have conceived a baby before their wedding and nor would they be the last.

The problem now was that Iris had no fiancé to marry and support her, and her baby would have no father.

'What am I going to do?'

'Try to remain calm to start with.' Hettie took hold of Iris's hand. 'Getting yourself into a state will not help you or the baby. Forgive me for saying this but do you want to keep the baby or have it adopted?'

Iris's eyes widened. 'Keep it, of course!' She put her free hand on her belly as if to protect her unborn child. 'He or she is all I have left of Frank. I would never give our baby away.'

'I understand,' Hettie said sympathetically. 'With that decision made, it helps make your path ahead clearer. As far as I know, you probably won't be able to stay in the Land Army if you're going to have a child to care for. I must check with Lizzie at the county office. Beattie and Stan will need to be told so they can get a replacement for you at the farm. I don't suppose you want to go back to your parents in Nottingham after what you've told me about them?'

Iris gave a bitter laugh. 'Even if I wanted to I know my mother wouldn't have me back. She'd say I'd brought shame on the family, that I had made my bed so I could lie in it.'

'Can you be sure of that?' Hettie questioned her. 'The baby will be her grandchild.'

'That won't matter to my mother!' Iris drew in a sharp breath and raised her chin, a determined expression on her face. 'I'm on my own in this. I will bring up Frank's child myself.'

Hettie squeezed Iris's hand. 'You're not alone, I promise you that. Whatever else happens, you have me. I won't let you down.'

'Do you really mean that?' Iris's blue eyes held Hettie's.

'Absolutely,' Hettie assured her. 'Now first things first, let me talk to Lizzie and find out where you stand with the Land Army. You tell Beattie and Stan. After that, we'll see how things look. You'll have me by your side each step of the way.'

'Thank you, Hettie. I'm so grateful and relieved. I've been so scared of what's going to happen.'

'It will be all right in the end.' Hettie said in an upbeat voice, determined to fulfil her promise to Iris, the baby and to Frank, who'd given his life in the battle for freedom. 'We must put our trust in the people around us, and not lose heart for even a minute.'

CHAPTER 43

The East End, London

Prue was no stranger to seeing the damage air raids could do to a city. Closer to home, she'd manned a WVS canteen in the aftermath of the Norwich Blitz and had even seen her dead husband pulled from the ruins of a bombed-out house. But the destruction here in the East End of London was on a wholly different and horrifying scale.

'It's heartbreaking, isn't it?' Peggy glanced over at Prue from the driver's seat of a WVS delivery van. 'I ought to be used to it by now but it still affects me. So many houses gone! And each one a family's home. Look what's left!' She gestured at the gaps like missing teeth in the terraced streets where only rubble remained.

'I've read about it in the newspaper but, until you see it yourself, you can't appreciate the extent.' Prue stared out of the window as they drove along, her vision blurred by tears for all the killed and displaced people each destroyed house represented.

It was now her third day working with the London WVS. She had spent the day before helping prepare meals at a British Restaurant. This morning she'd been paired with Peggy again and they were taking clothes from the depot to be distributed to families who had been bombed out in the latest attacks.

'All this,' Peggy said bitterly, 'and now these damned doodlebugs. Have you seen them?'

'I have,' Prue said ominously. Her first sight of one had shocked her to a standstill. Its horrible buzzing, like an angry wasp, sent her heart racing as it approached, along with a desperate hope the engine kept on running. She'd heard them while walking to and from work, and at night, had pulled aside the blackout and seen the fiery orange glow of a doodlebug's exhaust standing out against the inky black sky over London.

'Do you get many in Norfolk?'

'I've not seen any, but I've been told there's been a few, though nothing like you have here. They're truly terrifying.'

Peggy slowed the van and changed to a lower gear. 'They are, and they've made many people unsettled and wary. But we must still carry on, not give up. Right, here we are.'

Prue saw a church hall up ahead; there was already a queue forming outside it.

'Brace yourself,' Peggy warned her, 'we're in for a busy day!'

Prue checked the map that Violet had drawn for them. 'I think it must be down here towards the Tower of London,' she told

Max. 'Ambulance Station 75 is in a kind of courtyard off a street called Minories. Violet said to look out for an archway on the right.'

It was a clear August evening and Prue and Max were on their way to visit Violet at work.

'This must be it.' Prue halted as they reached a wide arched passageway big enough for an ambulance to drive through. 'I'm glad Violet warned me that Station 75 is tucked away. I'd never have known it was here otherwise!'

They headed through the passageway which opened into a wide courtyard. A crescent of tall, grand houses stood on one side. Opposite them were flat-roofed mews garages. The doors to the garages stood open and they could see a small fleet of ambulances inside.

''ello! Are you Prue and Max?' The voice calling out from above had an East End accent that reminded Prue of Nancy. She looked up and saw a young woman with auburn hair peering down at them from the garages roof.

'Yes, we are. We've come to see Violet – Station Officer Steele,' Prue corrected herself.

''old on a tick and I'll be down to take you to 'er,' the young woman called before heading inside.

Prue's eyes met Max's, a look of amusement passing between them at their arrival being spotted from the rooftop.

'I was not expecting them to keep a lookout,' Max said dryly, making Prue laugh.

Barely a minute later, the door to the side of the garages burst open and the young woman hurried out. She was wearing the same London Auxiliary Ambulance Service uniform as Violet wore, only with black trousers rather than a skirt.

'Welcome to Station 75. I'm Frankie.' She held out her hand and shook hands with Prue and then Max. 'The boss said to keep an eye out for you so I've been sitting up on the roof for a bit while I'm on my break, enjoying the last of the day's sunshine. There's a smashing view of the Tower from there if you would like to look while you're 'ere. I'll take you up to the boss's office.'

'Thank you – I would like to see the view,' Prue said as they followed Frankie in through the door and climbed the flight of stairs to an upper floor.

Frankie led them into a large room where there was a variety of old chairs and a sofa, plus a table and a wireless. 'This is our common room.'

Other crew members, both men and women, were sitting around occupied in various activities like reading the paper, knitting or playing draughts.

'Aye, aye, we've got visitors!' A man dressed in overalls called out as he lowered his copy of the *Daily Herald* newspaper.

'That's Sparky,' Frankie commented. 'He doesn't miss a trick.'

'Hello, Sparky,' Prue called over to him.

'Evening, missus.' He flashed her a grin and then returned to reading his paper.

Frankie led them over to a closed door and knocked. On hearing a voice call, she opened it. 'Your visitors are here, Boss.'

'Thank you, Frankie.' Violet appeared in the doorway and smiled warmly at Prue and Max, whom she'd met the day Prue arrived. 'I'm glad you found us all right. Would you like some tea? The crew are on a break so it would be no bother to rustle some up.'

'Not for me, but thank you,' Prue said.

'What about you, Max?' Violet asked.

'No, thank you, I'm fine too,' he replied.

'In that case, let me give you a guided tour of our ambulance station. Frankie,' Violet turned to the young woman. 'Will you stay in my office and mind the telephone for me for a few minutes, please? I'll send Winnie down to take over.'

Frankie gave them a small wave as she went into the office.

'Let's go up and start on the roof,' Violet said, 'then you'll get some perspective of where we are.'

Violet led them up another flight of stairs onto the flat roof of Station 75, where Prue was amused to see three deck chairs, two of them occupied, and a small, golden-haired dog sprawled out in the sunshine. Spotting their arrival, the dog leapt to its feet and hurried over, its tail wagging rapidly as it greeted Violet with obvious delight.

'Hello, Trixie,' Violet said fondly, bending down to stroke the dog's head.

Two crew women hauled themselves out of their deck chairs and smoothed down their uniforms.

'Good evening.' The tall, slim, blonde-haired woman, who wore pillar-box-red lipstick, spoke with a plummy voice. 'I'm Winnie and this is Bella.' She indicated her colleague, who was shorter, with dark brown curly hair.

'Hello,' Bella greeted them cheerily.

Violet continued the introductions. 'This is Prue, who's staying with me and is my friend Thea's sister, and Max, who's staying at Thea's home in Norfolk for a while.'

'Welcome,' Bella said. 'I remember when Thea came here.'

'My sister told me about her visit,' Prue said. 'She enjoyed it very much and it's lovely to be here and see the place for myself and meet you all.'

'Winnie, will you man the telephone, please?' Violet instructed, then checked her watch. 'Break time's over. Bella, please inform the others it's time to get back to work. Needs must,' she said, turning to Prue and Max. 'We have to run a tight ship if we're to be ready to do our bit to the best of our abilities. A call-out to an incident can come in at any time.'

Winnie lifted Trixie into her arms and then she and Bella went downstairs to resume their duties.

'So what do you think of the view?' Violet asked, casting her arm around.

'It's amazing!' Prue looked in awe at the imposing Tower of London. Just to the left of it she could see the magnificent Tower Bridge, spanning the River Thames. The vista extended off into the distance, downstream to where wharves lined the river's banks, and upstream into the heart of the city.

'We're most fortunate to have such a grand spot for our ambulance station. We even have an allotment in the Tower's dry moat,' Violet told them. 'We grow cabbages and potatoes on the site of so much history.'

'Where do you send your ambulances? Do you go all over?' Max asked.

'Not usually, each ambulance station has its own patch. Ours mainly extends that way into the East End.' Violet waved a hand to the left. 'Although if needed we will go to other areas. It depends on where the bombing occurs and how bad it is.'

'You were right in the thick of the Blitz here,' Max said.

Violet nodded, her face serious. 'We were indeed. Some of my crew were sitting up here as the Blitz began. They spotted the squadrons of bombers coming this way, like swarms of flies high in the sky guided by the river to their targets, and they saw the smoke curling up from where the first bombs fell.' She shook her head sadly. 'It was the beginning of a long and difficult time. I remember that was the day Thea came to visit us.'

Prue felt her mouth go dry as she recalled hearing about

the massive air raid on the wireless the next morning and her terrible worry about both her sister and her son Edwin, who'd been working for the Friends Ambulance Unit in the East End. Thankfully, they'd both come through it unscathed.

'But we dealt with it. My crews were magnificent,' Violet said. 'They still are. I count myself very fortunate to work here with them.' After a last glance around at the view, she added, 'Let me show you the rest of Station 75.'

After Violet's tour of the ambulance station, Prue and Max said their goodbyes and headed down to the Tower of London and the River Thames.

'Thank goodness the Tower is still standing after all those air raids and let's hope it stays that way too. It would be tragic to lose such an important historical monument,' Prue said as they walked by the centuries-old building, the August sunshine bathing the pale stonework in a warm honey glow.

'I like how part of it is being used to help Dig for Victory.' Max stopped to admire the neat rows of vegetables growing in the dry moat.

'They're adapting to the current desperate situation,' Prue commented. 'Like all of us. Shall we have a stroll by the river? I feel like enjoying some time by the water.'

Max turned to her, their eyes meeting. 'Excellent idea. I would like that very much.' He held out the crook of his elbow for her to take, his eyebrows raised. 'May I?'

Prue laughed as she hooked her hand through Max's arm and they walked down to the river wall, pausing there for a few moments to take in the sights and sounds of the Thames at low tide, and the smells – a pleasant, earthy aroma arose from the sunlit muddy banks.

Prue felt the breeze in her hair and on her face and closed her eyes, drawing in a breath of river air that reminded her of the river running through Great Plumstead and of the time she'd met Max walking there...

She felt his arm about hers and when she opened her eyes, he was watching her, his face as relaxed and happy as she felt herself.

'Where shall we go from here?' Max asked her.

It cost her an effort to remove her gaze from him. She looked to the left, then the right, and then back at Max.

'I'm all right just here,' she said.

CHAPTER 44

Rookery House, Norfolk

Hettie had just explained Iris's predicament to Lizzie Thornton on the phone. Lizzie was Norfolk's Land Army County Secretary as well as being youngest sister to Thea, Prue and Reuben.

'Iris isn't the first Land Girl to find herself in this situation and she won't be the last.' Lizzie's voice was sympathetic as it came down the telephone line from her new office on Prince of Wales Road in Norwich. 'However, I'm afraid it will mean she'll be discharged from the Land Army.'

'Straight away?' Hettie's heart sank, knowing how Iris's work was giving her some much-needed stability while she grieved for Frank. If she lost her job – and with it, her lodgings – what would happen to her? From what Iris had told Hettie about her mother, it was unlikely that the young woman would be welcome back at her family home in Nottingham with an illegitimate baby on the way.

'She can keep on working for as long as she's healthy and it is safe for her to do so. After that, she'll have to leave. She wouldn't be able to work as she gets closer to giving birth or when she has a baby to look after.'

'I understand,' said Hettie, feeling downcast.

Lizzie let out a sigh. 'It's such a pity for Iris – she's an excellent Land Girl and must be suffering terribly since losing her fiancé. I'd best come out and see her, explain to her what needs to happen.' She paused and Hettie could hear pages being turned. 'I've checked my diary and, if I do a bit of rearranging, I can visit Crossways Farm this afternoon. Will you go with me? I could pick you up on my way there.'

'Of course I will,' Hettie said without hesitation. There was nothing she had planned that couldn't wait. Helping Iris was her priority.

'Thanks, Hettie. I'll be at Rookery House at half past one. Try not to worry. I know how much you watch out for the Land Girls under your care. Iris will be all right, I promise you – we'll find a solution.'

'I'm nervous,' Hettie admitted as Lizzie turned her Austin 7 off the road and into the lane leading down to Crossways Farm.

Lizzie glanced at her. 'It will be fine. Nothing's going to happen immediately – there's plenty of time to sort things out.'

'It's just been such a difficult time for her,' Hettie said. 'I find it hard to watch the poor girl suffering.'

'We won't be heavy-handed,' Lizzie assured her. 'You and I are both sensitive to her needs and the Land Army has ways to help. Has Iris told Beattie and Stan yet?'

'I'm not sure. She hadn't when I saw her on Friday morning, but she's had the weekend since then.'

'Let's hope she has because otherwise they're in for a surprise today. It would be best if they are fully on board with helping Iris.'

'I'm sure they will be,' Hettie told her as Lizzie steered her car around in a circle in the farmyard and brought it to a halt by the barn.

Hettie spotted Beattie unpegging bed sheets from the line to the side of the house. On a warm, breezy August day like this they would have dried in no time, Hettie thought, her mind wandering.

'Ready?' Lizzie asked. She had her hand on her door handle.

Hettie was brought back to the moment. 'As I'll ever be,' she said, with a heavy sigh.

The farmer's wife stood with the basket of folded sheets in her arms as they headed towards her across the farmyard.

'Afternoon, Hettie, Lizzie,' she greeted them politely, though her usual smile was absent; Hettie was sure Iris had told her.

'Hello, Beattie,' Lizzie said. 'How are you? I was hoping to have a word with you.'

'About Iris's baby, I expect,' Beattie said. She sounded and looked tired and Hettie realised she wasn't the only one feeling the strain of the situation. It must be hard for Beattie and Stan too.

'Hettie told me this morning,' Lizzie explained. 'We've come to talk to you and Iris about what happens next.'

'Come on in.' Beattie led the way indoors and put the washing basket to one side of the kitchen. 'We've talked about little else here all weekend. Can we three speak first before you talk to Iris? She's out with Stan mending a fence.'

'Of course,' Lizzie agreed.

Beattie looked relieved. 'Sit yourself down and I'll make us some cordial.' While Beattie busied herself fetching glasses and pouring out their drinks, Lizzie and Hettie sat at the large wooden table in the middle of the kitchen.

'When did Iris tell you?' Hettie asked when Beattie joined them.

'On Saturday morning. I'd known something was up for a couple of weeks, but I'd thought it was because of Frank dying; Iris has looked so pale and tired. I was all up for calling the doctor. Though I wasn't thinking she was pregnant – it never crossed my mind.'

Lizzie made to speak but Beattie held up her hand. 'If you don't mind, I'd like to say my piece, I'm sure you understand.'

Lizzie and Hettie both nodded for her to go on.

'Iris expecting... with no mother and father to help... no husband... and I know what you're going to say, Lizzie, that she'll have to leave the Land Army and that means leaving here as well.'

Hettie watched Beattie's eyes fill up with tears.

'Stan and I don't want that,' Beattie said firmly. 'Iris has become like a daughter to us and she's brought a lot of joy to our lives. So we've made up our minds, it won't matter if she's not a Land Girl any more. Iris can stay, if she wants. She can have her baby here and live with us. *I'll* help her care for the child even if her own mother won't. And Stan's ready to do his bit too.'

Hettie's heart leapt at Beattie's words. Lizzie flashed a smile at her, then turned to Beattie.

'You're right. Iris will have to leave the Land Army once her pregnancy is too advanced for her to work. However your offer to have Iris keep on living with you is a generous and kind one, and the Land Army certainly won't stand in your way. Far from it – there may be ways we can assist you.'

'We both think the world of Iris,' Beattie said. 'I know there are some who'd throw her out, but if fate had been kinder, Iris would have been married soon. Iris and Frank's baby wouldn't have been the first to be on the way before its parents married. Stan and I were in the same boat with our son!' Beattie's cheeks grew pink at her revelation. 'Iris's family might not help her, but we will stand by her side and support her every step of the way.'

'Have you told Iris any of this?' Hettie asked.

'Not yet; we were waiting to hear what the Land Army had to say first.' Beattie smiled sheepishly. 'I was ready to fight them all the way to get what we want!'

Lizzie laughed. 'I'm glad to hear it! Now, do you want another Land Girl to replace Iris?' Lizzie asked. 'Stan can't manage this place on his own.'

Beattie looked surprised. 'You know, we haven't even thought about that. If we're allowed one, we could, or else perhaps a POW? Stan and I need talk it through.' Beattie took a sip of her cordial. 'First things first, we must talk to Iris.'

'Shall I go and fetch her in?' Hettie offered.

'No, I'll go,' Beattie stood up. 'I won't be long.'

Left alone in the kitchen, Lizzie said, 'What do you think of Beattie's offer?'

'It's a good one!' Hettie beamed. 'I'm hoping Iris will accept. She and her baby will have a wonderful home here and I'll still be able to help her too.'

'She's lucky to work for such kind people. Few of the other farmers I deal with would be so understanding.'

'It was a fortunate day for all when Iris was sent here,' Hettie said.

A few minutes later, Beattie returned with Iris and, after pouring the Land Girl a drink, she sat beside her at the table.

'I'm sure you know why I'm here.' Lizzie gave Iris a gentle smile. 'I need to tell you it is Land Army policy that expectant mothers must be discharged from the service when it's no longer safe for them to do their work.'

'I thought as much,' Iris said, matter of factly. 'I want to carry on for a while yet to help Stan, then I'll leave.'

Beattie took the young woman's hand. 'Stan and me don't want you to go. You can stay here and have your baby.'

Iris's blue eyes widened and then welled up with tears. 'You'd have me stay even though I'm expecting an illegitimate child?'

'Yours and Frank's child,' Beattie said. 'That's who you're having. Stan says this should be your home.'

'Thank you so much!' Iris flung her arms around Beattie and hugged her. 'I've been so worried about where I'd go. I would *love* to stay here with you both. This has been the happiest place I have ever lived in.'

'The Land Army Benevolent Fund will give you a grant to help with expenses for you and the baby,' Lizzie said. 'The WVS can provide you with a layette.'

Iris wiped her wet cheeks with the back of her hand. 'Thank you.'

'I'll knit you some things as well,' Hettie added. 'We'll get you prepared – you'll have everything you need.'

'Who will replace me on the farm?' Iris asked.

'We'll get another Land Girl or a couple of POWs,' Beattie replied.

'Thea's happy with Luca's work at Rookery House – I'm sure she'd be willing to talk to you about how she went about applying for POW help,' Hettie said.

'After the baby's born, I could do some work again on the

farm while it's sleeping,' Iris offered. 'I wouldn't be an official Land Girl but I could still help in the dairy or with the pigs.'

'Don't worry about that now,' Beattie said. 'The important thing is you know that you're safe with us.'

Iris nodded, unable to speak as her emotions got the better of her.

'We'll leave you to get on,' Lizzie said. 'I'll come and see you again in six weeks, but if you need anything before then, please let me know. Look after yourself and don't overdo things.'

'I'll make sure she doesn't.' Beattie squeezed Iris's shoulder. 'And thank you both for coming today. It feels like a weight's been lifted off us.'

Lizzie stood up. 'We'll see ourselves out.'

'I'll pop over next week.' Hettie got to her feet. 'Though you can ring me any time at Rookery House and I will get here as soon as I can.'

'Thank you,' Iris said. 'I'm so lucky to have you all looking out for me.'

Outside, Lizzie slipped her arm through Hettie's as they walked back to the car. 'I wish all my dealings with Land Girls and farmers worked out as well as that. Iris is going to be fine.'

'That's what happens when people pull together. Iris is part of an extended family now and we'll all be helping as much as we can. I'm looking forward to her and Frank's baby being born.' Hettie raised her head to bask in the warmth of the summer sun on her face. 'I shall start knitting something for him or her tonight!'

CHAPTER 45

London

Prue's last evening in London had arrived and she and Max were spending it dancing. They'd come to a hotel where there was a band playing and it was a delight to move together to live music under sparkling chandeliers.

After a morning peeling potatoes in a men's hostel followed by an afternoon spent washing up in a British Restaurant, Prue had been glad to put on a summer dress and go out to enjoy herself.

'You're looking happy,' Max said as he steered her around the dance floor.

'I am. I was thinking how lovely it is to be here after a busy day. I've never peeled so many potatoes before in my life. And I'm not sure I want to, ever again!' Prue laughed. 'But it was for a good cause. And it makes being out dancing all the sweeter.'

Max's mouth twitched with amusement. 'Have you

enjoyed your week volunteering? Has it been worth the effort?'

'I have, and yes, it has.' Prue's eyes met his. 'And I've enjoyed our time together very much too.'

The evening before, Max had taken her to the theatre. Prue had asked Violet to come along too but she'd declined as she had other plans. Prue had loved the variety show and it had been such a treat to go.

'It's been wonderful and…' She hesitated for a moment, unsure whether to say truthfully that she would miss Max when she went home. This interlude with him wasn't her real life, she reminded herself. She'd be foolish to think it might continue when they both returned to Great Plumstead. It couldn't, as their normal lives would resume. These evenings spent together would become merely memories of their time in London. 'Thank you for showing me around and taking me out.'

'It's been a great pleasure.' Max slowed their dancing until they were barely moving, his eyes holding hers.

Prue's cheeks grew warm. She blurted out, 'When are you going back to Rookery House?'

'In a few days, I hope.' He picked up the pace again, steering her around the other couples. 'I'm looking forward to returning to the countryside; I've missed it.'

'You've become accustomed to the ways of country life,' Prue teased. 'Did you ever think that might happen, when you first left London?'

'Not at all. I've always lived in cities. Amsterdam and then London. I've learned however that the countryside has its attractions.'

Prue laughed. 'It does,' she agreed.

～

Rather than go straight back to Violet's flat after the band played their final piece, Max suggested they take a last stroll by the River Thames. Prue happily agreed, not ready to end the day just yet.

Now, leaning on the cold stone of the wall overlooking the water, Prue breathed in the night air, which had a slightly salty, tarry smell coming from the river at high tide. She watched as some coal barges floated past, their movement sending faint, silvery ripples of reflected moonlight dancing across the water's surface.

'I love the wide, open space the Thames gives to London. It's a relief after the packed city streets on either side of it,' she mused. 'It feels as if there's more room to breathe down here.'

'I understand what you mean,' Max said, standing close beside her. 'The canals in Amsterdam give that same sense of openness. It doesn't feel so crowded.'

'Amsterdam sounds like a lovely place.'

'It is. Or was. I hope it remains so after years of being occupied.'

Prue touched his arm, which was resting on the wall as he watched the river. 'I hope so too.'

She looked up at the sky. A waxing cream-coloured moon hung overhead, painting London in monochrome tones of black and grey. An orange flickering light caught her eye, high above the city on the south side of the river. It was heading in their direction. Moments later, the unmistakeable buzzing noise of a doodlebug filled the air, making Prue's heart pound. 'Look!' She pointed to the fiery tail, which was coming closer by the second.

She saw Max open his mouth but before he could say anything the droning of the engine altered to a *phut, phut* sound and then cut out, leaving an ominous silence as the rocket began its deadly descent.

Prue was filled with a cold dread; she saw the blood draining from Max's face, his eyes widening in alarm.

'Quick!' He grabbed Prue's hand and pulled her to the ground in the lee of the wall, positioning himself on the outside of her, sheltering her with his body.

Prue closed her eyes, aware of the way her heart hammered inside as she waited for the rocket to land. All the while, Max kept a tight hold of her hand, his other arm wrapped protectively around her. She didn't know how long they lay there; it seemed like an age but must only have been a matter of seconds before there was a mighty *whoomph* as the doodlebug exploded on impact.

Max let out a long breath. 'Are you all right?' His voice was shaky.

Prue was unable to speak. It had missed them, landing further north of the river; how far, she couldn't say. Maybe just a street or two over. If its engine had cut out a few seconds earlier, it could have landed on them.

Max got to his feet and helped her up, then wrapped both his arms around her and held her in a firm embrace. Prue hugged him back, leaning her head against his chest, grateful for his comfort.

Then without speaking, he loosened his grip, cupped Prue's cheek with one hand and gently kissed her.

'I have wanted to do that for a long time,' Max said, his eyes meeting hers in the shadowy moonlight. 'I hope you don't mind, only after what we've just experienced, it's a reminder not to be afraid to take a chance on happiness.'

Prue returned his gaze. 'I didn't mind at all. If you like, we could do it again.'

So they did.

CHAPTER 46

Great Plumstead, Norfolk

'I wish I didn't 'ave to go back 'ome tomorrow,' Jess said. 'It would be lovely to 'ave more time with George and Betty.'

'You'd be very welcome to stay for as long as you want,' Thea offered.

Jess had been at Rookery House for the past few days and was due to return to London in the morning. Thea, Jess and the two youngsters were walking in the wood close to Rookery House, the children running on ahead of them, throwing sticks for Reuben's dog Bess, who'd joined them for their outing.

'Thank you, I appreciate your kind offer, but I've got to get back to work first thing on Thursday. Seeing how much my two 'ave grown since I last saw them, well…' Jess gave a long sigh. 'It brings it 'ome to me 'ow much I'm missing out on them. I can't bring them back to London yet, though, not with the doodlebugs raining down on us. It's not safe. The bombing raids were bad enough but at least we had a warning to get down to the underground to shelter.'

'Hopefully the war won't last much longer,' Thea said. 'The Allies are making progress in France, pushing the enemy into retreat.'

'The sooner it's over the better for all of us. I'm grateful my Bob ain't fighting over there. He's doing 'is bit in the dockyards, mind you.'

Thea hadn't met Jess's husband, though Jess often mentioned him. Thea found it rather odd that he hadn't visited George and Betty since they'd been evacuated out of London but then not all fathers were keen to spend time with their children. Perhaps for him it was a case of out of sight, out of mind.

'I'm fortunate to have my 'usband at 'ome with me, not thousands of miles away doing who-knows-what.' Jess gave Thea a quick look. 'Where 'e is, I can keep a close eye on 'im.'

Thea wondered if Jess had guessed she knew the real reason Jess had returned to London leaving her children at Rookery House. Nancy had told Thea that Bob had a 'wandering eye' and Jess wanted to be with him in London to stop him from straying. At least she had been sensible enough to leave Betty and George here, Thea thought. Their mother had put her children's safety first and Thea had huge respect for Jess for doing so.

'It's hard for wives with husbands away fighting,' Thea said, to fill the silence.

They walked on a little way, watching the children laughing and playing with Bess.

'Can I ask you something?' Jess put a hand on Thea's arm to halt her.

'Of course.'

The young woman drew in a deep breath before speaking.

'There ain't no easy way to say this, but if anything 'appened to me and Bob, would you keep looking after my children for me, please? Let 'em stay with all of you at Rookery 'ouse.'

Thea opened her mouth but the words didn't come. The request was so unexpected and not something she'd ever considered, though it was prudent of Jess to think of all eventualities no matter how unlikely.

'It's all right if you don't want to,' Jess said hurriedly, mistaking Thea's reaction. 'I appreciate everything that you've done already and perhaps it's too much to ask...'

'It isn't too much, Jess,' Thea told her. 'You've caught me by surprise, that's all. I'd be delighted to continue to look after your children for as long as they need me. However, I really do think it won't be necessary – you'll be able to have them home again with you once it's safe for them to go back to London.'

'That's what I 'ope, that we can carry on our lives just as we left off, before the war started. Only these new raids got me thinking about it and worrying. What if the worst does 'appen? I'd rest easier knowing my two were 'appy 'ere with you.' Jess's eyes filled with tears that quickly spilled over. 'I ain't being morbid, Thea, just realistic. These doodlebugs... well, one of them could 'ave mine and Bob's names on it.'

'I do understand your fears,' Thea said and, taking Jess in her arms, she hugged the younger woman. 'You're a good mother, Jess,' she said, 'and you're looking out for Betty and George as you always do.'

'I think about them all the time,' Jess admitted when Thea let her go.

'I'm sure you always will,' Thea replied, 'and I hope it will ease your concerns that they will have a home here at Rookery House for as long as they need it. That's my promise to you, Jess.'

'Thank you,' Jess said, wiping her cheeks with the back of her hand.

A thought occurred to Thea. 'What about your mother-in-law, though?' she asked. Jess and Bob had moved in with Bob's mother when their own home was destroyed in the Blitz. 'Wouldn't she want to have her grandchildren live with her?'

'She *might*,' Jess scoffed, 'but *I* don't want 'er to 'ave them! And neither would Bob.' Jess was keeping her voice low, glancing at the children to make sure they weren't in earshot. 'She ain't a nice woman, Thea, and the thought of 'er bringing up my two darlings chills my 'eart. It mustn't *ever* 'appen, Thea!' Jess grabbed hold of Thea's hand, her eyes pleading.

'She is their grandmother and so would have a legal right to her grandchildren,' Thea mused. 'If you want them to stay with me should anything terrible happen to you and Bob, then you will have to make your wishes known.'

"ow would I? I ain't talking to 'er about it, she'd 'it the roof!'

Thea squeezed Jess's hand. 'I think it would need to be written in a Will or some other legal document. Then there could be no doubt about where you wanted George and Betty to live.'

'You're right, Thea. Though I couldn't leave it in my mother-in-law's 'ouse, she'd destroy it to get 'er own way!' Jess's eyes suddenly lit up. 'I've got it! I'll get a Will made as soon as I get 'ome and I'll send you a copy and another to my cousin in Yorkshire. That way there couldn't be any dispute.'

'There couldn't,' Thea agreed. 'Though I hope there won't ever be a need to use it.'

A burst of giggling from the children caught their attention. Bess was racing around and through their legs while George waved a stick about just out of her reach.

Jess gave Thea a grateful smile. 'You 'ave done so much for us. When I think of them 'ere with you it warms my 'eart.'

'It's a privilege to have them here.' And it will be a wrench when they leave, Thea couldn't help thinking. 'Come on,' she said, putting her arm through Jess's and striding ahead, 'no more talk of doodlebugs and plans we hope will never be necessary. Let's enjoy ourselves.'

Jess laughed. 'Yes, let's make the most of it. George, Betty, wait for me!'

Letting go of Thea, Jess raced to catch up with her children.

Thea smiled as she followed on behind. Jess feared for her children's future but was taking action in case things should go wrong. Life was so uncertain but Thea hoped with all her heart that George and Betty would never have to face losing their parents at a young age. Should that happen, though, Thea would always be there for them, no matter what.

CHAPTER 47

'Is that you, Prue?'

Nancy's voice called from the kitchen as Prue closed the front door behind her.

'Yes, hello Nancy.' She put her suitcase down, then took off her jacket and hung it on the coat stand. She was glad to be home after a long journey back from London. After several delays, it was almost half past seven by the time she arrived at Great Plumstead station, much later than she'd planned.

'Ready for a cuppa?' Her friend gave her a welcoming smile as Prue joined her in the kitchen. Nancy was already pouring Prue a cup of tea from the familiar brown teapot which was barely visible under its colourful knitted cosy.

'Oh yes, please!' Prue pulled a chair out from the table and sat down. 'How have things been here? How are *you*?'

'All good. Though it's lovely to 'ave you 'ome again.'

'How are you feeling?' Prue observed her friend, who stood on the other side of the table. 'I'm sure you've grown bigger in the past week.'

'I 'ave and no doubt about it!' Nancy placed both hands on

her blooming stomach. 'I can feel it moving about in there, stretching its legs.' She sat down opposite Prue and opened her mouth to say more but halted as the kitchen door burst open and her daughters Marie and Joan came rushing in, both in their nightgowns.

'Auntie Prue!' the girls chorused and threw their arms around her as she stood up to greet them.

'We missed you!' Joan said.

'I missed you all too.' Prue hugged them back.

'What did you do in London? Where did you go?' Marie asked, releasing Prue and looking up at her, waiting for answers.

'Auntie Prue can tell you about 'er trip tomorrow,' Nancy said. 'You need to get back to bed and to sleep.'

'But...' Joan began but was silenced by a stern look from Nancy.

'Go on, do as your mother says,' Prue urged them. 'I promise I'll tell you all about what I did in London tomorrow.' She kissed each of them on the forehead. 'Now, off to bed. Sleep well.'

Sitting down at the table again after the girls had gone upstairs, Prue took a sip of her tea.

'They've been that excited about you coming 'ome,' Nancy told her. 'They wanted to stay up and wait for you. I 'ad to put my foot down.'

Prue smiled. 'It's wonderful to have such a warm welcome from them.'

'How did you get on?' Nancy asked.

'You want to know too?' Prue raised an eyebrow, her eyes meeting her friend's across the table.

'Of course I do!' Nancy let out a laugh. 'An' I don't want to 'ave to wait until the morning to 'ear about it either! Did the journey there with Max go well?'

'It did. I enjoyed having someone to talk to on the way. Hettie packed a delicious picnic for us to share and Max guided me to Violet's flat once we reached London. It was much easier than finding my own way and ending up getting lost,' Prue explained.

'I'm glad you 'ad help – I get lost down that way myself. Was it all right staying with Violet?'

'Yes, she's a lovely person. Although she wasn't at home much of the time as she works a twenty-four-hour shift pattern. I visited the ambulance station Violet's in charge of near the Tower of London. It was interesting to see what they do there.'

'What about your WVS work? What did you do?' Nancy asked, nodding eagerly for Prue to continue.

'I did something different every day and was sent to various places. One job that hit home was working in a WVS canteen at Paddington Station, providing tea and biscuits for the volunteers organising the evacuees. I saw evacuation from the other end, children leaving all they were familiar with and looking scared, not knowing where they were going.' She put a hand to her chest, recalling images of the lines of children arriving at the station. 'I'd only experienced it from this end so seeing the children leaving was eye-opening.'

Nancy's face grew serious. 'I know I was lucky that I could come 'ere with my girls – it would 'ave been 'eartbreaking sending them off on their own.'

'I'm glad you came too.' Prue gave her friend a smile. 'Anyway, altogether it was a wonderful experience volunteering with the London WVS. It is so different for them there as they work in a city under attack, be it from the air raids or these latest doodlebugs.'

'Did you see any?'

'Quite a few! Thankfully none landed where I was, but

they make you feel on edge that they might.' Prue didn't want to re-live her and Max's close shave by the Thames – it still seemed too real, and too terrifying. 'Anyway, I'll be back to normal tomorrow, on duty at The Mother's Day Club.'

'Everyone will be pleased to see you again and keen to 'ear 'ow you got on. It weren't the same there without you.'

'Sometimes it's beneficial to go away. Even a short trip makes us appreciate what we already have.' Prue stifled a yawn. 'Excuse me. I'm tired after a hectic week.'

'Do you want anything to eat?'

'No, I'm fine, thank you. I had some sandwiches on the train. I think I'll head up to bed early and catch up on some sleep.' Prue stood up. 'Thanks for keeping this place going for me while I was away.'

'My pleasure.'

Heading upstairs with her suitcase, Prue reflected on how it felt to be home in her familiar world of this house and the village of Great Plumstead. She was happy to be back but so glad that she had volunteered in London for a week. It had given her so much – her experiences there were both challenging and delighting.

CHAPTER 48

'Let me get those for you.' Chuck reached up and picked the ripe and plump cluster of blackberries that hung high above Hettie's head.

'Thank you!' She beamed at the tall American, who was enthusiastically embracing this morning's blackberrying expedition around the Rookery House hedgerows, which had been overloaded with ripe fruits since September arrived. Chuck, along with Walt, Earl and Gil had come over from the aerodrome to join Prue, Hettie and the others. They were harvesting berries to make jam for the WI market stall to sell. 'I'm glad you're here, Chuck,' Hettie told him, 'you can pick those that are out of my reach – and they always look like the best ones!'

Chuck tossed a berry into his open mouth and chewed. 'Mmm! They taste good too!' He dropped the rest into the filled basket she was holding. 'Shall I take that to the pram for you and fetch another?'

'Yes please, I'll pick into Thea's while you get it.' She

gestured towards where Thea was picking a little further along the hedgerow.

Hettie watched Chuck head off to where Marianne had left her pram by the gate to Five Acres field; it had been her idea to use her pram to transport the harvest to Rookery House and it was a good idea because many pounds would be picked today.

The sound of laughter coming from further around the field caught Hettie's attention and she turned to see Prue, who was picking beside Max, reacting to something he'd said to her. Prue's laughter was unusually open and carefree. It was a joy to see Prue so happy, Hettie thought, and kept watching her and Max. The two of them seemed so... she struggled to find the right word to explain what she'd observed... *together*. It was as if Prue and Max were a unit on their own, unlike the others who ranged around the hedgerows. While they picked over the brambles, Prue and Max remained close, their heads and bodies angled towards each other.

Aware that she was staring, Hettie turned away and trudged over to Thea.

'Have you noticed what's going on?' Hettie spoke in a low voice as she dropped a handful of berries into Thea's basket.

Her friend stopped picking and regarded Hettie. 'What do you mean?'

'Between Prue and Max,' Hettie whispered. 'Something's changed. You can see it!'

Thea turned to watch her sister and Max for a few moments. 'They appear to be enjoying their blackberrying,' she said simply. 'What am I missing?'

'There's more to it than that – take a closer look at Prue,' Hettie urged. 'She looks lighter and like she's glowing! I've never seen her that way. And Max is attentive to her. Keep watching.'

Thea shrugged. 'I see nothing unusual, Max is just...' Thea stopped talking mid-sentence. Max had put his hand briefly on Prue's waist, guiding her as they moved along. 'Ah,' Thea said.

'See what I mean?'

'I do. Prue hasn't said anything to me.'

'Not even while you're out together in the WVS canteen?'

'No, nothing,' said Thea.

'Well, unless I am very much mistaken, it looks like she and Max might be more than just friends. If they are, then it's a good thing, in my opinion. They're both lovely people, and after what Prue put up with being married to that swine Victor for all those years she deserves to find happiness with a decent man. What do you think, Thea? You're being very quiet about it!'

Thea smiled. 'I've been surprised again, that's all – unexpected developments seem to be following me around lately.'

Hettie knew she was referring to Jess's request about Betty and George; Thea had confided in Hettie, who had agreed that the children's future at Rookery House was secure for however long they needed to stay.

'Are you happy for Prue?' Hettie pressed Thea.

'I'm pleased for them both if it's what we think it is.'

'Good!' said Hettie, wholeheartedly.

'I don't know why she hasn't told me though,' Thea mused.

'There must be a reason for it. Maybe you should just ask her,' Hettie suggested. 'Prue might be worried about what people will say, especially her family.'

'She needn't have concerns there – we'd all be delighted for her, of course.' Thea looked thoughtful. 'Come to think of it, Max has seemed different lately. Have you noticed he goes for a walk every evening now? He heads off towards the village...'

Hettie chuckled. 'I think we can guess who he's going to see!'

'They can't be meeting at Prue's house without Nancy knowing and she'd have said something.'

Hettie heard Chuck striding towards them and turned to greet him.

'Here we go, Hettie, another basket for you!'

'Thanks Chuck. There are some beauties up there I'll never get.' Hettie pointed to a cluster of plump berries swaying tantalising just out of her reach a little way along the hedge.

'Okay, no problem.' Chuck handed Hettie the basket and went to get them.

Hettie whispered to Thea, 'Prue will be at Rookery House helping with the jam making this afternoon.'

'Then I'll ask her when I get the chance to speak to Prue on her own,' Thea said.

Hettie returned to her blackberry picking, wondering what the future held for Prue. There would be happiness – she felt sure of it.

CHAPTER 49

Now was a good time to ask her, Thea decided. She had observed Prue and Max throughout their midday meal and there was no doubting they had formed a close bond, sitting together at the kitchen table and chatting easily, oblivious to those perched around them. Even Flo seemed to have noticed, at one point catching Thea's eye and winking after she'd offered to top up Prue's cordial and received no answer. Prue's attention had been so firmly focused on Max she hadn't heard a word Flo had said.

Thea and Prue were standing at the table in the back garden of Rookery House, peeling and chopping windfalls from the orchard which would be cooked with the blackberries collected that morning. Luca and Flo had gone to collect more apples and everyone else was indoors in the kitchen, doing the preparations for jam making.

'Prue?' Thea stopped what she was doing and looked at her sister.

'Hmm?' Prue replied, busy cutting away a bruised bit of apple.

'Have you got something to tell me?'

Prue paused briefly, then carried on attending to her task. The bruise expertly removed, she plopped the piece of apple into the bowl of water before turning to face Thea. 'What do you mean?'

'Has anything happened you might want to share with me?'

Pink bloomed in Prue's cheeks and Thea saw a look in her eyes that she hadn't seen for many a year. Prue seemed so *alive*. Thea felt a surge of warmth for her sister. Was she in love? Thea found herself hoping that she was.

'I *might* have something to share with you,' Prue admitted and Thea could see that she was bursting to reveal all.

'Then share away,' Thea said, pursing her lips to hide her smile.

'What do you know already?' Prue asked.

'Nothing as such, only what I saw this morning when you and Max were picking blackberries together. You looked like you were enjoying… being with each other.'

Prue glanced around as if to check no one could hear her. 'All right, I'll explain all,' she said in a low voice, 'but what I'm about to say must be kept secret, at least for now anyway.'

'Can I tell Hettie? It was she who first noticed how you and Max seemed so close,' Thea said in a hushed voice.

'Very well, but *only* Hettie, and you must keep it between the two of you,' Prue agreed.

'You can trust us both, you know that.'

Prue drew in a steadying breath and then said, 'Max and I have been seeing each other. We walk by the river. We've become… very fond of each other.' She smiled suddenly. 'I never expected anything like this to happen to me! Thea, he's brought a joy to my life that I didn't know was missing.'

Thea held her younger sister's hands. 'This is wonderful! I'm delighted for you, I really am. Why the secrecy?'

'At the moment, we'd rather keep it between ourselves. It's no one else's business. That's how we both want it, for now.'

Thea nodded slowly. 'I understand and respect that,' she said. 'I promise it will go no further than Hettie and I. How long has it been going on?'

'Since Max returned from London last month. While we were there, we spent most evenings together; that was when...' Prue's face broke into an expression of amazement, 'we realised we felt the same about each other. That was the start. Being away gave us plenty of time to get to know one another. I'm so glad I volunteered – and that Max was going to the city too and so could accompany me.'

'Where might it lead, do you think?' Thea asked.

Prue lifted a shoulder. 'I honestly don't know. I'm not thinking about that, just enjoying our time together. He's a kind, caring man and I've never been in a relationship with someone like that before. It's lovely to be with a person like Max; it makes me happy. I...'

Prue halted as Hettie opened the back door and came hurrying towards them.

'Nancy has just telephoned – the baby's on its way!' Hettie announced, her cheeks flushed.

'I must go home to be with her.' Prue gave Thea's hands a squeeze before letting go. 'Where's Walt?'

'I'm here.' Walt came out after Hettie, buttoning his olive-coloured uniform tunic.

'I'll grab my things and then I'll be ready to go.' Prue hurried to go inside. Thea noticed her meet Max in the doorway and stop briefly to say something to him.

'I hope everything goes well.' Thea directed this to Walt. 'Will you let us know when the baby's born?'

'Sure, though I don't know how long it will take to arrive.

I'm looking forward to this, but I am nervous too,' Walt admitted.

'You'll be fine,' Hettie patted his arm. 'You've done it before.'

'I have, many times, but not for a while.' Walt saw Prue come back out with her bag. 'Okay, time to go.'

'Tell Nancy we'll be thinking of her,' Thea said as Walt and Prue collected their bicycles from where they'd left them earlier, leaning against the side of the scullery wall, and set off.

After they'd gone, Hettie pushed up her sleeves. 'While Nancy has a baby to deliver, we've got jam to make. How are you getting on with the apples?'

'There's plenty left to peel and chop yet and Flo and Luca are bringing more,' Thea said. 'I'm afraid Prue and I got distracted talking.' Her eyes met Hettie's and she lowered her voice. 'What you suspected is true but they want to keep it to themselves for now.'

Hettie beamed and whispered back, 'That's marvellous! Their secret is safe with me, they know that.' She clapped her hands together. 'Oh, I'm so pleased for them! Prue deserves all the happiness she can get.'

'She does,' Thea agreed. 'And I hope it works out well for them both.'

CHAPTER 50

'Thea, may I speak with you, please?'

Thea had just been to the orchard to check all the hens were inside the coop for the night and was walking past Reuben's railway carriage house as the light slowly faded. Hearing Max's voice, she turned to see him coming down the veranda steps towards her.

'Of course.'

Max glanced back at the house before adding in a low voice, 'Could we talk somewhere private?'

'Come with me to check on Primrose,' Thea suggested. 'It's quiet by the meadow – no one will overhear us there.'

'Thank you.'

They walked in silence and Thea was aware that Max didn't seem his usual calm, relaxed self. Her mind searched for possibilities as to what was the matter but, after Prue's revelation this afternoon, she guessed it was highly likely to do with his relationship with her sister.

'It won't be long before Primrose has to stay in the byre overnight,' Thea commented as they reached the gate. 'I'm making the most of these glorious September evenings as much as she is.' Her gaze was drawn to the light from the dipping sun filtering through the trees on the far side of the meadow; it bathed the air with a beautiful golden syrup glow.

Max didn't reply but stood nearby, shifting from foot to foot with his hands in his pockets.

'What did you want to talk to me about?' she asked.

'Prue and I,' he said.

'Ah,' Thea nodded.

Max swallowed before saying, 'Before Prue went home this afternoon to be with Nancy, she told me that you know we've been seeing each other.'

Thea nodded. 'That's right – we talked about it while we were peeling the apples.'

'I want to tell you I am serious about Prue!' he said, his voice suddenly filled with emotion. His eyes were bright as he met hers. 'I haven't felt like this about anyone for a long time… and I promise you, Thea, I will never mess Prue around or hurt her in any way. In fact…' he paused for a moment before declaring, 'I want to marry her!'

Thea's mouth fell open.

'I love Prue,' Max continued. 'Our relationship has surprised and enchanted me. I know it's not been very long, but I feel it in my heart that I would like to spend the rest of my life with her.'

'What does Prue think? Have you asked her if she wants to marry you?'

He gave a sheepish smile. 'Not yet. But I will. And soon. If Prue isn't ready, then I will wait until she is. I know what a terrible time she had with her husband. I won't rush her.'

Thea let out a long breath. It was a lot to take in. The news that Max and Prue were seeing each other had been enough of a surprise but now he was talking of marriage.

'Since Victor died, Prue has blossomed,' Thea told him. 'She's taken charge of her life and is happier than she has been for many years. I must be honest with you, Max, she told me recently that she didn't plan to wed again. That was shortly *before* she went to London with you, though, so I don't know what she would say now – she may have changed her mind. Being with *you* might have done that. There's only one way to find out and that's to ask her!'

Max nodded, his brow furrowed. 'If Prue does not wish to marry again, then I will respect her wishes. Her happiness is the most important thing to me.' He looked out to where Primrose was grazing before returning his attention to Thea. 'What would *you* think about Prue and I marrying, if it's what she wanted? I value your opinion, Thea.'

'I would be happy for you both,' she replied without hesitation. 'I will support my sister in whatever she decides though. I didn't agree with her decision to marry Victor, but she did it, and I was still always there for her.' She looked Max firmly in the eye. 'You are nothing like him,' she said, and for a moment she felt a flash of anger at Prue's former husband and what he'd put her through. 'Max, you're a far better, far kinder and thoroughly more decent man. I believe you would be a good husband for Prue.'

Max's face relaxed. 'I would have your approval then, Thea?'

'Is that what you are asking me for?' she said shrewdly. 'Is that why we are here?'

'It is.'

'Then you have it, though Prue is quite capable of making her own decision. If you want my advice, I would urge you to be patient. You've already told me you are prepared to wait if Prue needs time.'

'Life has taught me patience,' Max said, 'but I should tell Prue how I feel.'

'You should,' Thea agreed. 'When will you ask her?'

'Soon. Please, Thea, will you keep what I have told you secret?' he asked.

'Of course. It's yours and Prue's story to tell when you're ready, not mine,' Thea reassured him.

'Thank you. I bid you good night.' Max gave a small bow of his head and then headed off back to the railway carriage house.

'Good night!' Thea called after him, watching him go, wondering what Prue would say when Max asked her to marry him. It was her sister's decision and hers alone, but if she asked Thea's advice, it would be to say yes.

Thea leaned her arms on the top of the gate and gazed across to where swallows were diving and darting for insects over the grass. What a day it had been, she thought, first Prue revealing that she was secretly seeing Max, then Nancy going into labour and now Max declaring his wish to marry Prue. If her sister accepted his offer, then she would, in all likelihood, be with a man who'd love and cherish her for the rest of her life. It would be a whole new beginning for Prue, who deserved to be happy after her years of despair and misery. Prue's future was out of Thea's hands though; all she could do was watch and wait and hope that everything worked out for the best.

CHAPTER 51

The kitchen at Rookery House was quiet, the lamp on the table casting a low glow around the room. Thea was the only one still up, waiting for news of Nancy and her baby. She'd made herself a cup of cocoa and moved a chair closer to the range and was resting her socked feet against the still warm oven at the bottom. She checked the clock on the wall again – it was now quarter past ten. Knowing it could be tomorrow before the baby arrived, and that she had a full day's work ahead of her, Thea decided she'd give it another half an hour and then go to bed.

A gentle tapping woke her with a start. She had fallen asleep in her chair. Glancing at the clock, she saw it was a quarter past eleven. Rousing herself, she hurried to answer the back door and was greeted by a smiling Walt.

'Did I wake you?' he asked, stepping into the kitchen.

'I dropped off! Tiredness must have caught up with me. Never mind about that – has Nancy had her baby?'

'She has and mother and son are both doing well.'

'Oh, a boy, that's wonderful! I'm so pleased for her.'

'It was a straightforward birth and a real privilege to be there to help her.' Walt looked wistful. 'I was reminded of the work I did in my family medicine practice back home before the war. I want to thank you, Thea. It's because of you and getting to know you and your friends and community that I was able to be a family doctor again, even just for one night. It's what I love doing and I look forward to returning to it some day.'

'Nancy and I have both benefitted from your medical skills,' Thea said, smiling.

'It wasn't a great day for you when you broke your wrist, but it was a fortuitous one for me. Otherwise, we may never have met. I didn't just get a new patient that day; I gained a friend.' Walt grinned. 'And I now have a lot of other friends too, all through knowing you.'

'We're a friendly bunch around here!' Thea said. 'Which reminds me, can I offer you some refreshments? Tea?'

'That's thoughtful of you but it's late and I must get back to the base. I called by because I wanted to bring you the news.' He stepped forwards and planted a kiss on her cheek. 'Thank you for your friendship, Thea, and for giving another purpose to my life here in England. I'll see you soon. Goodnight.'

'Goodnight,' Thea echoed as he left, closing the door quietly behind him.

Standing alone in the dim kitchen, Thea took a moment to settle herself. This had been a summer of surprises – Walt's frankness being the latest of them. She wasn't used to men speaking so openly or expressing themselves with kisses to her cheek! He was an American, of course; they were used to doing things differently and Thea rather liked that.

She checked the range was banked up for the night and put her empty cup in the sink. Walt was right, she thought. Her accident had led to him becoming part of her life and a regular visitor to Rookery House. He wasn't the first and he wouldn't be the last to find friendship and community here – and that was exactly what she had intended when she bought the place.

Thea yawned. It was time she went to bed. Picking up the lamp from the table to light her way upstairs to her room, she was already looking forward to sharing the joyful news with the others in the morning.

CHAPTER 52

Sheringham, by the sea, Norfolk

'It was such a good idea to come here today, Max. Thank you!' Prue breathed in the salty air, her eyes drawn to the horizon. The blue sky was dotted with small, puffy clouds and the sea was a shifting pattern of turquoise and dark marine blue. 'Such a beautiful sight.'

It was the last day of September and Max had surprised Prue with a trip here to Sheringham by train to enjoy a day by the seaside. It was one of those precious days of warmth and sunshine, before the cooler months set in and the summer became only a memory.

'You mentioned coming here that day we first met by the river,' Max reminded her.

'I remember.' Prue looked up at him and smiled. 'And here we are, paddling hand in hand together.'

The tide had turned and was on its way in, gentle waves washing over the sun-warmed golden sand; Prue could feel the water warming as it washed around her bare calves and through her toes.

Max took both of her hands in his, their eyes meeting. 'Prue, what I'm about to say might ruin things between us but I have to say it.'

Despite what he'd said about ruining things he appeared assured, confident and happy and she felt she knew what he was going to say; she wanted him to say it.

'I know it hasn't been long since we got to know each other,' Max continued, 'but I think it's the right thing to do. I made up my mind a while ago and it hasn't changed.'

Another wave came in, and the sea deepened where they stood, wetting the hem of her dress and Max's rolled-up trousers. Prue ignored it, her eyes fastened on his.

'I love you, Prue. I want to spend the rest of my life with you and take care of you.'

To Prue's astonishment, Max went down on one knee as the wave went out.

'Will you marry me, Prue?'

Prue felt her heart race but kept her face calm. 'There's another wave coming in,' she warned.

'Let it,' said Max.

'Then yes!' Prue pulled Max to his feet just before the wave reached them. Even so, he was now soaked up to his knees, though he didn't seem to care at all about that.

'Yes, I will marry you, Max,' she told him again, drinking in the look of wonder on his face. Suddenly he let out a whoop of joy, picked her up and spun her around as wave after wave washed in around them.

'You have made me the happiest man on this earth, Prue.'

'I'm glad to hear it – now take me to dry land, please!'

Max carried her up the beach, the pair of them giggling.

When he put her down, she immediately embraced him, kissing him for all the world to see.

They sat on a bench, leaning into each other as they looked out over the water, her hands held in his. The tide had rolled in, changing everything. And all was well, Prue thought.

She'd never felt such a powerful conviction about a decision before. Accepting Max's offer felt as if all the jumbled pieces in her life had at last fitted together to make a whole. She had no doubts that marrying him would bring her great happiness – he was an honourable, kind, decent and loving man, who treated her as an equal, valuing her opinion and caring that she was happy.

'Let's get married in the new year,' she suggested. 'How would that suit you?'

'Perfectly,' Max replied.

'It will be a wonderful new beginning for both of us,' she said.

Dear Reader,

I hope you enjoyed reading *New Beginnings at Rookery House*! It was a delight to write about Prue finding happiness at last.

Prue, Thea and Hettie and the other residents of Great Plumstead will return in the final book of the series *Wedding Celebrations at Rookery House*.

I love hearing from readers – so please do get in touch via:

Facebook: be friends on **Rosie Hendry Books,** or join my private readers group - **Rosie Hendry's Reader Group**
X (Twitter): @hendry_rosie
Instagram: rosiehendryauthor
Website: **www.rosiehendry.com**

On my website, you can sign up to get my newsletter delivered straight to your inbox, with all the latest on my writing life, exclusive looks behind the scenes of my work, and reader competitions.

If you have the time and would like to share your thoughts about this book, do please leave a review. I read and appreciate each one as it's wonderful to hear what you think. Reviews also encourage other readers to try my books.

With warmest wishes,

Rosie

IF YOU ENJOYED NEW BEGINNINGS AT ROOKERY HOUSE...

It would be wonderful if you could spare a few minutes to leave a star rating, or write a review, at the retailer where you bought this book.

Reviews don't need to be long – a sentence or two is absolutely fine. They make a huge difference to authors, helping us know what readers think of our books and what they particularly enjoy. Reviews also help other readers discover new books to try for themselves.

You might also tell family and friends you think would enjoy this book.

Thank you!

HEAR MORE FROM ROSIE

Want to keep up to date with Rosie's latest releases?

Subscribe to her newsletter on her website.
www.rosiehendry.com

Subscribers get Rosie's newsletter delivered to their inbox and are always the first to know about the latest books, as well as getting exclusive behind the scenes news, plus reader competitions.

You can unsubscribe at any time and your email will never be shared with anyone else.

ACKNOWLEDGMENTS

A huge thank you to all my readers who have taken the Rookery House books and characters to their hearts.

Thanks to the fantastic team who help me create the books — editor, Catriona Robb and cover designer, Andrew Brown. Also to my author friends and especially those of the Famous Five whose friendship, chats and laughs together are such a joy.

Finally, thank you to David, who supports me in all I do.

ALSO BY ROSIE HENDRY

East End Angels series
East End Angels
Secrets of the East End Angels
Christmas with the East End Angels
Victory for the East End Angels
East End Angels Together Again

Rookery House series
The Mother's Day Club
The Mother's Day Victory
A Wartime Welcome at Rookery House
A Wartime Christmas at Rookery House
Digging for Victory at Rookery House
A Christmas Baby at Rookery House
Home Comforts at Rookery House
Christmas Carols at Rookery House
A Joyful Springtime at Rookery House
New Beginnings at Rookery House
Wedding Celebrations at Rookery House

Standalone
Secrets and Promises
A Home from Home
Love on a Scottish Island
A Pocketful of Stories

Rosie Hendry lived and worked in the USA before settling back in her home county of Norfolk, England, where she lives in a village by the sea with her family. She likes walking in nature, reading and growing all sorts of produce and flowers in her garden — especially roses.

Rosie writes stories from the heart that are inspired by historical records, where gems of social history are often to be found. Her interest in the WWII era was sparked by her father's many tales of growing up at that time.

Rosie is the winner of the 2022 Romantic Novelists' Association (RNA) award for historical romantic sagas, with *The Mother's Day Club,* the first of her series set during wartime at Rookery House. Her novels set in the London Blitz, the *East End Angels* series, have been described as 'Historical fiction at its very best!'.

To find out more visit **www.rosiehendry.com**

www.ingramcontent.com/pod-product-compliance
Lightning Source LLC
LaVergne TN
LVHW040134080526
838202LV00042B/2905